# "Faith Hartman?"

The unexpected sound of her name brought her head up and she found herself staring into ice-blue eyes. It took her a second to find her voice, because this guy—this tall, dark, trigger-inducing man—couldn't be pixie-like Debra's brother. Could he?

She cleared her throat and managed to say "Yes, I'm Faith" in a remarkably normal voice.

"Drew Miller."

Worst nightmare coming true. She somehow managed to force her lips into a smile as excuses started tumbling over themselves in her brain. Her schedule had changed...she'd decided not to take on clients...her job was taking up more time than she'd anticipated...

*Get a grip.*

She really hoped she could. More than once she'd left public places because of people who reminded her of her assailant. But grip or not, she wasn't going to be spending time with this guy. How could she if having him sit across the table from her made her heart race?

And the worst part was that he was her new neighbor.

Dear Reader,

We all have moments when we want to get away—to escape the reality of our lives, regroup and rejuvenate. In this story, both the hero and heroine have experienced life-altering traumas, escaped to heal and are now finding their way back.

Faith Hartman has spent a year recovering from an assault and is now actively working to put her life back on track and reclaim her place in the rodeo world. My hero, Drew, on the other hand, is still working through his pain and looking for strategies to help him build a life for him and his young daughter. When he approaches Faith for riding lessons, he never dreams that he'll end up traveling the state, acting as her bodyguard as she competes in rodeos...or that he's going to fall in love with her.

Drew and Faith had a rough journey toward their happily-ever-after, and they beat me up a little on the way. I didn't mind, though. It was worth it to get these two together.

Happy reading,

*Jeannie Watt*

# JEANNIE WATT

# Her Mountain Sanctuary

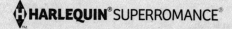

HARLEQUIN® SUPERROMANCE®

Recycling programs
for this product may
not exist in your area.

ISBN-13: 978-1-335-44919-1

Her Mountain Sanctuary

**Printed in U.S.A.**

www.Harlequin.com

**Jeannie Watt** lives on a small cattle ranch in Montana's beautiful Madison Valley. When she's not writing, Jeannie serves as the tractor copilot (aka the gate-opener/cattle-fender-offer). She enjoys horseback riding, reading, sewing and knitting.

Visit the Author Profile page at Harlequin.com for more titles.

I'd like to dedicate this book to those who stood beside me on my writing journey—Mom and Dick, Gary, Jamie and Jake, Mike Allen, Charlie Hauntz. Thank you for all of your encouragement. It helped so much.

# CHAPTER ONE

DREW MILLER WOKE as he hit the floor, a scream catching in his throat.

The brilliant orange yet eerily silent flash from the blast faded into the night as his eyes snapped open. Kicking himself free of the sheets, he lay on the cold floor next to the bed, taking deep, gulping breaths. Sweat beaded on his forehead as his eyes adjusted to the moonlit loft. He pushed up to a sitting position and took in the damage. The lamp had taken another hit, and the books he'd had on the nightstand were strewn across the room.

*Shit.*

He looked at his knuckles—no blood this time—then leaned back against the bed, drawing his knees up and resting his forearms on them, letting his head fall forward. It didn't take a whole lot of thought to connect the nightmare to the second anniversary of his wife's death, but he hadn't dreamed of Lissa.

He'd dreamed of the roadside bomb that had taken out his convoy a year ago. As always.

Drew never remembered the dreams themselves. Only the colors and invisible forces holding him down, shoving him back. Killing his friends. He fought back, of course. Violently.

After getting to his feet, taut muscles protesting, he scooped up the bedding, dumped it on the mattress and then started down the ladder that led from the small loft to the living room of his grandfather's cabin.

He crossed the room to the clothes dryer in the alcove off the kitchen, pulled out pants, socks and a flannel shirt. After getting dressed, he turned on the generator, made his coffee. When the brew had finished percolating, he poured a cup and took it out onto the porch where he sat on the step, letting the early morning sun warm him. Calm him.

Deb, his sister, had set up the meeting for him that morning with the equine therapy lady. He was going to go, with the sole objective of saying he *had* gone—but not today. Not when he looked like the crazed hermit his sister seemed to think he was. He'd call Deb, change the meeting. She'd be upset, but grudgingly oblige, because there wasn't much else she could do other than hound him. He had no intention of engaging in any kind of therapy that was not of his own choosing. He'd done months of it before being discharged from the military and moving back to Eagle Valley to be close to his daughter. With the help of the counselors, he'd cleared up a few matters, developed some strategies, but he hadn't been able to shake the nightmares— unless he was taking the drugs that left him useless during the day.

Deb didn't know about the nightmares— thank goodness. She only knew that her brother was sullying her reputation as one of Eagle Valley's social elite by living off the grid in a rustic cabin. Well, he loved this cabin. He and Lissa had spent their honeymoon here. She'd drawn up plans to renovate it, and he was going through with them, so that someday, maybe, his daughter could actually live with him.

Although…maybe renovating the cabin, following Lissa's diagrams, tracing her handwriting with his finger, was also triggering nightmares.

Drew didn't know, but he'd damn well bet

that hanging around horses wasn't going to help him one iota. Nevertheless, he was taking the meeting, eventually. It would get Deb off his back—for a while anyway.

HE WASN'T GOING to show.

Faith Hartman stirred cream into the coffee the waitress refilled on her way by, wondering how long she needed to wait before returning to the college and telling her boss, the registrar of Eagle Valley Community College, that the meeting was a no go. Not looking forward to that. Debra Miller-Hill hadn't been happy when her brother had canceled the first meeting, and she'd probably be less than thrilled about him not showing up for this one.

Faith dipped her spoon into the cup, then looked up as the door to the café opened and a big man in a dark gray flannel shirt stepped inside.

Faith's heart thumped as she dropped her gaze.

*Damn.*

She pulled the spoon out of her coffee, carefully setting it on the napkin before chancing another look at the man who was now casually surveying the café. His gaze passed over her and she felt a rush of relief.

Not the guy she was waiting for. She could see now that he was older than the man she was expecting, and certainly not a walled-off hermit with a thousand-mile gaze, which was exactly how Debra had described her brother.

That didn't slow her heart down one bit. Faith knew from bitter experience that she wouldn't feel totally safe until either the man left the café or she did. And here she'd thought she'd made such progress over the past several months.

The guy started moving, and Faith lifted her cup with both hands, concentrating on the warmth of the ceramic against her fingers, the aroma of the coffee—anything to bring her heart rate down before the guy she was *supposed* to meet arrived. If he did arrive.

"Faith Hartman?"

The unexpected sound of her name brought her head up and she found herself staring into ice-blue eyes. It took her a second to find her voice, because this guy—this tall, dark, trigger-inducing man—couldn't be Debra's brother. Could he?

She cleared her throat and managed to

say, "Yes, I'm Faith," in a remarkably normal voice.

"Drew Miller."

Worst nightmare coming true. She somehow managed to force her lips into a smile as excuses started tumbling over themselves in her brain. Her schedule had changed…she'd decided not to take on clients…her job was taking up more time than she'd anticipated…

*Get a grip.*

She really hoped she could. More than once she'd left public places because of people who reminded her of her assailant. But grip or not, she wasn't going to spend time with this guy. How could she if having him sit across the table from her made her heart race? And the worst part was that he lived relatively close to her.

Debra seemed to think that the fact that they were neighbors was a sign from above or something. *It would be so handy for both of you…*

Faith had agreed to the meeting and now she was in a situation.

"Are you okay?"

The abrupt question brought her back, and Faith did her best to infuse some warmth into her smile and a look of surprise into her eyes as she squeezed her hands together under the table. "I expected someone younger. Like… midtwenties?"

"Why's that?" he asked as he eased into the booth.

"From the way your sister spoke of you, I guess."

She certainly hadn't expected a guy in his mid- to late-thirties who looked as if he was in command of everything around him. But she wasn't a trained psychologist— just a woman who had helped run an equine therapy program as part of her former job. A program that Debra thought might help her brother.

Now it was his turn to fake a smile. "My sister…yes." The smile faded. "I'm curious as to how Debra described me."

Time to pick words carefully. Hard to do when her brain was shouting at her to leave the café. Now. "She said that you were ex-military. That you'd just moved back into the area and that you were interested in horseback riding." Not the total truth, but tactful.

He snorted through his nose. "Did she tell you I was a basket case?"

"Uh…"

He cocked his head, no longer bothering with the smile. "Or a hermit with post-traumatic stress disorder?"

Faith swallowed. "The second."

He gave a nod and dropped his gaze to regard his hands. "I guess that's something I'll have to put up with if I plan to stay in the area."

"Do you?" According to Debra, he lived on the mountain a couple of miles from Faith's house. Now that she knew how she reacted to him, she'd feel better if he didn't stay.

He raised those icy-blue eyes. "I was raised here. What's left of my family is here. So yes."

An uncomfortable silence settled between them, and Faith took hold of her cup with both hands again, more for something to do than because she was going to drink the rapidly cooling contents. Drew Miller looked up again, those amazing eyes zeroing in on her.

His saving grace, those eyes. The reason she wasn't already gone. The man who'd slammed her to the ground, put a knee on her back and cut off her ponytail with one slice of a very sharp knife had green eyes.

Black hair, green eyes. A striking combination that she'd noticed at the bar an hour or so before he'd assaulted her in the rodeo ground parking lot as she'd walked back to her truck. His attack had been stopped short by a couple of men driving by, so she could only imagine what might have ensued had he not been caught…and sometimes her imagination could be brutal.

She shook off the thoughts as best she could, made a heroic attempt to sound normal as she said, "Do you want coffee or something?" He shook his head and once again the ball was in her court. "Debra said you might be interested in…" She trailed off before saying the words *equine therapy*. Something to do with him knowing that Debra had described him as a hermit with PTSD.

"Horseback riding?" He spoke ironically, telling Faith that he wasn't fooled by her attempts at tact.

"Equine therapy." There. Now the record was set straight and he wouldn't think that she was a woman who pussyfooted around the truth. Not that it mattered, but she had her pride.

He settled back in the red upholstered seat

and regarded her for a long moment. Faith made a conscious effort to meet his gaze, hold it. The guy let off an aura of power, coupled with something Faith couldn't quite put her finger on. She didn't want to put her finger on it. She wanted to end this uncomfortable meeting and be on her way.

Drew shifted in his seat then, making her jump. Inwardly cursing, Faith met his gaze dead-on, silently challenging him to say something.

He did.

"Do I make you nervous?"

"No." It wasn't him, per se. *All* guys like him made her nervous…although again, she'd thought she'd moved on. Her reaction to him proved otherwise. Faith let go of her cup, dropping her hands back into her lap so he couldn't see her twisting her fingers—a habit she hated.

He didn't believe her. It was more than obvious from the way one corner of his mouth tightened and his eyebrows lifted. His reaction stirred something in Faith. She would hold her own. She had nothing to fear from this guy. He wasn't her assailant and they were in a public place. She squared her shoulders.

"Before we go any further, I need to tell you that I'm not actually a certified therapist."

"I know. You worked under a therapist. Debra briefed me."

"What else did Debra tell you?" Because she didn't feel comfortable having total strangers being briefed on her, although, to be fair, Deb had given her a lot of information about Drew. Information he probably would prefer his sister didn't give to a perfect stranger.

"I know that you're new at the college, new to the Eagle Valley. I pass your house when I drive to town." Her heart kicked at his last statement. Even though she'd known that he lived near her, she hadn't realized until this meeting that he was a walking trigger-fest. "And...I know that Deb hopes you'll make me 'normal' again. Not much else."

One corner of his mouth tilted up, but there was no humor in his expression. His eyes were cool, watchful, giving Faith the feeling that he noticed *everything*.

"Do you have PTSD?" Asking the point-blank question made her feel a little more like her old self—a woman who had control of her life.

"I have grief." A flat statement of fact, spoken without any sign of self-consciousness, but Faith felt his withdrawal. She took it to mean, yes, he had PTSD and no, he wasn't going to talk about it.

"Are you in therapy?"

"I was. I deal with it on my own now."

Which was why Debra was concerned. Her brother had lost his wife, survived some kind of military disaster and was now living alone in an isolated cabin, dealing with his symptoms on his own. So she had urged Faith to meet with him after discovering Faith's equine therapy background.

Faith had been torn about meeting Drew Miller, but had agreed because she believed in the healing power of contact with animals. If he hadn't shared the same body type as her assailant, if he'd been smaller or blonder or geekier, she might have encouraged him to try "riding horses." He wasn't any of those things. He was tall and muscular and powerful and Faith was allergic to masculine power. She didn't want to risk having to spend more time with this guy.

She gave up trying to fake things. "I don't think this is a good fit."

"Because I make you nervous."

"I said—"

"I heard you. I don't believe you."

"That's blunt."

"And truthful."

Anger sparked deep within, giving her a dose of courage. "It's not a good fit because *you* aren't really interested in equine therapy." Her right hand was squeezing her left hand so tightly now that it was going numb from the pressure. "Right?"

He settled back again, regarding her as if she was a puzzle he needed to solve. She could cut things short—simply agree that he made her nervous and explain why, thus solving the puzzle—but the words froze in her throat. It was none of his business and, just in case he did talk to his sister, she didn't want her coworkers to know. Her attack was nothing to be ashamed of…but it was personal. Something she held close in hopes that it wouldn't color her entire life.

As it was coloring it now.

Faith drew in a breath, but before she could speak, he said, "Why did *you* agree to meet with *me*?"

"I thought I could help." She hoped her

nose didn't grow. The truth was that she wanted to remain on her boss's good side.

He smiled a little, a faint lifting of the corners of his mouth. "You wanted to get Debra off your back."

Her face went warm. "No."

"Don't worry. I won't tell."

"I don't know you, so I don't know if that's true," Faith snapped.

"And it doesn't look as if you're going to know me."

She was in a situation. She liked her job working in the registrar's office, digitalizing the old records and updating the new. The people she worked with were friendly, but not too friendly, allowing her to work alone without a lot of interruptions. And her office was in the basement, where she felt as if she had an extra layer of security. It wasn't easy to find her and she liked it that way.

"I'm not going to talk to Debra." He moved then, easing out of the booth and getting to his feet, towering over her. "You can tell her I wouldn't agree to therapy."

Faith would have gotten out of the booth, but she didn't want to face him without the safety of the table between them. So, she kept her neck craned upward as she said, "Maybe you should tell her."

"I avoid my sister at all costs. But, if she does manage to track me down, I will."

"You avoid her, yet you stay in the area because of her?" He frowned at her, looking perplexed, and she said, "You said you were here because of your family."

"Deb isn't my only family."

Faith opened her mouth, closed it again. Debra had made it sound as if she and Drew were the last of their line.

Not something Faith wanted to get into.

"I'm sorry to have wasted your time."

There was only the slightest hint of irony in his voice, but Faith caught it. And she didn't think it was necessarily directed at her. He saw her as his sister's puppet. Which she was.

A moment later he was on his way out of the café, and Faith's limbs went weak with relief when the door closed behind him. She propped an elbow on the table and pressed her hand to her forehead as a wave of depression followed relief. Sheer adrenaline had gotten her through the meeting, but now… wet noodle.

She'd thought she was doing better. She'd

even managed to deal with the big guy on the college grounds maintenance crew who had tried to hit on her. He wasn't as close to her assailant's body type as Drew Miller was, but he was big. And muscular.

But not powerful.

Drew Miller exuded an aura of power, and that was the difference.

"YOU DIDN'T EVEN give it a chance, did you?"

Somehow Drew refrained from rolling his eyes at his sister. That would only lengthen the time he had to spend in her uncomfortable-feeling McMansion, defending his desire to run *his* life *his* way. He'd been truthful when he told Faith Hartman that he avoided his sister at all costs, but sometimes offense was more effective than defense with Deb. She needed to forget the therapy idea and accept the fact that he could handle matters on his own. He took a deep breath, spoke calmly.

"I know you mean well—"

"Of course, I mean well," Deb snapped.

"However, after talking with Ms. Hartman…" He shook his head. "It won't work out."

Deb's mouth tightened as if he'd given exactly the answer she'd expected. "I know you feel as if Eric and I are interfering, but, Drew…you've changed."

Huh. Losing his wife and having his convoy hit by a roadside bomb had changed him. Losing his comrades while grieving his wife had changed him. Coming home to a daughter he hadn't been there to support during the roughest time of her short life had changed him. Go figure.

"And for Maddie's sake, I think—"

"Leave my daughter out of this." They'd discussed this before. Maddie had been hit with a double whammy in a short period of time and was not to be dragged into any of Deb's half-baked schemes to keep up appearances. "I know I'm different, and here's the deal, Deb. I'm not going to magically change back to the guy I once was. Not even if I pet a couple of horses."

"It's more than petting."

"I know it's more than petting." He did his best to tamp down his growing irritation.

"If it *looked* like you were doing something to help yourself, then…"

"Then…?"

Deb's mouth snapped shut.

"Then people wouldn't be so wigged out about my living alone in Granddad's cabin?" The further tightening of her lips answered his question. "I don't care what people think, Deb. It doesn't matter. It's not like I'm building an arsenal or writing manifestos—"

"Don't talk like that."

"People do live in cabins without being nuts, you know."

Deb looked as if she'd like to argue the point, making him wish he hadn't come, even if it was a necessary trip. Otherwise she would have hounded him via text. One of the drawbacks of his place was that even though it was isolated and didn't have conventional power, it did have an excellent cell phone signal—if he remembered to plug his phone in and charge it when the generator was on.

"You know that Eric and I are just…concerned." Always *Eric and I*, even though Drew had a feeling his brother-in-law couldn't care less about his living on the mountain alone.

"I'll act as normal as possible when I come to town, okay? That way people won't talk."

Deb took a step forward. "I think you're afraid of this therapy."

Change of tactic. And not a bad one. "What if I am?"

"Then you need to meet your fears head-on." She sounded as if she were rallying troops.

"Noted. I have to go."

"Pete's shop?" Deb said his late wife's brother's name with a faint sneer.

"Yeah. He's swamped. I told him I'd help out." And he made it a point to be at the shop when Maddie got home from school, so they could spend time together. Deb didn't seem to have a maternal bone in her body, so he didn't bother mentioning that.

Drew started out the door and then looked back at his sister. "This matter is closed, by the way."

Deb's jaw shifted sideways as it always did when she was thwarted. It'd looked cuter when she'd been five and he'd been ten. "You are never going to segue back into society if you spend all of your time either in the cabin or Pete's shop. You're never going to be able to give Maddie the support she needs."

"That's none of your business, Deb." The first sparks of serious anger started to burn deep in his belly. "I'm not kidding about that.

Not even a little bit. Stay out of my life. No therapy, no interventions. Got it?"

She pulled in a breath through her nose, lifting her chin. "You're my brother. If I see you driving off a cliff, I'm going to stop you."

He gave a small snort as he pulled the door open. Sometimes talking to Deb was literally like talking to a wall.

FAITH HADN'T SEEN the Lightning Creek Ranch prior to the fire that had destroyed the house two years ago, but she'd studied enough photos to know she was living in a carbon copy of the place—on the outside, anyway. She doubted that the original house had had the same open layout, or the state-of-the-art appliances, yet the house she rented retained a homey farmhouse-feel that warmed her every time she walked through the door.

She dropped her purse on the sofa near the door and shrugged out of her coat. She was lucky to have this place—and a job. After the attack eighteen months ago, she'd given up barrel racing and quit her day job as an administrative assistant at a high school. She'd moved into a small over-the-garage apartment belonging to her friend, Jenn, an equine therapist who owned the stable where Faith boarded her horses.

It'd taken almost two months and the constant presence of a canine roommate before she'd felt safe enough to go to work for Jenn, helping with equine therapy classes, going to therapy herself. And she'd healed—to the point that when an assistant registrar job opened at the Eagle Valley Community College three months ago, and her friend Jolie Brody Culver had called about it, she'd successfully applied. It was a records job—something where she didn't have to be in constant contact with people—and it was also a huge step forward.

Now she'd taken a step back.

It happened.

Drew Miller had triggered her. She sensed he was a decent guy—damaged, as his sister had said, but decent. That hadn't kept her primitive survival instincts from kicking in. It was unfair and illogical, but she kind of hated him for driving home the point that she wasn't as far along as she'd thought. That she probably would never fully recover.

She went to the back door and opened it, allowing her overgrown Airedale and personal bodyguard, Sully, to bound inside.

"Yes," Faith said as the dog sniffed at her, then rubbed his curly head on the side of her leg, "I had a rough end to my day." Sully always managed to read her and react accordingly. She wouldn't be surprised if he tried to sleep on the foot of her bed that night, crushing her feet with his reassuring weight, as he always did when she'd suffered a fright or a setback.

The house was darker than normal due to the blue-gray clouds that had rolled in as she drove home from work, so she snapped on a light and headed over to the gas stove to flip the switch. A cheery blue fire began playing over a fake birch log.

There was a low rumble in the distance as she went into the kitchen and pulled a bottle of merlot out of the cupboard next to the fridge. After the meeting with Debra's brother, she deserved a glass of wine. Maybe two. Her lips curved humorlessly as she uncorked the bottle.

She left the wine to breathe and walked to the window, staring out at the dramatic sky. Across the field, Jolie and Dylan's lights were on. They'd chosen to build on the far side of the property, while the older Brody sister, Allie, and her husband had built a custom home in the trees at the base of the mountain, leaving the main house for their sister Mel and her husband. Only Mel had chosen to stay in New Mexico for another year while she and her husband, KC, wrapped up their business there, so the house had been empty, waiting for a temporary occupant—and her horses.

Jolie had been a lifesaver. And now, even though Faith didn't see much of the Brody sisters due to their work schedules and busy home lives, she knew they'd be there if she had a problem. She went to the window and stared out at the lights at the opposite end of the field.

Drew Miller was also her neighbor. She'd watched through the café window to see what he drove, and sure enough, she recognized the red Jeep he'd climbed into. It had passed her a time or two as she'd ridden her mare along the county road toward Dani Brody Matthews's place. Dani was the only Brody sister who didn't have a house on the Lightning Creek Ranch. Instead she and her husband lived in a beautiful stone and glass house on the road leading to the trestle bridge—the road to Drew Miller's house.

The thought of him being near shouldn't bother her. He wasn't her attacker—just a guy with a similar build, who probably had PTSD.

Lightning forked through the sky on the other side of the valley and Sully abandoned his chew toy to follow Faith into the mudroom where she slipped into her barn coat. She still had to feed the animals and it seemed wise to do it now, before the storm hit for real. After all the hungry equine mouths had been fed, she'd come back in, nuke a TV dinner, sip her wine and do her best to forget about having to deal with Debra Miller-Hill, whose brother she wouldn't be helping. She would have loved to tack on "through no fault of her own," but she'd been the one to back off.

Faith had no idea whether Drew Miller would discuss the matter when his sister brought it up, but she hoped that if he did, it wouldn't affect her job. Debra had been registrar for less than a year, but she already had a reputation for being hyperaware of everything that went on in her department. In other words, she tended to micromanage anyone who was on her radar, and she was all about appearances. And loyalty. The woman was insecure and defensive, and Faith had a bad feeling that she was sitting right smack in the middle of Debra's radar screen.

DREW SLOWED THE open-top Jeep as he passed the Lightning Creek Ranch, though he would have preferred to have gunned it. He could see the rain coming in the rearview mirror and he had no desire to get caught in a downpour. He shot a look at the ranch buildings as he passed. Lights shone in the windows of two of the houses—the main house closest to the road and a small house on the far side of the pasture. His would-be therapist's house, no doubt.

He fixed his eyes back on the road, swerving to miss a pothole. One reason Deb had been so adamant about trying the horse-petting program, aka equine therapy—he really hated the word *therapy*—was because he and Faith were practically neighbors. Like that affected anything. But his sister was one to grab at anything she could find to win an argument.

Usually, she didn't win so much as wear him down. This time she didn't win or wear him down because he wasn't going to have her poking her nose into his mental health, especially when he was convinced that her concern was more about blowback on herself than because she gave a rat's ass about him.

And then there was Faith Hartman. He'd expected her to be like his sister—superficially concerned about him, ready to "help" in exchange for remaining in his sister's good graces *and* receiving a healthy session fee.

She hadn't been anything like he'd expected. She'd appeared serious, honest, sincere.

Jumpy as hell.

She'd visibly drawn into herself when he'd taken a seat on the opposite side of the booth and even though she'd squared her shoulders and met his gaze, it had cost her. There'd been a haunted look in her wide green eyes, giving him the feeling that Faith had a few issues of her own. What made a woman who appeared to have backbone go pale at the sight of him?

Drew slowed again as he passed the beautiful stone, wood and glass house where his nearest neighbors—his former classmate, Dani Brody, and her husband, Gabe—lived. *Near* being a relative term. Drew's cabin was another three miles up a road that rapidly degenerated from maintained gravel to rutted dirt. And regardless of what his sister thought was best, he liked living on a rutted, unmaintained road. Maddie was good with it, too. In fact, she loved the bouncy ride to the cabin on the weekends.

He'd talked about the situation with Pete and Cara and they'd agreed that when summer vacation started, Maddie would stay at the cabin more often but return to their place at night. She didn't know about the plan and still thought she'd be at the cabin full-time, but hopefully, between Drew and Pete and Cara, they could help her understand why this was the best course of action—why he didn't want her at the cabin if he came unhinged during the night. The thought of Maddie being there if he woke up yelling or punching a wall ruined him.

The sky was getting darker and he could smell the rain that was going to catch him if he didn't step on the gas.

Thunder cracked behind him as he negotiated a corner, and then the rain started, spattering on the windshield, the seat beside him, his jeans and shoulders. He dodged a couple ruts and accelerated. Another two miles.

Lightning flashed as he rounded a corner, illuminating the white-tailed buck standing in the middle of the road. Drew swerved hard to the right, just missing the animal, then cranked the wheel back toward the road too late.

The front tire caught the berm, jerking the rig sideways. It teetered on the edge of the embankment before crashing down on its side and then rolling over onto its top.

Drew was thrown sideways and he smacked his head on something, making stars explode in his vision as the Jeep came to a rest on the roll bar. He hung from his seat belt as the rain began to pound.

# CHAPTER TWO

FAITH HAD JUST thrown the last of the hay when she heard the crash. She turned toward the sound, pushing the damp hair back from her forehead. She wore a hooded raincoat, but the wind was now blowing sideways, driving rain into her face and down her back.

Too loud and metallic to be a gunshot. Too close to ignore.

Lightning flashed and when the sky darkened again, she saw the odd lights pointing into the sky where there should only be darkness. Mini floodlights…or headlights.

Her heart started pounding as she raced to the two-passenger ATV parked inside the open barn. Sully abandoned the kittens he'd been playing with and bounded over the door into the passenger seat. Faith's phone was still in the house, so she stopped at the end of the walk, raced inside and grabbed it, dialing 911 as she headed back to the vehicle and climbed onboard. She pushed Sully farther onto his side of the seat so she could move her arm without bumping him.

The call put her straight through to sheriff dispatch. She explained that she'd heard a crash and now there were lights pointed into the sky. The operator promised to send a deputy as soon as one was available. Did she need an ambulance? That would take time, too. There'd been an accident on the rain-slicked roads just outside of town.

"I'll update you when I get there." Faith dropped the phone in her pocket and roared past the dark house Dani Brody and her husband called home. It was close to six o'clock. People should be getting home soon, but right now she was the only game in town.

Rain pelted the windshield and blew in through the open sides of the ATV. Faith's wet fingers were getting numb from the cold. She followed the tracks that the rain was rapidly washing away, rounded a corner and saw the lights carving their way through the dark sky, pointing toward the tops of the tall fir trees ahead.

The ATV slid sideways in the slick mud as she approached the place where the tracks headed over the edge of the road, and she slowed, then stopped. She told Sully to stay, then jumped off the vehicle and headed toward the embankment. As she got closer, she heard the sound of rolling rocks over the rain. A few seconds later, a head appeared over the top of the berm.

Faith rushed forward and the man slid backward before his feet regained purchase on the slippery bank and he heaved himself upward again. Taking hold of his wet jacket, Faith set her feet and leaned back, counterbalancing the man as he made his way up and over. She staggered sideways as he regained his footing on the muddy road.

He was big and broad and once he had his balance, he towered over her. Just as that guy in the parking lot had before he'd spun her around and knocked her down.

Faith's chest constricted. For one long moment, she and Drew Miller faced off in the lights of the ATV.

*Move. Say something.*

Instead she stared at him as the rain pelted her face.

"I'm not going to hurt you." He stepped

backward and one of his knees buckled, snapping her back to her senses.

Of course he wasn't going to hurt her. "Can you get in on your own?" She pointed at the ATV and he gave a slow nod before advancing. She pulled her phone out of her pocket and he stopped.

"What are you doing?"

"Calling dispatch."

"No."

He spoke adamantly and Faith lowered the phone. "I already called them. I promised an update."

"No ambulance."

"I can take you to the hospital," she said, assuming it was the cost that had him concerned.

"No hospital."

"Do you want me to leave you here?" she snapped.

He angled his head as if discerning whether he'd heard her correctly. "I'd appreciate a ride to my place. It's a couple of miles up the road."

"Fine." Faith wiped the water off her face. She wasn't about to try to force him to seek medical care. She'd take him home. Drop him off. Hope that he didn't have a concussion or something.

Once they were both in the close confines of the side-by-side and Sully was in the open cargo space at the rear, she put the vehicle in gear and headed up the road, weaving in and around the ruts. "What happened?"

"Deer."

She gripped the wheel tighter. A couple of miles. She could do this. It wasn't as if he was her attacker. Just a close physical facsimile…and, maybe because she was in the role of rescuer, her tension seemed more directed toward the shock of the accident rather than knee-jerk fear. She maneuvered around a corner and then another. He lived at the end of a very windy road. "I know the hospital is out, but do you want me to call your family? Tell them what happened?"

"I'll do it."

Faith forced herself to release her death grip on the steering wheel. *Just another mile. Then you can breathe. Go back home. Climb into the tub. Drink your wine…*

"Thank you."

The words surprised her and it took her a couple seconds to say, "Not a problem."

"I think it is."

She frowned but resisted the urge to look at him. They covered the last mile in total silence, rounding one final corner before the headlights of the ATV illuminated a very small cabin with a metal shop building next to it. The shop dwarfed the cabin.

"Cozy," she murmured. It couldn't have more than three rooms, tops. Her money was on two.

"It's home," he spoke as he climbed out of the ATV.

She nodded, waiting for him to start toward his dark house, her nerves humming with the anticipation of escape.

"I'd appreciate it if you didn't tell my sister about this."

Faith was about to tell him that she didn't see any way around telling Debra, when he swayed a little. "Are you okay?"

"Fine." He abruptly turned, started for the cabin. He made it almost three feet before he crumpled into a heap in the muddy driveway.

"Blast." Faith jumped out of the ATV and raced to him. She used both hands to take hold of his broad shoulder and roll him over so that he didn't drown in the mud puddle he'd landed in.

He let out a groan as he flopped onto his back.

Okay. He was breathing. And he was done calling the shots. She pulled the phone out of her pocket, water beading on the screen as she punched in 911. "I need an ambulance at the top of the Trestle Road." She answered the dispatcher's rapid-fire questions and was assured that a deputy was on his way.

"No ambulance," Drew muttered from where he lay.

"An ambulance will follow," the dispatcher said.

She hung up without asking if she could move him. She was going to do it anyway. He couldn't lie in a mud puddle until help arrived and he'd already moved quite a bit under his own steam.

"If I help you, can you get up?"

He nodded, grimacing, and rolled over to bring himself up to his hands and knees. Faith crouched close to him, taking hold of his arm. She braced herself as he put his weight on her and slowly got to his feet. He swayed again, but Faith kept him from going down.

"Is your house locked?"

"Key under the mat."

"Very original," Faith murmured. As they made the slow journey through the mud, she supported less and less of his weight and by the time they reached the small, two-post porch, he was walking on his own. But Faith noted that he did not bend to retrieve the spare key and that he took firm hold of the post as she unlocked the door. Sully remained next to her, pushing his way into the cabin before Faith stepped inside. He wasn't going to allow her to be alone with Drew, and his presence gave her a small measure of security.

She flipped on a light switch as Drew followed her and Sully inside, but nothing happened.

"The storm must have knocked out the power," she said.

"I don't have power."

Her eyes widened. "No power?"

"Generator." He stepped over to a box next to the light switch and pushed a button. Lights flickered a few times, then lit as the machine outside roared to life. She glanced around the cabin—so it was three rooms. A combined kitchen and living room with a back exit and two interior doors. A half loft. The place was old, the floorboards warped. The kitchen barely had any counter space or cabinetry. A rustic, minimalist place that somehow seemed to fit the man living here.

"You live with that sound?"

"No." He pressed his hand to his head as if the answer had cost him.

"Sit down." Faith motioned to the surprisingly nice leather sofa, then took a couple of steps back as if giving him room. In reality, she was giving herself room. He did as he was told, sinking down with a low exhale. "I'll stay until the ambulance gets here."

"I'm sending them back down the mountain."

"No insurance?"

He shook his head. "No hospitals."

"Do what you have to do. I'm staying until they get here."

"No wonder you're friends with my sister," he muttered.

"We're not friends." Faith's face grew warm at her clipped comment. "What I mean is that she's my boss. Best not to blur lines."

He lifted his gaze, one hand still pressed against his forehead and Faith took a step back, settling her hand on Sully's wet curls. Logically, she knew Drew wasn't a threat in his present condition, but survival instincts, once triggered, were strong. Exhaustively strong. He frowned as she moved back another step, and she had a strong feeling that it wasn't from pain. He was trying to read her. Figure out what was wrong with her. Just as he had in the café.

He didn't say a word, and neither did she. The rain beat on the roof, and a tree branch brushed lightly against the windows, but the silence inside the cabin seemed louder than the weather outside.

Finally, Drew broke the silence. "If you're not friends, then maybe you don't need to discuss this with her."

She gave him an incredulous look. "And when she finds out? I can't see where that would be good for either of us."

"I don't want her to scare my daughter."

"You have a daughter?"

She had no idea why that revelation stunned her, but it did.

He closed his eyes without answering, letting his head rest on the cushion behind him. Faith stayed standing, hugging her arms around her middle. She scanned the room, which was sparsely furnished, ridiculously neat. A photo on the desk caught her attention and she glanced at Drew before leaning closer to get a better look. A much younger and carefree-looking Drew smiled down at the dark-haired woman in his arms. She smiled directly at the camera, joy lighting her face. A tremendous capture. Her contentment, his adoration. A couple deeply in love.

Faith pulled her gaze away, feeling as if she were intruding on a private moment. Drew's eyes remained closed when she gave into impulse and checked the hands resting loosely on his thighs. The ring he wore in the photo was no longer on his finger.

The sound of an engine brought his eyes open again, catching her midstare. Faith quickly averted her gaze and moved to the window. A sheriff's SUV pulled to a stop next to Faith's ATV. A few seconds later, she opened the door to let a young deputy wearing a black raincoat and a plastic cover over his hat.

She gave him her statement while Drew sat silently on the sofa. The deputy turned to him.

"How are you feeling, sir?"

"I'm fine."

"He fell face-first into a mud puddle." Faith figured the deputy might as well have all the facts before he left.

"Is that true, sir?"

"I'm not going to the hospital."

"You're refusing medical care?" the deputy asked.

"I am."

"The paramedics are almost here. What say we let them check you out?"

Faith held her breath, releasing it when Drew grunted consent. "Then they leave. Everyone leaves."

"I'll leave now." She couldn't *wait* to get out of here. The deputy had her contact information and there was nothing to keep her. She headed toward the door, Sully at her heels, giving the deputy a quick nod before pulling it open. She didn't look at Drew Miller.

The seat of the ATV was soaking wet, but so were her pants, so Faith climbed on and turned the key. In fifteen minutes, she'd be at her house, warm and dry.

She saw the lights of the ambulance turning onto the road leading past the Lightning

Creek as she started down the mountain. *Good luck to you guys.*

The headlights of Drew's vehicle were no longer cutting through the darkness as she rounded the corner where he had crashed. She eased to a stop, despite the rain, directing her headlights so that they illuminated the place where the tracks left the road. Easing her way through the muck, she peered over the bank. An open Jeep rested on its roll bar. Faith shuddered and headed back to her ATV.

When she put the machine into gear, her hands were shaking so badly it was hard to get a good grip on the gearshift. It was cold and wet out. Of course her hands were shaking.

It had nothing to do with Drew and that Jeep sitting squarely on the roll bar that had saved his life.

DREW STRUGGLED OUT of his wet clothes, which stuck to his damp skin. After dealing with the deputy and the no-nonsense female paramedic who could have taken him in a fair fight and then climbing the ladder to the loft, he barely had the energy left to do battle with his clothing. Finally, he kicked the last bit of his jeans free and collapsed onto the bed.

He hurt.

He had a hellacious bruise where the seat belt had cut into him, a large bump on the side of his head where he'd hit the doorframe and general soreness from tensing up during an adrenaline spike.

He was going to hurt more in the morning, once the shock wore off. So be it. Pain was an old friend. At one point, he'd embraced physical pain because it distracted him from the real anguish in his life, and, because of that, he now had a huge stash of unused meds. A scary stash. One that he should have gotten rid of a long time ago, but kept as a remembrance of surviving when he wasn't certain he'd wanted to. But he'd soldiered on for his little girl. And for Lissa, who wouldn't have wanted him to give in to the pain.

He closed his eyes, thinking that he'd pull the blanket up over him in a moment. The next thing he knew, gray light was filtering in through the windows and he was shivering on his side. He reached out for the blanket and groaned as his body rebelled.

Maybe he wasn't remembering correctly.

Maybe he'd been hit by a truck instead of rolling down a hill. It certainly felt as if he'd made close contact with a Peterbilt. There was no way he was going back to sleep, so Drew swung his legs out of bed, then sat for a moment before forcing himself to his feet.

He didn't pee red.

Now he didn't have to stop by for that checkup that Brunhild the paramedic had insisted on. He'd pop a few ibuprofens and wait for Deb's call—because Faith had made it clear that she wasn't going to keep her mouth shut. He comforted himself with the knowledge that Pete would intercept any call from Deb to Maddie, to keep Deb from upsetting her. Drew didn't want his daughter to know that he'd come close to buying it again. She was insecure enough about loss as it was.

Drew pulled a pair of sweats out of the antique armoire that served as a closet. No jeans today. He struggled into them, jammed his feet into his moccasins and gingerly pulled a long-sleeve T-shirt over his head. He got stuck halfway through the process. He let out a breath, gathered his strength and managed to pull the shirt into place.

Once dressed, he sat back on the bed and caught his breath.

He had a Jeep to winch up the side of a mountain. Probably some serious bodywork ahead of him. The radiator had been hissing and spewing when he'd started climbing the hill, so add that to the list. He'd call Pete in a bit, arrange to haul his sorry rig up the mountain and tow it to the shop. Pete was a hell of a lot better at bodywork than he was, so he'd offer a trade of some kind.

Drew preferred paying in cold hard cash, but Pete would have none of it. Ironic that Pete needed the money and wouldn't take it, and Drew had the money and wanted to give it.

He got to his feet and stiffly descended the ladder into the living area, swallowing a groan of pain as he stepped off the last rung. The silence pressed in on him, but he didn't start the generator. His gaze drifted over to the photo of him and Lissa. He'd caught Faith studying the photo the night before, as if she were surprised that a woman might get that close to him.

Twenty-four hours ago, she'd been a name on a slip of paper that his sister had pressed upon him. An unwanted meeting. Now she was his rescuer. Yes, he might have gotten to the cabin under his own steam, but he also might have passed out in the road, and then died of exposure during the rainy night.

Once upon a time, dying hadn't seemed like a bad option, but he'd always been clear on the fact that it wasn't an option for him. He was a survivor. His methodology might suck. He might not have the greatest existence, but he was carving something out for himself and Maddie. After all he'd been through, it would have sucked to die in a mud puddle.

He owed the woman.

He needed to thank her…even though he had the very strong feeling that she didn't want to be thanked.

Didn't want any contact with him at all.

# CHAPTER THREE

FAITH DREADED GOING to work the day after she'd helped Drew Miller back to his cabin. She had to say something to Debra when the other woman returned from her morning meeting in Helena. But what would she say?

*Hey, did you hear that your brother had a wreck on the mountain? No? Well, let me fill you in.*

It was a damned-if-she-did, damned-if-she-didn't kind of situation. If he'd told his sister, fine. But she truly doubted he was going to do that, which left it up to her to say something. Word of the accident would surely get out in the small community. Even if the paramedics or deputy didn't say anything, a wrecker would certainly be called to haul the vehicle back up onto the road.

What was the worst that could happen if she kept her mouth shut?

Once Debra found out about Drew's accident, Faith would be in a very awkward spot. The woman had accepted the fact that Drew wasn't going to be partaking in equine therapy, but she'd also said in a wistful way that she wished Faith had "tried harder" to talk him into it.

Now she was stuck in the middle of a situation not of her making. All because she'd agreed to take a meeting with the guy. If she hadn't done that, he wouldn't have known who she was when she'd shown up to rescue him. She wouldn't have known who he was. If they figured it out later, it would have been one of those odd coincidences that they could have marveled over.

But they did know each other. Debra had wanted her to work with Drew so she could get the scoop on how he was doing from Faith at work. She hadn't said that last part, but Faith had understood that was part of the deal. Debra was worried about her brother. And now that she'd met the man, Faith believed that Debra had cause. He'd come off as being in control, comfortable in his surroundings at the café. But the isolation in which he lived, his insistence on no medical treatment, the photo of him in younger, happier days…

The man who'd smiled out of that photograph was not the guy she'd dealt with.

And he had a daughter who didn't live with him.

Yes, Debra had reason to be concerned. And now that he'd wrecked his Jeep, she had more reason. Although Faith was certain that Drew was fine. She'd left him in good hands before escaping down the mountain.

Debra came breezing in from her trip to Helena as Faith left the main office after dropping off some files.

"Uh… Debra…?"

Debra turned, her expression falsely bright. "Yes?"

"Do you have a moment?"

"Only a few. I have to report to the dean."

Faith smiled apologetically and shook her head. "We can talk later."

She was steaming as she headed to the basement archives an hour later without seeing Debra again. How dare this guy put her in a position like this? The thing to do was to wait until Debra returned to the office instead of heading to her car at quitting time, sit Debra down and tell her what had hap-

pened. Then Debra could be outraged or hurt
or whatever, but Faith would be out of it.

Yes.

After unearthing a handful of ancient
transcripts that had yet to be digitized, she
marched back up the stairs to the administrative offices, paused to take a deep breath,
then walked into the registrar's office, only
to find Debra's inner-office door closed and
dark.

Damn and double damn.

Back to her truck she went. After tossing
her tote bag onto the passenger seat, Faith
sat at the wheel for a long moment. Should
she call?

She could only imagine giving Debra the
news over the phone when she hadn't given
it to her in person. Faith cranked on the ignition.

*No biggie. She'll find out, ask why you
didn't say anything. You'll say that Drew
wanted to tell you himself. She'll know that's
a lie...*

Faith gripped the wheel harder as she drove
to the Lightning Creek Ranch. After the assault, she'd developed the habit of overthink-
ing and manufacturing anxiety. Over the past

few months, she'd gotten a handle on the problem, but maybe she was reverting to old coping mechanisms.

No. She wasn't. Her anxiety was the result of a real-life situation. She was in an awkward spot and she wasn't happy about it—to the point that instead of slowing to turn into the drive at the Lightning Creek, she continued on up the Trestle Road toward Drew's house.

*What is wrong with you?*

Faith set her jaw, gripped the wheel, dodged potholes and ruts.

*A lot of things.*

But she had to do this. She went over the scenario. When she got there, he'd come out of his house.

*What if he doesn't?*

He would if there was a vehicle with the engine running parked next to his cabin. If not…she'd honk.

*What if he's passed out due to pain meds?*

Faith skipped over that part. He'd come out. She'd leave the truck running, roll down the window and tell him to call his sister and explain what happened, because he was affecting her life and her livelihood and she needed this job.

*"Clear things up with your sister! Now!"*

Faith sucked in a breath. Yes. That's how it would go. Then he would call Debra and she'd never have to see him again, except for when he drove past the Lighting Creek Ranch.

She slowed as she rounded the corner where Drew had driven off the edge. The vehicle was still down there. Her heart sank. Drew was probably passed out in his cabin and she was about to rouse him.

There was no place to turn around, so she had no choice but to continue up the road. The first open spot was in the clearing where the cabin sat. In for a dime, in for a dollar, as her dad liked to say.

The cabin door was propped open when she pulled into the clearing, but there was no tall, dark-haired guy in sight. Faith pulled up next to the truck parked beside the shop building and left the engine running as planned.

Nothing.

She gave the horn a quick honk, her nerves jerking at the sound. What she wouldn't give to have Sully in the truck with her. She should have stopped to pick him up...but if she'd stopped, she might have lost her nerve.

No sign of life.

If her shoulders weren't so tight, they would have sagged in defeat. Did she sit and pound the horn, or suck it up and knock on the cabin's open door?

She'd check the shop. Faith got out of the vehicle and slowly approached the building, as if afraid that something—or someone— would burst out of the door before she got there.

*Suck. It. Up.*

She knocked on the metal door, then after waiting a few seconds, pushed it open to find a thoroughly organized work area. Everything was in its place, the floor swept, the benches clear. If Drew worked on projects here, he didn't currently have one in progress, although there was a big stack of lumber along one wall and a table saw set up close by. Faith closed the door again and turned toward the house, then stopped.

She couldn't do it. The anger that had propelled her up the mountain had dissipated. No...it had been beat into submission by the knee-jerk fears that were forcing their way into her brain. She was alone, on a mountain, with a stranger. The stranger was related to her boss. She'd saved him from a mud puddle, but he was a stranger all the same and she needed to get the hell out of there.

"Can I help you?"

Faith nearly jumped out of her skin as the low voice sounded from behind her. She whirled to find Drew standing on the porch outside his open front door, buttoning a shirt over his broad chest.

Again she felt very close to hating him for making her feel this way. Her reactions were not his fault, but it was demoralizing to discover she hadn't healed as much as she'd thought she had.

"Yeah, you can." The words sounded choked as she fought to control the fight-or-flight instinct. She pressed a hand to her chest, her voice sounding slightly more normal as she said, "Tell your sister about the accident. You've put me in a hard situation by not telling her."

She moved toward her running vehicle as she spoke, keeping her eyes on Drew and doing her best to look as though she was casually sauntering. He frowned deeply as she opened the door and took refuge behind it. Once the barrier was between her and the man on the porch, she felt better.

"I need this job," she continued.

"Deb won't hold it against you for not telling her about this."

Faith wasn't so sure.

He started down the steps, then stopped as her back stiffened. "She'll hold it against me," he said. Faith's chin came up, but before she could speak, he added, "I'll talk to her and mention that I wanted to explain before you said anything to her."

One corner of his mouth moved, quirking up into a humorless half smile that drew her attention to the fact that he had a nice mouth. She did not want to notice things like that about Drew Miller. It felt too dangerous.

"I would appreciate that very much." She gave him an unsmiling nod and prepared to duck into the cab of her truck.

"Thank you."

She straightened, looking at him over the top of the door. "Excuse me?"

"I owe you a thank-you."

"Yes. You do." She saw no reason to deny it. She got into the driver's seat when he moved toward her, pulled the door shut and locked it, hoping he would think it was an automatic feature of her vehicle—which it was not. He was her boss's brother, after all.

As he got closer, she rolled down the window a couple of inches, doing her best not to look like some kind of weirdo barricading herself in a car—although she'd do the exact same thing if she had a do-over. Fear and survival instinct trumped hurt feelings or seeming paranoid.

He tilted his head so he could see her face through the window, his frown more perplexed than threatening.

"Why are you afraid of me?"

Her heart stopped as she stared into his cool blue eyes. Knowing she looked frightened bothered her.

Faith moistened her lips, noted how his gaze followed the movement. This guy noticed details. He read people. He'd read her.

"I need to go." She owed him no explanations, and she didn't want to say anything that would come back to haunt her later. Such as, *You remind me strongly of my assailant.*

She didn't talk about her attack. Didn't want it to define her, didn't want it to control her life any more than it already did. So she would drive away and deal with Debra tomorrow.

"I know you do."

There was something in his voice that made her hand pause on the gearshift.

"How?" The old Faith, the confident, bulletproof Faith, popped her head up.

He shrugged his broad shoulders, making the fabric ripple. "I served long enough to know scared people when I see them. Hell, I was one of them sometimes."

She swallowed dryly, her hand still on the gearshift. "I see."

"What scares you, Faith?"

She blinked at him. Giving up secrets meant giving up power. Or at least it felt that way. Her cheeks went cold, then warm. She was astonished to find that she was tempted to blurt out the truth. To a stranger. "How do you feel today?" she asked him instead.

The sudden change of topic seemed to surprise him. It surprised her, but it also put her back in control of a situation she'd been in danger of losing control of.

"Sore as hell. But alive. Thank you for rolling me onto my back last night."

She gave a small snort. "Least I could do."

Something changed then. Momentarily lightened. Emphasis on momentarily. Faith was no longer a woman who allowed herself to be lulled into a sense of false security by a charming remark or smile.

"I'll call my sister."

"I'd appreciate it."

He shifted his weight. "I don't know what it is about me that sets you off, but I promise you I'm not an ax murderer or whatever my sister led you to believe."

Relief washed over her as Drew provided a logical motivation for her fear. An excuse. She grabbed it with both hands. "She didn't say anything to make me think you were… that." But her inflection made it clear Debra had said things about his "issues"—which she had.

"Maybe not an ax murderer, but she paints me in a way that makes people wonder if I'm one step away from going postal."

And what was she supposed to say to that?

She'd called Jolie from work that afternoon to ask about Drew. Jolie said he was a stand-up guy.

*Was.*

Jolie hadn't talked to him since he'd returned home, since life and the military had changed him.

Faith took hold of the gearshift again.

They were neighbors. She worked with his sister. She was going to see Drew Miller again, and she didn't want this situation hanging over her head. She put the truck in Reverse but kept her foot on the brake as she forced herself to do the hard thing. "The way I act around you has nothing to do with your sister."

His gaze narrowed, but other than that he didn't move a muscle. He waited for her to continue, which made her wonder if he was afraid of spooking her. "Almost two years ago, I was attacked by a man in a parking lot at a rodeo. A…big man."

An expression of dawning understanding transformed his features. Softened them to a degree.

"And I'm a big guy."

"You are."

He gave a very slow nod, his gaze dropping as he once again folded his arms. When he brought his gaze back up, she was surprised at how open it was. "I'm sorry to hear that happened to you."

Faith gave a jerky nod, but didn't answer.

"It explains a few things."

"I didn't want you to blame your sister for putting ideas in my head."

"You know that we're going to run into each other from time to time. I might…" he casually shrugged his heavy shoulders "…drive off the mountain or something."

She didn't crack a smile at the unexpected joke, even though a small part of her wanted to. "I hope that time will make things better," she said stiffly.

"One can hope."

She started to ease her foot off the brake, needing very much to get out of there. To escape not only the situation, but the odd feeling that she'd just found someone who understood.

"I'm sorry I make you nervous, Faith."

"Yeah." Her voice was little more than a throaty whisper, because she hadn't expected empathy and didn't know how to deal with it. "Me, too."

With that, she stepped on the gas, swung the truck in a wide arc, then started back down the rutted road to the Lightning Creek Ranch and safety.

# CHAPTER FOUR

DREW FOLLOWED THROUGH on his promise to Faith and drove to Eagle Valley Community College where he would confess to his sister that he'd rolled his rig off the mountain, thus freeing Faith from her dark secret. He wouldn't have told Deb at all if Faith hadn't been involved.

Deb left him cooling his heels in her outer office with her long-suffering associate, Penny, as she finished a phone call and made another. Finally, she welcomed him into her personal space, which was decorated in the same minimalist, yet expensive-looking style as her house. Lots of leather and glass. Single orchids. That kind of stuff. Drew was more of an overstuffed-chair, coffee-table-you-could-put-your-feet-on guy, so he'd never felt comfortable in his sister's sphere.

"How are you feeling?"

Drew managed to keep a straight face, despite her solicitous tone. "I'm sore."

"Have you intensified your workouts?"

"No. I rolled the Jeep night before last and got banged up."

The gold pen Deb had been holding fell out of her hand and rolled across the desk. "Were you drinking?"

Drew scowled at her. "What the hell kind of question is that?"

"A reasonable one," she defended. "People with your affliction tend to self-medicate."

"Deb...stop with the affliction talk, okay? And I'm not self-medicating." He was afraid to. He was afraid of disappearing down a rathole if he started depending on substances to help him through the long days and longer nights. He hoped like hell that he wouldn't be driven back to the nightmare drugs that had made him feel like the walking dead. "I swerved to miss a deer and over-corrected. It was rainy and slick."

She studied him for a long moment, as if trying to make him squirm like one of her employees. He wondered if Deb could make Faith squirm. She had backbone, but she was new on the job, and probably on probation.

She was also the reason he was there, having yet another uncomfortable meeting with his sister. "Are you all right?" she finally asked.

"Yeah. Faith Hartman heard the wreck and came to my assistance."

Deb's eyes widened. "She didn't say a thing."

"I asked her not to."

"Why?"

Drew cocked an eyebrow. "Because I didn't want you peppering her with questions that should be directed at me…like whether I was drinking." Deb flushed. "I told her I'd tell you in my own time."

"She did ask to speak with me yesterday," Debra said with a thoughtful frown.

He got to his feet. "Let's leave Faith out of this. She's my neighbor, your employee. Period. She shouldn't be in the middle of family matters."

And he didn't want to add more stress to her life. She'd remained in his thoughts the night before, long after she'd confessed her past, and he'd woke up thinking about her. He told himself it was because his protective instinct was kicking in. He had an idea of what she was going through and he felt for her. That was all.

When Deb remained silent, he assumed she accepted his logic and decided to make good his escape. "See you around."

"I heard there was a lumber delivery at the cabin."

Drew stopped with his hand on the doorknob and turned back. "How?"

"That's not important. What on earth are you doing up there?"

*None of your business.*

Except it was half her business. She and Drew had inherited equal interest of their grandfather's mountain hideaway years ago, and he now leased her half of the property.

"Do you really care?"

"I'm interested."

"I'm not building a bunker or anything."

"That's not funny."

"Wasn't meant to be." He let out a breath that made his shoulders sag. "I'm going ahead with the renovations that Lissa mapped out."

Deb's eyebrows came together. "Is that a good idea?"

Drew pretended to consider for a moment before saying, "Yes. I think it is. It's something Maddie and I can work on together over the summer."

Deb gave a brittle laugh. "Oh, I'm certain she'll *love* that."

Deb knew next to nothing about Maddie. She was the most hands-off aunt he knew of. Maddie was acknowledged on her birthday and at Christmas, and Drew was certain that was only because it was expected.

"She will. And so will I."

"Drew...you need to think about this. If Maddie comes to stay with you full-time, is she really going to want to live in a mountain cabin? Even if it is renovated?" Deb cleared her throat. "Wouldn't it be fairer to her to move to one of those nice neighborhoods they're building on the west end of town?"

Drew gave his sister a long, hard look, wondering what her objective was. Did she honestly care about what was best for Maddie? Or was she just trying to make him fit the mold so he wouldn't embarrass her?

"I don't know. I'll cross that bridge when I come to it, and in the meantime, I'm renovating the cabin." He let himself out of the office before she could say anything else to add to his already bad mood.

The door clicked shut behind him and after giving Penny what he hoped was a pleasant nod, he headed down the hallway toward the exit. Nobody raised his blood pressure like his sibling. He gave a small snort as he unlocked the truck. She probably thought the same about him.

Drew parked next to his brother-in-law's shop a few minutes before Maddie's school bus was due to arrive at three thirty. Pete, who was elbow-deep in a trash pump repair, gave him a grunt of greeting.

Earlier that morning, as soon as Maddie had caught the bus to school and Cara had taken off for work, they'd winched the Jeep up the side of the mountain and towed it to the shop, where it now sat, listing sadly on its axles.

Drew was going to have to explain to his daughter about the accident and he wasn't looking forward to it. Maddie was a resilient kid, but she'd lost her mother, had nearly lost her father, and she didn't need to hear that she'd almost lost him again. He wouldn't exactly lie, but he was going to gloss over a few things. Pretty much, he'd almost hit a deer and had a little accident. Then he'd come up with a way to distract her.

"Doing okay?" Pete asked as he finished ratcheting a bolt into place.

Drew idly rubbed his left shoulder, testing for pain. The bumps and bruises from his deer encounter were nothing compared to the percussion injuries he'd suffered in Afghanistan. Injuries he'd ignored as he'd done what he could to help pull his buddies from the wreckage—it was only afterward that his body had shut down. The doctors had been amazed at what he'd managed to do despite a gaping head wound, broken ribs and a punctured lung. Sheer adrenaline had carried him through—then abandoned him. He'd gone into shock, waking up in the hospital to the news that he'd lost three friends.

He swallowed dryly. "I'm good. Not looking forward to explaining to Mads."

"Understandable." Pete put down the wrench and got to his feet, dusting off his hands on his jeans.

Maddie essentially had three parents now. Pete—Lissa's brother—and his wife Cara had taken Maddie in after Lissa's death, with the idea that she'd stay with them until Drew's tour of duty ended. Then came the blast, the hospital stay, followed by five more months of duty. And the nightmares. He'd had to confess those to Pete and Cara when he'd arrived back in Eagle Valley four months ago, and he'd confessed about the one he'd had a few nights ago—which was why Maddie wouldn't be staying with him as much as she hoped during the summer.

Pete jerked his head toward the line of lawn mowers near the bay door. "Those are all yours."

"I'll take a few with me today, pick the rest up tomorrow."

The school bus rumbled up to the end of the driveway and the door opened with a hydraulic hiss. A few seconds later, Maddie came around the nose of the bus and headed for the shop, her expression brightening when she saw Drew step out of the bay door.

"Dad!"

His heart twisted, as it always did at the sight of his beautiful daughter. "Hey, tiger." Before he'd left for his last tour of duty, he'd swung her up in the air when she got home from school and she'd thrown her head back and laughed. Now she was twelve, almost thirteen, and swinging in the air was no longer the thing to do. Instead they bumped fists and then she gave him a bear hug.

"Can I stay with you this weekend?" she asked, tilting her head back to look up at him. It was all Drew could do not to push her glasses a little farther up her nose. Lissa had had the same problem. Glasses simply hadn't stayed in place.

Before he could answer, tell her that she wouldn't be staying overnight, her eyes went wide. "What happened to the Jeep?"

Pete and Drew exchanged quick glances, then Drew said, "I swerved to hit a deer yesterday."

"And wrecked the Jeep?"

Maddie sounded horrified, so he made an extra effort to sound casual. "It was rainy. It slid off the road."

Maddie headed for the vehicle, her backpack bouncing on her back. She inspected the damage with a critical eye, making Drew glad that the Jeep was topless. As it was, she had no way of knowing it'd rolled. "Are you going to be able to fix it, Uncle Pete?"

"It'll be better than it was when I get done with it."

"Good." She turned back to Drew. "Is the deer all right?"

He almost laughed. "Yeah, honey. I swerved, remember?"

"Good. Sorry about the Jeep, but glad about the deer." She gave her father a side-long look. "Does this mean I won't be spending the night this weekend?"

Maddie knew about his nightmares, knew why he spent his nights alone. She was also convinced that if she moved in, then he wouldn't have them anymore. "Because you'll have me there," she'd told him a few months ago, after his discharge.

"I just…think it would be best. But we can have pizza tonight, and I'll get you first thing in the morning."

Maddie didn't argue. She didn't look happy, but she didn't argue. "Okay, but it really has to be first thing."

"How does 6:00 a.m. sound?"

"Horrible," Pete muttered.

"Ignore him," Maddie said with a grin. "I'll be waiting on the porch."

THIRTY MINUTES TO quitting time. Faith pulled her attention back to the open folder in front of her. A big part of her job involved pulling old files and scanning the information into digital format so that alumni who'd graduated prior to the digital age could have easy access to their records.

Faith doubted that she would have liked the job before the assault. She'd enjoyed interacting with people, but now she preferred being alone, having minimal contact with her fellow employees. Working her way through the archives while listening to music. Essentially hiding from the world. The job made her feel safe, but the hours did seem to drag on.

"Faith?"

Her head jerked up at the sound of her boss's voice, and her heart did a guilty double beat—which wasn't fair. It sucked being caught between a rock and a hard place. But if push came to shove, she owed more loyalty to Debra than to her brother…even if, hands down, she preferred the man who reminded her of her attacker. What did that say about her?

That she liked having a job in safe surroundings.

"Yes?" She forced a bright note into her voice while wondering if she was about to be taken down for hiding vital information from her superior.

Debra glanced at the clock. "Would you stop by my office before you go home?"

"Certainly. I'll be there in twenty minutes."

"Thank you." Debra didn't bother with her fake smile, which made Faith's stomach tighten a little more. After Debra left, she closed the file. She'd worked through her break, as she often did—it wasn't like she really needed to sit in the small staff room and socialize—so she wasn't cheating the college by leaving early. She'd put in her hours.

What now? She let her head fall back, tried to remember a time when she hadn't automatically expected the worst.

Actually, it was very easy to remember that time—it was her entire life up until the assault had shifted her perspective. She was getting damned tired of shifted perspective.

Faith set the closed file on top of her Done pile and pushed her chair away from her desk. Why wait to find out what Debra wanted? If it was bad news, then she might as well get it now. She grabbed her purse, locked the door to her small basement office and headed for the stairs rather than the elevator. When she reached the registrar's office, she gave a quick rap on the open inner-office door. Debra looked up, then waved her inside.

"Please close the door."

Faith already had it half-shut.

"My brother told me about his accident—and your part in aiding him. Thank you."

Relief washed over her. Drew Miller had been as good as his word. "I'm glad you understand. I didn't feel right keeping the matter quiet, but he wanted to tell you himself."

"I do understand." Debra gave her shoulders an odd little roll before meeting Faith's gaze. "However…in the future…if something of a serious nature occurs, I would very much appreciate a heads-up. Just a hint that I should be aware that all is not well in my brother's life. You don't have to spill all the beans—just let me know I need to look into things."

The warm feeling of relief had started evaporating at the word *however*, and by the time Debra was done speaking, Faith was once again in defensive mode.

"I can't get involved in your family matters." She should have made this position clear from the very beginning, shouldn't have agreed to meet Debra's brother, but she'd caved to stay on Debra's good side—and because she believed in equine therapy. Now she regretted that decision.

"I'm not asking you as a boss. Please understand that." Faith's eyebrows rose. "Drew is not the man he used to be and until he is… well, it would help me to know what's going on. So that I can help him."

A hard knot was forming in Faith's stomach. "I doubt I'll see your brother again."

"That's very possible. But…" Debra's expression became even more serious and there was a faint pleading note in her voice as she said, "You are his neighbor, and if you notice anything unusual, will you please tell me? I'm worried about Drew. I want him to get better."

Faith sucked in a breath. "I don't think I'll see Drew," she repeated, hoping that Debra would believe her. "However, I will tell you if I notice anything disturbing."

As in *very* disturbing. Call-the-sheriff disturbing. Otherwise, she was not getting involved.

"Thank you." Debra smiled in a grateful kind of way.

"Of course."

Faith was almost to the door when Debra said, "Faith? Please understand how much I appreciate this. I won't forget your help."

Faith gave a quick nod and left the office, wondering what would happen if she did know about something and kept her mouth shut. Deb might not take overt action, but she could make Faith miserable. That said, Faith knew with a certainty she wasn't going to spy on Drew. Her perspective of the man had shifted since the accident. Drew was nothing like her attacker. He was a guy who'd been through hell and was fighting his way back. Even though she'd automatically locked her truck door during their confrontation the night before, she'd started to feel a connection with the man. He understood. She knew that instinctively. And he was hurting, just as she was, which made her wish she hadn't needed to lock the door to protect herself. That she could allow herself to trust him. That maybe they could share insights.

*Nice fantasy, Hartman.* Like she was ready to open up to a virtual stranger.

*But you did. Last night.*

Faith shushed her small voice, unlocked her truck and got inside, tossing her tote onto the passenger seat. She'd continue to handle things in the safest way possible—alone.

As soon as she got home, Faith set up the barrels in the arena and saddled Tommy, her black-and-white paint barrel horse. She needed to blow off some steam after the unsettling day. She had a job where she could earn a decent paycheck with no unexpected triggers, because no one except for Debra and the occasional administrative associate ever ventured into her realm. And because her job seemed so perfect, maybe she was imagining threats where there were none.

No *maybe* about it. She was overreacting. Manufacturing trouble. It wasn't like Debra could fire her because she didn't spy on her brother. That was a lawsuit waiting to happen.

If she could prove it.

Tommy was in the mood to run and Faith let him do his thing, losing herself in the moment as she tried to make every run perfect. She'd only run the barrels once or twice a week when she'd been in serious competition, spending most of her training time working on flexing, bending and speed. But she was no longer in serious competition, so she could essentially do whatever she wanted, and tonight, she wanted to run.

When she was done, both she and the gelding were sweating. Their times were improving, and as Faith dismounted, she felt a familiar stirring of resentment. She'd been on track to make the National Finals Rodeo when the attack had taken her out of competition. It was supposed to have been her year. And then her world had been turned inside out by a sicko.

Faith returned to her too-quiet house, Sully close by her side, reminded herself that she liked the quiet and then turned on some music. Maybe it was her encounter with Debra, or maybe it was simply the summer stretching ahead of her without a lot to fill it that had her feeling antsy—at loose ends.

Last summer, she'd been focused on getting her feet back under her, even though it felt like a year should have been a long enough time to get it back together. It hadn't been.

She'd made two attempts to compete in small rodeos after the anniversary of her attack had passed, having convinced herself everything would somehow be better after the one-year mark. On her first attempt, she hadn't even made it out of the driveway. On the second, she'd driven to the rodeo, but once there, the sights and sounds—the smells—had brought on a full-fledged panic attack. She'd tried to force things too soon.

Would she try again this year?

She wanted that part of her life back. Deep down, she was still as competitive as hell, and resented not being able to do what she once did so well.

Solution?

She needed to suck it up. Sign up for some rodeos even if she didn't go…and, if she was serious about returning to competition, she needed to face the unpleasantness of demanding her custom barrel racing saddle back from her ex-boyfriend. The saddle she rode in now was perfectly adequate, but it wasn't the saddle she'd bought with her winnings. The saddle she'd waited a year to be made and which represented her as a professional. The saddle that she bet Hallie Johnson was probably riding in right now. It hadn't taken long for

Faith's ex to hook up with the hottest girl on the circuit.

She reached for the phone, then put it back down.

Did she really want to ruin her evening by contacting Jared?

No.

Which was why she didn't have her saddle back. No night ever seemed worth ruining. A year ago, she hadn't needed the saddle, so she'd never called. This year…she wasn't letting herself off the hook.

Faith picked up the phone, found Jared's name in her contacts and pushed the number. It rang and her heartbeat ratcheted up ever so slightly. Even small confrontations were harder for her than they'd once been. The call went to voice mail, and Faith wondered if it was because he didn't recognize the number. Or because he did. Maybe Jared didn't feel like discussing saddles with his ex.

She hesitated, then left a message. "Hey, Jared. It's Faith. I'm calling to set up a time to get my saddle. Call me back."

She hung up, glad on the one hand that she'd gotten the ball rolling, nervous now about the return call—which came within minutes.

"Faith! How are you?"

"I'm…better." Her voice sounded totally normal as she spoke to the guy who'd let her down when she needed him most.

"Still working at the riding stable?"

"No. I got a job at a college. Benefits and everything."

"Excellent." He spoke a little too jovially. "You're calling about the saddle."

"Yeah. I am."

Before she could ask him about setting up a time and place to meet, he said, "You know, I've been meaning to call you about that saddle. I'd kind of like to buy it from you."

"Starting a new rodeo career?"

It took him a second to catch on, but when he did, he laughed. "No. I'm not barrel racing. But since you won't be using it—"

"Who said I won't be using it?"

There was a healthy pause, then Jared said, "You're going to start competing again?"

"I might. And even if I don't, it's still my saddle and I want it back. For sentimental reasons if nothing else."

"On the other hand, you could have some cold hard cash, and that trumps sentiment every time, right?"

"Who has my saddle?"

"Uh…"

"Who, Jared?"

"Does it matter? If you don't want to sell, I'll get it to you."

"Ship it."

"Ship it? That gets into some serious bucks, babe."

"You gave my saddle away. Get it back to me or I'll see you in small-claims court."

Her heart was hammering, but she also felt empowered. Like her old self.

"Faith—"

"Send it to Eagle Valley Community College. The registrar's office. I'll give you the street address when you're ready."

"All right." There was a sullen note to his voice—almost as if he were dreading the task of retrieving her saddle from whomever he'd given it to. Tough. "Give me the address."

Faith rattled off the address, made him read it back to her, then asked, "When can I expect to receive it?"

"Soon."

"Give me a ballpark."

"Give me a break. We both know you're not going to use it."

Faith just stopped the *screw you* from dropping from her lips. "You have two weeks, or I'm going to file the court papers." Even if it meant traveling to Flathead County, where he now lived.

"Fine." He hung up without another word, leaving Faith holding her phone, amazed at how good it had felt to stand up for herself.

# CHAPTER FIVE

TAKING MADDIE DOWN the mountain to Pete and Cara's on Saturday afternoon was as hard as ever.

"Next weekend," he promised as she trudged out of the cabin to the truck.

"Unless something happens."

There was a sullen note in her voice that Drew chose to ignore. They'd had a good day and would hopefully have another good day on Sunday. After picking her up early that morning—seven, as opposed to six—he'd laid out the drawings Lissa had made of the cabin renovation on the kitchen table and they'd gone over them together.

"I like her handwriting," Maddie said at one point, and Drew agreed. Lissa had had a funky offbeat style, half-cursive, half-print. And, crazy thing, if he closed his eyes, he swore he could smell her scent on the paper. It was as if the three of them were together again.

They hadn't had enough time as a family, and if he had it to do over again, he probably wouldn't have gone career military. He would have done his first tour, then found work as a contractor or something.

But he'd made his choice, back when he was young and invincible, and his only regret, really, was the time he hadn't gotten to spend with his family. That was now one giant regret.

"If something happens, we'll deal with it."

"I want to spend more time with you."

*And I want to stop feeling like a failure of a dad.* They were a family again, but they weren't.

"I'm not afraid of your stupid dreams."

*I am.*

"Maddie… I can't explain everything, because I don't understand everything, but give me a little more time, okay?"

"One of my friends told me that you're crazy. That's why I don't live with you."

"I'm not crazy." *Even though your Aunt Deb thinks I'm close.*

"I know *that*." Maddie shifted in her seat. "That's my point. We should live together once the cabin is done. Because you're not crazy and that way everyone will know it."

Maddie's words made him die a little inside. "I agree."

"You do?"

"I want us to be a family as soon as possible."

"But it won't be all that soon." Before Drew could answer, Maddie asked, "Are you seeing a head doctor?"

Drew choked back a laugh at her overly serious tone. "I have."

"He couldn't fix the nightmares?"

"No. He told me some things to try, and I did and they helped, but they didn't cure me."

"You're probably going to tell me not to get my heart set on anything, right?"

Drew gave his daughter a quick sideways look. "I want to be a family," he said quietly. "And we will be."

"Yeah." She turned her head to look straight ahead, but Drew caught the sheen of tears in her eyes. He reached over and touched her knee. Almost immediately, she leaned across the seat so that her head rested on his arm. "I want us to be normal."

Drew blinked back his own tears. "We will

be. We just need to give it time. We'll build the cabin and…"

She raised her head, staring expectantly at him, the tears making her eyes look a darker brown. Like her mother's eyes.

"And we'll think of more things to do."

It took her a moment to say, "I'm almost thirteen, and in five years, I'll be going to college."

The thought made his throat start to close. Five years. A heartbeat.

Yeah. They needed to get normal. Fast.

THE MORE FAITH thought about Jared giving her saddle to some unknown woman, the angrier she got. Although she'd bet a dollar the woman was Hallie Johnson…unless Hallie had gotten tired of him.

*We both know you won't use it.*

Even if she never used her saddle at a rodeo, she'd use it again. Out of sheer spite, if nothing else.

After running Tommy through his patterns, then feeding the horses, she went to her computer and looked up the Montana rodeo schedule. Her hands froze on the keyboard when the search came up, but she forced herself to open the page, just as she'd done last year, and look for a rodeo close by. One that still had entries available.

There were several small rodeos still looking for contestants. All she wanted was a small venue where she could get her feet wet. Run a slow pattern, load Tommy and go home. Once she survived that, then she could think about more serious competition. She might not get to the level she was at before, but she could reclaim the part of her life that the asshole had stolen away from her.

A part she'd been hiding from and missed dearly.

Faith closed her laptop. Why couldn't she get back to her old level? Tommy still had some good years left in him. He was only eight.

*We both know you won't use it.*

Yeah, Jared? We'll see about that. All she had to do was make it through that first rodeo and she'd show Jared who would and would not be using her saddle.

On Sunday morning, Jolie stopped by on her way to the family's ranch supply store where she worked afternoons doing the books. She was six months pregnant with twins and assured Faith that she was certain that she and her husband were stopping at two kids.

"What if I got pregnant with twins again?" she asked, pressing her hand against her lower back. "We'd have to get a bigger truck."

Faith laughed as she poured herbal tea. Between jobs and pregnancies, she and Jolie didn't see each other much, but they had the kind of relationship that was easy to pick up whenever they found themselves together.

She'd thought about asking Jolie to go to her first rodeo with her, but her friend would be seven months pregnant by that time and, honestly? Faith preferred to handle matters alone. It was her way, had always been her way, and when her therapist had encouraged her to reach out to those close to her for help, she'd shuddered at the thought. Faith liked people, loved socializing—or rather, she had—but she dealt with trouble on her own.

*And how's that working?*

Faith told her inner voice to kindly be quiet and focused on having tea with her friend, catching up on the Brody sisters and anyone else Jolie could think to talk about. She hadn't mentioned Drew's accident on the mountain yet, so Faith brought it up, to avoid another situation like that with Debra.

"He wrecked his Jeep?" Jolie asked on a gasp. "That beautiful classic Jeep?"

"It looked repairable."

Faith went on to describe the wreck, the night, glossing over pretty much everything, and when she was done, Jolie sank back in her chair. "I'm glad he wasn't hurt. Glad you were there to help."

"So am I," Faith replied. And she was. He would have been in trouble without her. It was the aftermath with his sister that had caused her grief.

"I know you know Drew, but what about his sister?"

"Your boss?" Jolie asked with a quirky half smile.

"That's the one."

"She was on the cheer squad with me. Tried to be everyone's boss. I didn't like her."

Faith bit her lip.

"Go on. You can say it. You don't like her either."

"I guess I'm asking if her bark is worse than her bite?"

Jolie considered the question for a second

or two. "For the most part, yes, unless she's embarrassed in some way. Then she seriously lashes out. Or she used to. Maybe she's changed in the last decade." Jolie brought her cup to her lips, took a sip, then asked, "Trouble?"

"No. She asked me to meet with Drew about equine therapy. He turned me down. I'm thinking I shouldn't have said yes to the meeting. That it would have been better to keep everything on a professional level."

"It's a small town, Faith. Hard to do that sometimes. I think it was perfectly natural to agree to help."

"Good to know. And maybe I shouldn't have mentioned the equine therapy."

Jolie put her cup down. "Honey. Everyone knows that Drew Miller has been through hell and back." She gave a small snort. "I know quite a few ladies who'd like to help him through his recovery, but he's having none of that."

Faith gave a slight nod. She didn't like the idea of ladies offering Drew 'help,' which was both startling and unsettling. She looked up to see Jolie regarding her with a questioning expression and changed the subject, asking whether she could borrow a couple of Jolie's goats. She needed them to eat the weeds around the barn.

"Say the word and Dylan will drop them off."

"Word."

Jolie laughed and promised that her husband would bring a few goats by the next weekend. When Faith and Sully walked her to her car, Jolie stopped just outside the gate and looked around the place. "Are you doing all right here?"

"I am."

"I kind of worried about you living alone after the incident."

Faith automatically reached down to touch Sully's head. "I have a protector, and…I'm moving on. Doing okay."

Jolie studied her face for a moment, then gave a quick nod. "Good to hear. But if you ever need anything, remember we're just on the other side of the field."

"I know."

Jolie slipped on her sunglasses, then tilted them down to look Faith in the eye. "And by anything, I mean talking, too." She glanced at the house, then back at Faith. "Sometimes it's easy to spend too much time alone. Don't."

Faith ruffled Sully's fur as Jolie walked to her truck and awkwardly hefted herself into the driver's seat. She started the truck, waved, then headed down the drive.

It *was* easy to spend too much time alone. But right now, Faith didn't have a cure for that—not one she was comfortable with.

AFTER SPENDING THE weekend with his daughter, Drew had the proud feeling that Maddie could grow up to be an engineer or an architect. She had no trouble visualizing Lissa's carefully drawn plans for the cabin—the small addition, which would add sleeping space and privacy for a teenager, the improved kitchen and bathroom—and was all about starting construction immediately.

When they were done staking out the area for the concrete slab that would form the foundation of the additions, they headed to the shop to continue work on the lawn mowers he was repairing in return for the Jeep repairs.

Maddie happily chatted away about school, her friends, her teachers—a world Drew was fairly removed from. He'd met with the teachers after returning home, but he needed to know more about her life, become more involved in it. Except asking questions drove home the point that he hadn't been there for his family. He didn't know what other dads, more conventional dads, did. He decided to ask the questions anyway. A penance to pay.

"I thought your best friend was Maia."

"She was my best friend until Casey moved here. They're next-door neighbors, and Maia and Casey do *everything* together now."

"Do you miss her?" He and Pete had been best friends since the age of nine and nothing had shifted there—not even when Drew married Pete's little sister.

"We still see each other." Maddie's lips pressed together as she worked to undo a screw holding the shroud onto the mower. She was his official screw-loosener. "She was one of the ones who said I couldn't live with you because you're crazy."

"Sometimes people say things—"

Maddie's gaze flashed up. "Not to their friends. Not when it's mean."

"Good point."

Maddie went back to her screws. "That's what Aunt Cara told me."

"She's right." And she had more of a hand in raising his daughter than he did.

"Now I'm best friends with Shayla. She has horses."

"Do you like horses?" Something he should probably know.

She gave him a *duh* look. "Everyone likes horses, Dad."

"I'm kind of intimidated by them." He took the wrench that Maddie set down and loosened the carburetor.

"How come?"

"Because," he said without looking at her, "I tried to show off for a girl once by riding her horse. It bucked me off, and I broke my wrist. The only time I'd ever been on a horse barely lasted ten seconds and I ended up in a splint."

Maddie rolled her eyes. "You must have done something wrong."

"Does no saddle or bridle qualify?"

Maddie started laughing. Drew loved the sound. There was just enough Lissa in her laughter to make him feel as if he would never truly lose his wife.

After they finished the last lawn mower, Maddie helped him clean up the bench, then dragged the mowers to the truck so Drew could load them in the back. "Why don't you get a real job?" she asked after he'd hefted the last mower into place.

Another question from Maia?

"I will. Right now, I want to work on the cabin. Get a few things in order." He closed the tailgate. "It has nothing to do with my accident." Which was what he called the blast. His accident. He hoped that made it more palatable for her. And that she would never look up any information about roadside bombs or ask pointed questions. He glanced away as the memories flashed.

"I told Maia that you didn't *have* to work and that you were a lot luckier than her dad."

Drew smiled and held out his fist. She grinned back as she bumped it with her own. "Nice comeback." Even though he hated that his daughter had to undergo cross-examination from her "friends."

"It's true, right?"

"I have enough that I don't have to go to work until I find a job I really like." He had a healthy savings account, and while his pension wasn't huge, it was enough to cover costs—food, fuel, materials for the cabin, as well as the yearly lease he paid Deb for her half of the mountain property and the check he gave Pete and Cara every month for Maddie's needs.

Those needs would grow as she matured. He wondered what a prom dress went for these days. The cost of Lissa's dress for their official first date had seemed astronomical at the time, but she'd looked so damned amazing in it. Nothing like the quiet girl who'd hung around the shop, watching as he and Pete tore into their latest project. That prom had become Drew's last first date ever. He and Lissa were never apart after that.

Things had been a little strange with Pete at first—suddenly, Pete's little sister was a bigger part of his best friend's life than he was—but eventually the weirdness subsided. Drew enlisted, Lissa went to college. They married and traveled from base to base…it had seemed like a good life at the time.

"You want to grab a pizza before I take you back?"

Maddie shook her head. "Let's reheat the mac and cheese." As they walked toward the house, she gave him a sidelong look. "Did you have a nightmare last night?"

He smiled a little. "No."

"Then I can stay next weekend?"

"Maddie..."

"Just checking. One of these days, you'll say yes."

Damn, but he hoped that was true. Five years was not long enough when he only saw his daughter part-time.

THE BLAST BROUGHT Drew rearing up out of bed. He tried to run for cover, but the sheets tangled around his legs, stopping his progress. He twisted, writhed, fought before hitting the floor face-first, jarring himself to full consciousness. The dust in the bedside rug filled his lungs as he took a deep gasping breath. No smoke.

The cabin wasn't on fire. No explosion, none in the offing.

He let out a shuddering breath and lowered his forehead back to the floor, blinking back tears. The twilight dreams were the worst; the dreams that came between sleep and waking, when the horrors of the past mixed with the reality of his present.

Finally, Drew pushed himself to his hands and knees, then rolled to sit on the floor with his back against the mattress. The room was intact. He hadn't struck out with his fists, fighting for survival. Good sign?

He let out a grim, choked laugh and then dropped his head back.

No.

He wasn't certain how long he sat that way before rubbing his hands over his face, then slowly getting to his feet. His body was stiff—from fighting demons as much as from his recent tumble down the mountain. He headed to the john in the dim morning light, took care of business, then splashed water on his face. The man who looked back at him from the mirror was not the man he wanted his daughter—or her friends—to see. Ever.

*Shit. Shit. Shit.*

He tore his gaze away from the gaunt-cheeked, hollow-eyed man in the mirror and stumbled toward the kitchen. He had ten hours to get it together before heading off the mountain to see his daughter. They were going to shop for supplies for a school project that evening—the last one for this school year—and it would probably be best if he didn't look like the walking dead.

MONDAY MARKED A change in Faith's attitude at work. Maybe it was the fact that Jared had given Faith's saddle away. Or maybe it was because enough was enough and she wasn't going to live her life choked with anxiety. Whatever the cause, Faith wasn't her usual diffident self when dealing with her boss on Monday. When Debra showed up in her office demanding that three files be found before the end of the day, Faith pointed out that the files had been marked "lost" several years ago.

"I'll try, but I can't guarantee success," she said simply, instead of making promises she couldn't keep and then confessing her failure at the end of the day, as she'd had to do the last time Debra had asked for the impossible.

"You've found other lost files," Debra pointed out.

"I go through the storage boxes, looking for misfiled folders when I have spare time." She gestured at the open door of the archives. "There are a lot of boxes in there."

She spoke calmly, respectfully, but with a no-nonsense tone that she'd never used before with her boss.

Debra blinked at her, and Faith assumed

that she was going to be told to find the folders regardless, but instead Debra said in a tight voice, "I would appreciate it if you did your utmost to find these folders ASAP."

Then she turned and left Faith's office, the sound of her heels echoing off the cinder block walls as she headed for the stairs.

Faith leaned her palms on her desk. The last thing she'd expected was for Debra to back down. Lost transcripts were an embarrassment to the college, and Debra hated anything that reflected negatively on her position as registrar.

But perhaps she'd sensed that Faith had had enough. Living in fear sucked, and transferring fear to all aspects of one's life sucked even more.

She was no longer going to do that.

She would be cautious, she would be careful, but she was not going to kiss ass or be pushed into doing things she didn't want to do, to be involved in things she didn't want to be involved in out of fear.

Her screw-you mood lasted until she returned home and, just as she'd finished her practice runs, Drew Miller's truck pulled into her driveway. Then screw-you shifted toward caution…but it wasn't because of Drew's physicality. It was because she'd yet to have an interaction with the man that wasn't fraught with tension.

And because she'd been thinking about him.

A lot.

She rode to the fence and waited as Drew got out of the truck and walked toward her. He stopped a few feet short of the rails, hooked one thumb in his front pocket in a gesture that telegraphed self-consciousness. So, (a) why was he here? And (b) what did he have to feel self-conscious about?

"Hi." He shifted his weight again, lifted his chin to meet her gaze.

"Hi."

Drew looked past her to the field where Buck and Freckles grazed. He frowned a little as he did so, which spiked Faith's curiosity. She dismounted, looped Tommy's rein over his neck and took a few steps forward. Giving up her position of power was huge, so maybe she was once again on the mend.

"I have a question," Drew began.

Now she was doubly curious. "Shoot," she said in an offhand way.

"Do I still freak you out?"

*Yes, but not in the same way as before.*

She still found his size intimidating, but equally disturbing was the fact that she was starting to see him in a different light. That she hadn't liked the idea of women offering him solace, which was illogical and unsettling.

"Not as much. I've seen you rolling in a mud puddle."

Instead of smiling, he met her gaze, his expression dead serious. "Could you work with me?"

Her heart almost stopped. Drew had refused help from the willing ladies Jolie had spoken of, but now he was coming to her? Why?

"On what?"

"I...uh...want to do something with my daughter. Something that she can continue to do, even if I don't." Faith frowned, and he continued, "Maddie has been living with my brother-in-law and his wife since my wife died two years ago. Since we don't live together, I want to do something with her that she enjoys."

"Does she ride?"

"No. But she has a friend who does. I thought she could learn the basics and maybe I can tag along and—"

"Pet some horses?" she asked mildly.

He gave her a you-got-me look. "I rode once in my life and I got bucked off. Maybe I need to face my fears."

"All of them?"

Her question seemed to surprise him. But after a second, he gave a grim nod. "Maybe. But most of all, I want to do something with my kid. If she likes it, I can buy her a horse. I think she'd like that."

Faith considered for a moment. "There's one reason I hesitate to do this."

"My size?"

"Your sister."

He rolled his eyes, then caught himself. "I'll handle Deb."

She moved closer, separated from the man by two feet of ground and three sturdy fence rails. "Here's the thing. I didn't want to meet with you about the equine therapy, but I agreed to the appointment to do my boss a favor. That turned out to be a mistake." She let out a breath, then told the hard truth. "I don't like my professional life and my personal life to entwine."

"What you do outside of work is your own business."

"I know."

"Deb knows it, too. She's pushed things because she's always gotten away with pushing. Push back."

She already had pushed back—today—and now she was waiting to see if there were consequences.

"What if she makes my life misery?"

He smiled grimly. "I'll speak with her." He shifted his weight again. "I understand if you say no…but I'm hoping you won't."

Faith closed her eyes, then opened them to find Drew watching her, his body tense, as if the answer she gave really mattered. As if it wouldn't be that easy for him to find another activity for him and his daughter to do together.

Maybe he really did want to do the therapy, which was essentially riding and caring for a horse. Finding comfort in a nonjudgmental animal.

"You could bring your daughter by next

weekend. Saturday." He didn't exactly burst into smiles, but his cheeks creased as the corners of his mouth lifted. And there was a warmth in his expression that hadn't been there a few seconds ago. He was truly glad she'd said yes.

"Morning or afternoon?"

"Morning. Nine o'clock, unless that's too early."

"Nine is fine. I pick her up at seven."

"Then it's a date."

His smile faded. "Yes. A date." He reached into his shirt pocket and pulled out a slip of paper, which he held out to her.

"What's this?" She gingerly took the paper from him.

"My phone number. If you change your mind, give me a call. No harm. No foul."

*Well played, Mr. Miller.* Because he'd been smart enough to give her an out, she might not need one.

"It's unlikely I'll call," she murmured. "But…thank you."

## CHAPTER SIX

FAITH KEPT DREW'S phone number under a magnet on her refrigerator as a reminder that she didn't have to do anything she didn't want to do—or that she wasn't ready to do.

She *could* do this. There might be some tense moments, but if she could make it through these lessons, then perhaps she would be able to compete in a rodeo. Start the long road back to competition—to practice accessing her rational brain even when her protective instincts were trying to kick in. And besides that, Drew didn't trigger her as he had upon first meeting. They'd been through quite a lot together in the short time she'd known him, and, while Drew and her assailant were similar in size and build, there were differences she hadn't keyed in on during their first meeting.

Her assailant had swaggered when he walked. Watched the bar with a cool, almost predatory gaze that she would recognize in a heartbeat now but had been oblivious to at the time. Drew was watchful but not calculating, and he walked with the confidence of an ex-military man—no swagger, no need to prove anything to the world. He appeared to have everything in his life under control, but according to his sister—hell, according to him—the picture wasn't real. He'd lost his wife, been injured overseas. He had demons. There were things about Drew she didn't know. Couldn't know.

But she also had a sense that, because of their backgrounds, they shared an understanding, which was why she thought about him so often. He was an unexpected kindred spirit. She wasn't ready to proclaim best-buddy status or anything, but she would work with him. And his daughter, whom she was curious to meet. Drew as a father created an interesting picture.

She had no idea if Debra was aware of the arrangement. Since Faith had stopped being so complaisant in her manner, Debra's attitude had also shifted. When they interacted, it was cooler, more professional, and Faith no longer got the feeling that Debra looked at her as a lesser being she could easily manipulate. Debra was a user, and Faith wasn't going to let herself be used.

Not anymore.

When she got home from work on Friday, she gave Tommy a short workout, riding the perimeter of the field after his suppling exercises, then released him to eat with his buddies. The house felt empty when she went back inside, even with Sully lying next to the table while she scrambled eggs for dinner. Maybe that was a good sign, a signal that she was ready to move forward, but the thought of doing something about her solitary state froze her up. She knew the Brody sisters, but was reluctant to impinge on their busy lives. Which meant she needed to make friends. Which meant putting herself out there.

Which was too damned scary to consider right now.

Okay…she was moving forward, but still had a long way to go.

"I CAN'T BELIEVE you did this," Maddie said for the sixth or seventh time since Drew had told her that he was going to do something about his fear of horses, and that she may as well learn to ride at the same time—if she wanted to.

Maddie wanted to.

She was still hammering on him to move to the cabin for the next school year, and he was still trying to make her understand that as soon as he felt ready, they would live together.

"It isn't like you're going to go off on me, is it?"

No. That was not an issue. "After I have a…dream…" such an inadequate word for having his world explode around him "it affects me physically. It takes me a long time to come down. I need to be alone then." *I don't want you to see me panting and near tears. Don't want to put you through that.*

"Are you, like…embarrassed?"

Drew thought about it. "That's part of it." Although he felt more vulnerable than embarrassed.

"Well, I guess taking riding lessons is a good way to be together." She cast him a sidelong look. "You aren't squeezing me out of the construction, are you?"

"Wouldn't dream of it." He gave a quick eyeroll at his use of the word *dream*, but

Maddie didn't seem to notice. "And if all goes well, you'll get to sleep in the room Mom designed for you."

"And you know as I get older, I'll be able to handle more stuff. Right?"

Drew gave a noncommittal nod and asked, "Have you got everything?" as they got into the truck to drive down to the Lightning Creek Ranch.

"I have my boots," Maddie held up her foot, showing him the new Western boots she and Cara had shopped for that week. "And a good attitude. What else do I need?"

"Mom used to say that," he said softly. It was the first time he'd heard Maddie say what had practically been Lissa's mantra.

"I know." Maddie gave him a small smile. "I miss her."

"Yeah. Me, too."

WHEN THEY GOT to the ranch, Faith had three horses tied up to the fence near the barn. Maddie sat staring through the windshield at them after Drew had parked.

"You ready?" he asked.

She sent him a nervous look. "I guess."

He reached out to pat her leg. "I'm the one who's supposed to be nervous."

Maddie gave him a candid look. "Are you?"

"Damned straight."

She laughed, her stiff shoulders giving a little as she reached for the door handle. "Then I'll have to be the brave one."

He wasn't lying about being scared—but it wasn't only horses. He was scared about his future with his daughter and, if he was honest, he'd have to admit to being a little afraid of the woman who'd just come out of the barn, her curly-haired, brown and black dog by her side. He'd been noticing a lot of little things about her when they were together, and that made him uneasy.

Faith gave him a quick nod to acknowledge his presence, then held out a hand to Maddie, a welcoming smile softening her features. She had a nice smile. A nice mouth, soft-looking and sweetly curved.

"Hi. I'm Faith. Glad you could stop by." She spoke to both, but her eyes were on Maddie.

"I'm Madison."

"Let's go meet the horses," Faith said. "And you can tell me how much experience you have." She looked over her shoulder at Drew and he saw a flash of unexpected amusement as she said, "I already know how much experience your father has."

"That's why we're here today," Maddie said in a surprisingly dry tone. His baby was growing up. Fast. Five years and she'd be gone. "I've been on a horse twice. I just walked around."

"Well, that's a start. Today we'll be on the ground the entire time. If you like it, you can decide if you want to come back."

"I think I'll want to come back," Maddie said as they approached the animals. "I've always liked horses. I just never had a chance to be around them."

Faith gestured to the open door of her tack room. "The first thing we do during lessons is to put on a helmet."

Drew didn't hesitate. He moved forward and picked up one of the three helmets hanging from coat hooks near the door. He tried it on, adjusted it, put it on again and tightened the chin strap. Maddie and Faith did the same.

Once they had their helmets on, Faith led the way toward the horses, stopping a few feet from the fence to start her safety talk. "You always let a horse know that you're coming up behind them…"

The lesson lasted for forty-five minutes, during which time Drew and Maddie approached horses, brushed horses, learned to pick up feet and then led the horses, making certain they walked at a respectful distance. "Never let a horse walk up on you," she told them.

*Same goes for a sister.* Although Deb hadn't been in contact lately, so maybe she'd accepted the hard fact that Drew was going to deal with matters on his own…or maybe Faith had told her about the lessons, and Deb thought she'd won. Didn't matter as long as she gave him his space.

His daughter seemed to be a natural around horses, cooing and talking as she groomed her mare. Drew was more matter-of-fact, as if he was washing a car or something.

"You should connect with him," Faith told him as he worked the brush over the horse's coat. Drew frowned at her and she said, "Horses have personalities. Feelings."

"I know that," he said quietly. "I just don't know how to connect."

"It takes time, but it helps if you talk to them a little."

"Fine. I'll talk." He moved toward the horse's head. "Hello…"

He shot Faith a look over his shoulder and she said, "Freckles."

Drew let out a pained breath, then turned back to the horse. "Hello, Freckles."

After they'd learned to lead, back and bend the horses—who knew horses had to bend?—they released the animals into the pasture. Maddie let out a happy sigh, then stopped in her tracks as a kitten poked its head out of the barn.

"Oh my gosh!"

"There's a litter of six in there," Faith said as Maddie scooped up the little ball of fur and tucked it under her chin. "A pregnant cat showed up a few weeks ago, and this is the result."

"Can I see the rest?"

"Sure."

As Maddie made her way through the open door, Faith casually leaned an arm on the rail fence next to the barn and raised a cool gaze to Drew. As long as there was some distance between them, she seemed okay. The few times when they'd gotten close during the lesson, he'd felt her stiffen, but she'd held her position rather than retreating. That made him a little crazy. It was hell having her be afraid of him because of something he didn't do.

"Want to see the kittens?"

"Will you think me a monster if I say no?"

She laughed, the sound making him feel oddly warm inside. Maybe because he was used to seeing her either serious, stressed or anxious.

"Feeling better about horses?" she asked.

"A little. Feeling better about having me around?"

"Yes."

*Yes.* No explanation. No discussion. He wanted to know more.

"Facing your fears?"

"It's not exactly that. I'm not afraid of you anymore, but I'm still reacting sometimes. Since it stands to reason that I'm going to cross paths with…" Her mouth tightened. "I don't want to say, 'guys like you,' but that's pretty much it."

"No offense taken."

"I figure I need practice handling the reactions." She didn't quite look at him, as if talking about her fears was more challenging than she expected. "It's like my body is responding to cues my mind isn't able to control."

"Are you sure you want to control your reactions? I mean, after all, they keep you safe."

"Yes. They do. And I've given some thought to that."

"Personal question—you don't have to answer."

She raised her eyebrows.

"Have you had any kind of counseling?"

"About a year's worth."

"Takes time."

"Are you speaking from experience?"

"I'm not a big talker."

"So, no. Not speaking from experience."

"I had counseling. When I was in the hospital, recovering from the blast, I had… I don't know…anger issues. A manifestation of survivor guilt, maybe. And a head injury. So yeah. I had counseling."

"Are you still angry?"

"I'm not all the way happy." His instant response surprised him. He opened his mouth, closed it again. Finally, he said, "And I'm also not complaining. I'm doing okay. Handling things in a way that feels right to me. I have the anger thing under control." Except when he slept.

She didn't say anything, which made him feel as if he had to. But he didn't have a chance, because Maddie appeared at the door, four kittens cuddled against her chest. The Airedale came with her, looking up at her as if afraid that she was going to kidnap his charges. "Look at these little guys!"

"Yeah." He smiled and rubbed a couple tiny heads with his forefinger. "Cute. We should hit the road if we're going to get the footings poured."

"All right." She returned the kittens to the barn, then came back out dusting off her hands. "Dad and I are building an addition on the cabin, so that I can have a room of my own."

Drew looped an arm around his daughter's slim shoulders. "I'm raising an architect," he said with a smile. "She's good."

"I think she's going to be good with horses, too. I think you both are." Faith took a step back and turned to latch the barn door. "See you next week?"

"Yeah," Maddie said happily. "You'll see us next week."

Drew felt a swell of satisfaction as he drove home. The riding lessons had been a genius idea—at least according to his daughter. Maddie was practically dancing on air by the time they reached the cabin.

"So you're saying you enjoyed yourself," Drew said. They walked to the back of the cabin so he could show her the pad he'd poured for the addition while she'd been at school during the week.

"Totally. You didn't get very far," she said, propping her hands on her hips and frowning at the concrete square.

"Waiting for you."

"I think I'm the only kid in school building her own bedroom."

Drew wasn't sure if that was good or bad, so he kept his mouth shut and waited for a hint. He hoped it was good, because he loved spending the time with his daughter.

"Shayla wants to see it when we're done."

"Would she like to help?"

Maddie wrinkled her nose. "I don't think so. This isn't a real normal thing to do."

It wasn't?

"Do *you* want to do this?"

"Of course." She looked surprised. "I like

doing this. But I don't think my friends would get it."

"That's too bad."

She gave a casual shrug. "My life is kind of different from theirs." Before he could answer, she added, "At least I get to spend time with you. There are some kids I know who don't get to see their dads because of custody issues."

She spoke so matter-of-factly that it kind of broke his heart. "My time with you is the best part of my day."

She beamed at him, then stuck her closed hand out for the fist bump.

SCHOOL CAME TO an end the week after the first riding lesson and suddenly Maddie had an endless summer stretching before her. By the end of August, she expected to be a top-notch horseback rider and to be living at the cabin full-time. She'd even researched school bus schedules and discovered that she could catch a bus at the Lightning Creek Ranch, which was the turnaround point for Lightning Creek Road.

"Nice sleuthing," Drew said as he drove Maddie to Pete's after a day at the cabin. Now that she was out of school, they'd be spending more time together, and he hoped that Maddie could eventually move to the cabin full-time. On the plus side, he hadn't had a nightmare in almost two weeks. On the negative side, he'd gone this long before only to get hit out of the blue when he felt safe.

If he had a clue as to what triggered him, it would help, but despite keeping a journal, there was no obvious cause. Things built up, and despite all the calming stuff he'd do before bed, some nights he'd get slammed.

It was enough to make a guy not feel like going to bed.

"Are you and Shayla making any plans to ride during the summer?" he asked casually.

"I asked, but she said only one of their horses is trained good and her sister uses it for junior rodeo. Her sister doesn't share."

"That's too bad. But if you ever do decide to ride with a friend, I want an adult there. And you need to wear your helmet."

"Dad…"

"Not negotiable. I don't want you to end up with a head injury and nightmares." He shot her a serious look. "Do you?"

"No." She twisted the edge of her flowery

tunic. "Shayla says they might get another good horse."

"If she does, adult and helmet."

Maddie let out a sigh. "Agreed."

"We'll buy you a helmet this afternoon."

"And maybe a bling belt like Shayla has?"

Drew shot his daughter a frown, then instantly caved. "Yeah. A helmet and a bling belt. And you can help me clean the shop and take apart some carburetors." Maddie looked at the sky. "Wait. Let me guess. You're the only kid in your class who has to take apart carburetors."

She gave a small laugh. "I'm the only kid in my class who knows what one is."

"Well, we'll keep your carburetor work quiet for now, but trust me, honey…someday, some guy is going to realize just what a catch you are."

FAITH DID A foolish thing on Sunday night. Instead of getting her work clothes ready for the week or reading a book and drinking a glass of wine, she looked up old YouTube videos of herself running the barrels. And she drank that glass of wine as she watched.

She and Tommy were not only fast, they

were dead-on when it came to the turns, which was why, for the most part when she entered a rodeo, she came away with at least part of the purse.

She'd had sponsors, a travel budget. A plan. A goal.

And when the guy knocked her down and sliced off her hair, he'd destroyed all that. Her sponsors had found new riders, and she no longer needed a travel budget because she didn't go anywhere. Her plan then was to hide out, her goal was to survive.

It had taken her a year of therapy before she'd begun to see little parts of her old self emerging. Her first trips to stores immediately after the attack were painful, every person she met a potential assailant. Her first solo car trip to Missoula two months after the attack? She wouldn't have tried it without her hundred-pound Airedale, a healthy canister of pepper spray and a taser that may or may not have been legal. When Jenn's brother had given it to her, he'd told her not to show it around. She hadn't asked him where he'd gotten it, and she'd never tried to discover if she was a criminal for carrying it. She was grateful to have it and still kept it next to her bed. Just in case.

She'd lost so much she'd never get back, but she was gaining ground. Becoming a different version of her old self.

Faith spent a good part of the evening sipping wine, watching the tapes, sometimes smiling at what she'd once been. The NFR was now out of reach. She couldn't afford to do it without sponsors, but she had a full-time job and could afford to compete in the Montana region on her days off. Maybe win the region next year. Regain some of what she'd lost.

And a big part of her wanted to do it because that ass Jared had told her she wouldn't.

Yeah…deep down, Faith was still competitive as hell.

"YOU HAVE GOATS!" Maddie gave a delighted cry as she spotted the small, lop-eared animals nibbling weeds next to the barn, their little tails moving a mile a minute. She shut the truck door and went to get a closer look.

"Those are my lawn mowers," Faith said.

"How do you control them?" Drew asked with a dubious frown.

Faith sucked air through her teeth. "That is a bit of an issue. I stake them out where I want them to eat. Otherwise, they eat everything—especially if it's shaped like a flower."

"They are so cute," Maddie gushed.

"Are they your only lawn mower?" Drew asked.

"The real one is broken, so for now, these guys are it. Although, I let the horses take care of the grass around the house."

Maddie's smile widened as she glanced at her father. "Gee, Dad. Faith has a broken lawn mower."

Faith bounced a look between father and daughter, wondering what they found so funny.

"My brother-in-law runs a small engine repair shop," Drew explained. "I've been helping him out by fixing lawn mowers. Everyone has a broken lawn mower this time of year."

"Add me to the list," she said. She dusted her hands on her pants. "We should get started. Today we're going to catch the horses. Bring them in, groom them, then saddle them up and ride."

"Yes." Maddie put on the helmet she'd been

casually dangling from one hand and Faith nodded approvingly.

"Nice helmet."

"Thank you. Dad still needs to borrow one."

Faith smiled a little and met his eyes. "Dad knows where to find them." She waited for Drew to get back from the tack shed before saying, "We're only going to walk today and learn some balance exercises. Patience is an important part of working with horses. People need to be comfortable with each level before they move on. It saves a lot of grief in the future."

"And that keeps them from being bucked off." Maddie sent her father a look. "Right, Dad?"

"Right, Maddie," he said with an air of exaggerated patience.

As they groomed, Faith found herself watching Drew interact with his daughter as much as she watched him interact with the horse. He was different around his daughter, his expression softer, his movements somehow gentler.

She picked up a soft brush and stepped forward when he started grooming the off side of the horse. He gave her a quick look when she started brushing beside him. "Are you comfortable riding today?"

"I don't know if I'll ever be comfortable riding."

"It can be hard to come back after a bad experience." The irony of her words struck her hard. Drew was coming back from multiple bad experiences.

"To be honest, I could happily live my life and never get on a horse again."

"Are you going to drive your Jeep again?"

He opened his mouth, then closed it as he appeared to realize he had no comeback. Or chose not to give one.

"You never have to move out of your comfort zone…but don't let knee-jerk fears keep you from trying stuff." As she'd been doing.

"Of course I'll get on the horse. I'm doing this for my kid." He spoke in a low voice so Maddie wouldn't hear.

"Obviously, you wouldn't want to do it for yourself."

He turned his head to frown at her as if uncertain he'd heard her right. He had.

"You really aren't afraid of me anymore," he said gruffly.

No. Because she was seeing the gentle side of him as he spent time with Maddie. "Not unless you come at me from behind."

"Not much of a chance of that."

She shot him a look. From his tone, it sounded like he'd just slammed her—and here she'd been kind of admiring his body and been pleased that she'd been able to do so. He seemed to read her thoughts. "That's not an insult. I meant I will take pains not to startle you."

Her cheeks started to heat. "I wasn't insulted." She gave the horse's shoulder one final swipe of the brush, then moved on to Maddie's horse.

She'd been insulted, which was utterly illogical.

After the horses were groomed, Faith tacked them up. "You'll learn to do this," she told Maddie, "but today I thought you'd like to spend your time riding."

"Yeah," Maddie said on a soft note of excitement, stroking her horse's nose.

Faith handed her the reins and told her to walk the mare so she could tighten the cinch again. Once the girl was out of earshot, she went back to Drew, who was waiting next to his horse, watching his daughter lead the mare toward the barn.

When she got closer, he shifted that blue gaze to Faith, and for a moment she felt as if he could see inside of her. That he somehow knew she was becoming aware of him for reasons other than caution. That she noticed his build in a different way than before. It felt good to admire a guy's ass again, but not so good if said guy knew what she was doing.

She cleared her throat, dove into her speech. "Sorry to be judgmental earlier. What I meant to say was that while it's commendable that you're here for Maddie, maybe you can get something out of it, too."

His lips curved ever so slightly. As if he'd just figured something out. About her. "When you fall off a horse, you get back on?"

"Exactly."

His smile broadened, the first relaxed smile she'd ever seen from him, and it made her feel like something had just broken free inside of her.

She turned toward the horse as a spiral of warmth began to spread through her body. "Watch closely while I saddle the horse. You'll do it next time."

After she'd pulled the latigo through the cinch ring, she beckoned him closer and handed him the leather strap. "Pull it up slowly." He pulled the leather and she showed him how to make certain the cinch was tight but not too tight. "Now you walk your horse, then we tighten it one more time."

He gave a nod but didn't move. "Do you want me to look at your broken mower after we get done?"

She was shaking her head almost before she was aware of moving. "I have goats."

"It's probably the carburetor. Did you leave gas in it last winter?"

"I wasn't here last winter."

"Old gas," he said as he started leading the horse away.

"Old gas to you, too," Faith muttered before she pasted a smile on her face and headed over to give Maddie's cinch one final check.

Mounting was easy. Both of her mares had been used for Jenn's therapy classes and they knew the drill. Stand quietly and put up with whatever came their way. Her girls were paragons of patience.

"Sit in the center of the saddle, push your heels down, don't let them curl up." Faith adjusted Maddie's leg, pulling it down and positioning her foot, and was about to do the same with Drew, who'd grown stone-faced once he was atop Freckles. But she decided to keep her hands off the man.

"Okay. Lift the reins and give a little pressure with your legs. Do not kick."

The horses moved forward as soon as the reins were lifted, and Maddie's face broke into a wide smile. "Look at you, Dad. Still on the horse."

"Thanks, kid."

"Relax your bodies—but don't let your backs slouch. The horse reads your energy through your seat…"

Faith ended the session with balancing exercises, then helped them dismount. Drew looked pleased to have his feet back on terra firma.

"Well. That was fun." He led the horse to the rail.

"You did great, Dad."

Drew smiled at his daughter. "Yeah. But it was kind of spooky at first."

"Not for me."

"You're a natural," Faith said.

"Really?"

"Yes. You have great balance. You'll move along quickly."

"What about Dad?"

*Yes. What about Dad?*

"I can see where you get your balance." Drew was closest, so Faith took the reins from him. "Walk the horse for a few minutes, Maddie, to cool her down." She dropped the reins over the rail and started uncinching the saddle.

"I can do it." Drew moved in from behind her and gently took the latigo from her. She let him have it, hoping he didn't notice how her body had stiffened at his unexpected approach.

"Sorry," he murmured, telling her yes, he'd totally noticed. "I said I wouldn't do that."

"No worries," she muttered back, moving past him to help Maddie. She hated seizing up like that, but there was nothing she could do about an instinctive reaction. Except hate on the stranger who had done it to her. And that got her exactly nowhere.

After the horses were untacked, brushed and released back into the pasture, Maddie went to check the kittens, leaving Faith and Drew to walk back to his truck together.

"I honestly will look at the mower," he said.

"I have goats," she repeated, glancing down at the gravel.

"Faith." She looked up, a faint frown drawing her eyebrows together. "I'm sorry I startled you."

"And I'm sorry I was startled," she said darkly. "I'm trying so hard not to be, but it just happens." She tightened her mouth. "That wasn't a bad one. At work the other day…a colleague came into my office when I was in the back room and I about wet myself when I found someone in what I thought was my empty office. My logical brain understood that the unexpected person was a colleague—"

"Yeah. I know. That other part of your brain beats logic to the punch."

"That other part is probably always going to be there, as much as I'd like to believe it will someday go away."

"It might not be all bad."

She turned to him with a frown. "How so?"

"You will always be at the ready."

"Small blessings? Silver lining?"

He leaned back against the truck, folding his arms over his broad chest as he watched the open barn door, waiting for his daughter to reappear. "Platitudes. So helpful."

"There is truth to them…but they sting."

"Time heals all wounds." Drew lifted his eyebrows as if encouraging her to supply a platitude of her own.

"Things happen for a reason."

"At least you experienced true love."

"Just get over it already."

He frowned at her. "Someone said that to you?"

"Tough love, I guess. My boyfriend at the time."

"I hope you slugged him."

"We broke up."

"Your boyfriend was an asshole."

"I didn't see that side of him until he didn't know how to handle what had happened to me. He saw it more in terms of how it affected his life."

"Jerk."

"I chose him. I'm equally to blame."

"My assessment stands."

"Not everyone is cut out to help someone through a trauma."

Why was she defending Jared? Maybe because she was embarrassed and hurt by how he'd abandoned her. Made her feel as if she wasn't worth caring for when times got rough.

Yeah. That was pretty much it.

"True."

She was relieved that he took her words at face value…even though she was convinced he didn't fully accept her defense of Jared.

"By the way…I can take your broken mower with me today."

"You persist," she said mildly.

"Last offer. And I'm only persisting because you're doing me a favor with these lessons when I know you didn't want to do them. I'd like to do something for you." He met her gaze. "Just so you know, when push comes to shove, I'm a no-means-no kind of guy."

"Just not with lawn mowers."

"I'm serious."

She believed him. There was no way she could look at him and not. "The reason I said no is because I have trouble being beholden to people. I always have. My go-to answer when offered help is usually no."

"Sometimes you should consider yes. People like to help." He raised his dark eyebrows. "*You* like to help."

"Yes. I do."

"Think about it."

Her lips parted as she drew in a long breath and when his gaze slid down to her lips, her lungs seemed to seize up.

They both jumped at the sound of the barn door closing. "How long until they can leave their mother?" Maddie asked as she and Sully came toward the truck.

"A couple weeks."

Maddie waggled her eyebrows at her father, who immediately started shaking his head. "You know Pete's allergic to cats."

"But you aren't."

"We'll talk later."

"Dad…"

"Maddie…"

Maddie blew out a breath, but she didn't seem one bit disheartened, which meant that Drew might have a scuffle on his hands over the next several weeks as the kittens became cuter. Giving her father a *we'll see* look, she headed to her side of the truck.

"You can take the mower," Faith said as he reached for his door handle.

"I'm not strong-arming you into a free repair, am I?"

She smiled and pointed at the barn. "It's in there. Next to the kittens."

"Which are so cute," Maddie said.

A moment later, Drew returned with the mower. He easily hefted it into the back of his truck without bothering to lower the tailgate.

"See you around."

"Next week," she said. The guy left her feeling breathless in a number of ways that she was going to have to analyze once she was safely alone.

He got into his side of the truck and Maddie leaned forward to wave. A few seconds later, they were driving out of the ranch, leaving Faith and Sully staring after them.

What had just happened during her lesson? Who was schooling whom?

# CHAPTER SEVEN

DREW AND MADDIE spent the rest of Saturday and all day Sunday hammering two-by-fours together to frame her room. When the weekend ended, they had the walls framed in. The entrance would be the current back door to the cabin, and after the room was complete, he and Pete would cut and finish a new back door on the opposite side of the kitchen.

According to Lissa's plans, the appliances would remain in place, but the cupboards and cabinets would be moved to the opposite wall, allowing access to Maddie's room and creating a better flow through the small cabin. The half loft, where Drew currently slept, would become an office area, and the storage room would be enlarged and a sliding door and porch attached, thus creating the master bedroom.

Drew didn't know if he would follow through with the last renovation. The thought of a master bedroom and no one to share it with was too hard to deal with. He focused on Maddie's room and the revamp of the kitchen space, the bathroom remodel. He would re-evaluate later.

Late Sunday afternoon, he and Maddie put down their tools and headed to the truck for the trip down the mountain to Pete and Cara's place. He loaded Faith's newly repaired mower in the back of the truck, and Maddie told him to take a close look at the kittens when he dropped it off.

"I think I'm allergic, too," he said.

"Why don't you want kittens?" Maddie demanded as they drove down the winding road.

"Was that kittens, as in plural?"

"Does it matter?" she asked brusquely.

"Because I've never had a cat and I'm afraid of doing it wrong."

"Seems like you're afraid of a lot of stuff lately." Drew sent her a frown. "What I mean," she continued patiently, "is that you're afraid to have me live with you, and you're afraid of horses."

"I rode the horse." And kind of liked it,

although the feeling that the animal could do anything at any minute still freaked him out. But in case Maddie didn't understand, he added, "I enjoyed it. I like lessons."

And his instructor interested him, in a way he hadn't been interested in a long time. Not that he was going to do anything about it, but it felt good to know that there were parts of him that, despite lying dormant, were not dead.

"And maybe you'd like having a cat or two," Maddie continued.

He wasn't going to win this fight, so he kept his mouth shut. They passed the ritzy wood and glass house and rounded the corner to the Lightning Creek Ranch. The arena where they rode came into sight and then Maddie pointed. "Look. Faith is barrel racing. Can we stop?"

"I think she's training, so maybe we can ask her about it next week."

"You have to drop the lawn mower off."

"I'm not going to drag her out of the field to do that."

"Fine. But I want to watch her barrel race some time."

"You can—when you get invited. It's nice that Faith is giving us lessons. Let's not push things."

"All right." Maddie let out a loud sigh. "I hope we get to trot next week."

"And lope the week after?"

"That was kind of my schedule."

Drew was pretty sure that barrel racing would be scheduled the week after that.

"But…" Maddie added, "I don't want to learn bad habits. Faith says it takes a long time to unlearn them and I need to be patient."

"If you learn to be patient, you'll have an easier time in life."

"How did you learn patience?" Maddie asked innocently.

"The hard way. Best to pick up the practice now."

"I'll try."

"You won't regret it."

For once the lights were off in the shop when Drew turned into Pete's driveway. He parked at the end of the walk and walked with Maddie to the kitchen door.

"Hey, guys," Cara called from the sink,

where she was elbow-deep in suds. "Have a good day?"

"Not as good as yesterday, but good," Maddie said as she headed down the hall to her room.

"She really loves the riding lessons," Cara said, lifting the sweater she was washing out of the suds, then pushing it back in again. "That was a good call."

"Facing a few of my own demons in the process."

Cara's shoulders seemed to tighten and then she pushed the sweater deeper into the sink. "About that…"

"Yeah?"

She let out a sigh and pulled her hands out of the water, then reached for a towel. "I know you're enjoying building the room with Maddie. She's loving it, too."

"But…"

"Try to be realistic about the possibility of her moving up there with you. She was crushed when she thought she was going to stay and then couldn't."

"You know why she couldn't."

"Yes." Slowly, she wiped suds from her

forearms. "But rather than tempt her with possibilities, why don't you make it clear that she won't be able to live with you?"

"Because then she and I would be wasting our time building the room."

"Maybe you are," Cara said gently. She held up a hand. "I'm not telling you to stop, but I am saying that until you feel confident that she can safely live with you, don't keep promising her 'maybe next weekend.'"

Drew put a hand to his forehead and squeezed. "I want her to live with me."

"And we both want her to not be upset by things you can't control." Her expression softened, but she didn't look one bit less resolved to do what she thought was best for his child. Cara couldn't have children of her own; she'd raised Maddie for the past two years, so of course she felt she had a stake in Maddie's future. But his stake was bigger.

"I won't make promises."

"I think you should tell her that you don't see her moving in the foreseeable future." Her tone grew gentler. "It would hurt, but it would be easier on her in the long run if she could simply enjoy what she has without wanting things she can't have."

"She's always going to want those things." It would kill him if she didn't. "She's my daughter."

"But we were the ones there for her when her world fell apart."

"I know." His voice started to break and he had to stop. Start again. "You guys saved our lives. I know you want what's best for Maddie."

"We love her, Drew."

"Me, too." And he'd dare to say that he loved her in a different, deeper way than Cara and Pete. Had loved her to the depths of his soul from the moment the nurse had handed him the squirming pink bundle and she'd stilled when she met his gaze, her eyes wide as they stared into his, her mouth a tiny O. His daughter. His little girl. Whom he'd left to fight a war. It'd all been part of a bigger plan that hadn't worked out—not even a little.

"I've already talked to Maddie about the schedule this week," he said. "She has a lot of end-of-school-year stuff, so I'm going to see her on Tuesday and Thursday. I'm going to her awards thing on Friday, then I'll pick her up on Saturday in the morning as usual."

Cara went to the fridge and traced a finger over the magnetic calendar. "Yes. That seems about right." She turned back to Drew, pressed her lips together. "I only want the best for both of you. You guys are our family."

"I know." For a moment, they faced off, worried aunt, worried father. "I'll see you on Tuesday."

He called for Maddie and she came running down the hall to say goodbye. "Tuesday for pizza," she said.

"Yep." He leaned in to kiss her cheek. "See you then."

He ran into Pete on the way to his truck. His brother-in-law took one look at him and said, "Cara talked to you."

"Yeah."

Pete pushed back his ball cap. "She's worried. Maddie is the closest thing she has to a kid."

Drew almost said, "She *is* my kid," but managed to keep the words inside. He owed Cara and Pete a debt he could never repay. "I know."

"Here's the thing. She ran into your sister

at the community board dinner and Deb kind of did a number on her."

Drew's blood pressure started to spike. "What kind of number?"

"Pumped her for information about you. Asked if we thought a guy in your condition should be living alone on a mountain." Pete folded his arms over his chest. "What's she after?"

Pete knew Deb almost as well as Drew did, having been Drew's best friend forever.

"I think she's afraid people will talk about her wacko brother on the mountain and it'll reflect on her."

Pete bobbed his head. "Sounds about right."

"You know that I'd never do anything that wasn't in Maddie's best interest, right?"

"Well, yeah."

"Just checking. I'm starting to feel like I'm fighting a one-man war here."

"We got your back. Cara's just a little wigged out by Maddie hitting the teen years."

"So am I."

Five short years.

IT WAS DUSK by the time Drew pulled into the Lightning Creek Ranch. He could have dropped off the mower the following day, but Faith's lights were on, and as out of character as it was, he didn't feel like going home to his empty cabin. A short stop at Faith's would delay the inevitable. Cara's request had been an arrow to his heart.

Not have Maddie live with him? Ever?

Unacceptable. He was reading the books the therapist had recommended. Again. Trying his damnedest to address the root cause of his issues—although it was hard when the root cause was back-to-back tragedies.

He unloaded the mower and put it in the dark barn in the same place he'd gotten it from. From across the dark interior, he heard a low *maaa* from one of the goats, who'd been put away for the night.

"Sorry, bud. You're being replaced by technology."

"I don't know if talking to goats is a good sign or bad."

Drew about jumped out of his skin at the unexpected voice. "Whoa, shit. You scared me." Faith's Airedale trotted closer and poked his snout at Drew, who automatically ruffled the dog's curly fur as he regained composure.

"That's supposed to be my line," Faith said

as she stepped into the barn. "I thought you knew I was here. I left the house when you drove up."

"I didn't. I was...preoccupied."

"Ah." An awkward silence hung between them, broken only by the goats discussing life with one another.

"You want to come in for a minute?"

The invitation surprised him. "Why?"

Faith gave a short laugh. "One thing I like about you is that you don't play games."

"Yeah. Never been good with them."

"I wasn't exactly a game player in my former life, but I did like to have fun."

"And now?"

She let out a sigh. "It's hard to forget a guy grabbing your hair hard and then slicing it off with a knife."

Drew grimaced, thinking of what might have happened if the attack hadn't been interrupted. "That's heinous."

"He swore at the trial that all he wanted was my hair." She gave a stiff shrug. "It might have been true. I had hair to my waist at the time. It kind of fascinated some people."

And that was effing creepy. No wonder she couldn't handle people coming up behind her.

"Your hair is still long."

"That's a choice. On the one hand, do I want hair that can be used as a weapon against me? On the other, do I want his actions to dictate how I wear my hair? I chose the former." Faith folded her hands over her chest. "You want to come in or not? I opened a bottle of wine a few minutes ago."

"You're inviting me in for wine."

"Or you can get your ass on up the mountain. I don't care which."

It was his turn to laugh. "I…will come in. For a minute."

She gave a nod, stepped away from the barn door.

Drew followed Faith to the house, thinking it was one of those Twilight Zone moments that later he would wonder how he'd gotten himself into. But right this second, Twilight Zone seemed better than going to his lonely cabin. It was always hard after Maddie left, but Cara's talk today had given him a whole lot more to brood about.

The house was brand-new. He'd heard about how the main house had burned in the fire that had missed his cabin by a mere half mile, and now he could see that whoever had rebuilt it had been good.

Faith led the way through the sparsely furnished living room to the cozy farm kitchen, where, yes indeed, a bottle of wine sat open on the table, a fancy wine stopper lying beside it.

"Red? I was hoping for white."

Faith smirked at him. "Forgive me for not believing that."

She went to the cabinet and pulled out a second wineglass. A few seconds later, the wine was poured and she motioned for him to take his glass. Maybe she didn't want to risk having their fingers brush if she handed it to him. She lifted her glass in a small toast.

"To survivors everywhere."

He smiled as he lifted his glass. Drank. He was no connoisseur, but he liked the wine. Sully flopped down on the floor at his feet and gave a gusty sigh before closing his eyes. Drew had a feeling that if he made one move toward Faith, the seemingly mellow dog would have him by the throat.

"You…uh…seem a little spunky tonight."

Faith gave a small laugh, her pretty mouth tilting up at the corners, charming the hell out of him. "Spunky? I like that." She took another drink, set her glass down on the table and waved Drew to the seat opposite where she stood. As he sat, so did she.

"I called my ex tonight."

"The asshole?"

She gave her head a rueful shake. "He has my barrel racing saddle. Gave it to another woman. He is supposed to send it back, and he's hedging."

"And that pisses you off."

"That's an excellent summary of the situation." She lifted her glass back to her lips and Drew found himself following the movement of her glass.

"Maddie saw you practicing. She wanted to stop and watch, but I told her to wait for an invitation."

"I only run Tommy once a week. Otherwise he'd sour. But the next time I run him, Maddie can come by...except that you have to be careful she doesn't get the bug."

"What bug?"

"The barrel racing bug."

"Do you have it?"

"I've had it since I was fourteen. Barrel racing consumed me...right up until the attack." She set down her wineglass. "I was on my way to the National Finals, which was like my ultimate dream…and then…you know." She picked the glass back up.

"Sorry to hear that."

"Yeah. Yet another thing that jerk stole from me. Besides my sense of safety and well-being. My general trust in humanity. Now I automatically look twice at everyone."

"I think you looked at me three or four times."

"Six," she said with a straight face.

Drew fought a smile. He liked this woman. "Are you still on track for National Finals?"

She gave her head a small shake. "Qualifying involves so much time and travel. A lot of money. I no longer have the resources—or the time. But I have my eye on a prize."

"What's that?"

"I want to win the Region next year."

"Sounds worthy."

"Yes." Her mouth flattened, as if she was thinking of something unpleasant. "It won't be the same as going to the NFR, but it'll be enough, all things considered. It'll make me feel a little more whole."

Drew planted his elbows on the table. "I

think the trick to understanding our situations is to accept that a little more whole is a good thing."

She gestured at him with her glass. "Very intuitive."

"Only took months of bemoaning what would never be."

"Is that a fact?"

He smiled a little. "Is this what you were like? Before?"

"Yes." She gave a ladylike snort through her nose. "I was not the terrified person you met at the café. I used to tell guys a lot bigger than me to bug off. But after the attack… I didn't dare."

"Before I lost my wife…before the roadside bomb… I was a very driven man."

She raised her gaze. "Yeah?" she asked softly.

"I left my wife and went to war. The idea was that in twenty years, I'd have a decent pension and could pursue a civilian job. Then we'd be together full-time. Twenty years of being apart almost as much as we were together and then we'd cash in…except that Lissa didn't make it. And I almost didn't."

"And Maddie is collateral damage."

Drew's throat tightened as she spoke a very real truth. "Yes. And I'm trying to fix that. As much as it can be fixed, anyway."

"Why don't the two of you live together?"

"I have nightmares. I never know when they're coming." He was surprised at how easily the words slid off his tongue. The wine? "They affect me physically afterward and…sometimes they can be kind of violent."

Faith frowned, and if he wasn't mistaken, leaned back, putting just that much more distance between them. For a moment, he regretted his confession.

"You make me feel a little ashamed."

Not what he'd expected. "How's that?"

"Losing a barrel racing career is nothing compared to what you lost. Or what you're dealing with."

"It's not a contest."

She glanced down. "I know. But my trauma is more a case of what *could* have happened than what *did* happen." She brushed a few loose tendrils from her face before settling her hand back on the table. "I lost some hair. My faith in humanity. You lost people."

Without thinking, he reached out and covered her hand with his. Faith jumped, her startled gaze meeting his at the unexpected contact. Then he felt her hand relax beneath his. "Fear is fear," he said. "It's all valid."

She smiled and slowly pulled her hand away. "Thanks."

He wished now that he hadn't touched her. That she hadn't made it so clear that she didn't want to be touched. "How are things going with my sister?"

"I'm happy to report that our relationship is entirely professional."

He smiled grimly. "Keep it that way."

"No worries there."

Drew finished his wine in one big swallow that would have offended a sommelier and then pushed back his chair. "I should get home. Big day tomorrow fixing engines and tearing down cupboards."

Faith also got to her feet and the Airedale raised his head, as if checking to see if she might need him for anything before collapsing back onto the floor again. "Sounds exciting. I'll be searching out old files and scanning them."

"Double exciting."

Faith laughed and walked with him as far as the door. "Thank you," she said softly.

He didn't know if she meant for the mower repair or the conversation. "Anytime."

Faith waited until he was halfway down the walk before calling after him, "Was it old gas?"

He smiled at her through the darkness. "Yeah. It was."

WHEN WEDNESDAY CAME and her saddle hadn't arrived—no big surprise, given Jared's track record—Faith decided to give him a nudge. He didn't pick up her call, which told her that her saddle was not in the mail.

Annoying, to say the least. She'd signed up for her first rodeo and wanted her saddle. Somewhere in the deep recesses of her mind, she'd convinced herself that if she had her saddle, she would be able to follow through on her entry. She'd get further than she had last time, when all she'd managed to do was drive to the rodeo, unload her horse and then have a panic attack before driving back home again.

*You'll follow through. This year will be different.*

She hoped. She was doing well around Drew—but that might not count because he no longer frightened her. His aura of power seemed different now that she knew he'd been hammered by life and was fighting to regain his equilibrium. Now that she'd seen him with his daughter. He was her neighbor. The brother of her boss. Her student.

An attractive guy.

Something of an enigma.

Faith put on the kettle and went back into the living room as she waited for it to boil. Would being around Drew, getting used to being in close proximity with a big man, make it easier the next time she encountered a guy who reminded her of her attacker?

Would she be able to hold her ground when startled, as well-trained horses were taught to do, and assess the situation before reacting? To face her fears without letting the fight-or-flight instinct overrule her brain?

When horses shied in place, it was because they trusted their rider to take care of them in crisis. Faith was too self-protective to ask someone in her life to share the burden. She'd barely been able to let Drew fix the lawn mower. Besides, she had no idea when the next crisis would occur. It wasn't like she could have a bodyguard walking around with her, just in case she triggered.

She wasn't the bodyguard type. She stood on her own two feet.

*But sometimes you need to be propped up. Fact of life, like it or not.*

She went back into the kitchen and looked out the window. Toward the mountain, she could see the faint glimmer of light from Drew's cabin through the timber. Drew and Maddie. Father and daughter.

Maybe they would like to go to a rodeo…

And maybe then she'd make it all the way through the competition.

Faith pulled her phone out of her back pocket, went to the fridge and dialed the number Drew had written on the paper now trapped under her I Heart Airedales magnet. She assumed Drew would allow the call to go to voice mail, since he wouldn't recognize her number, but on the fourth ring he answered, making her jump.

"It's Faith." *Who has temporarily taken leave of her senses.*

"Is everything okay?"

"Yes." She gripped the phone a little tighter, wanting very much to hang up. She might have if she didn't believe he'd be down the mountain in an instant if he thought something was wrong. "I...have a proposition." Good. So far.

There was a note of open curiosity in his voice as he said, "Yeah? What kind of proposition?" When he said the word *proposition*, it sounded sexual. Or maybe the deep timbre of his voice made her think of sex, which she hadn't done in a long, long time. And maybe it was easier to think about sex when he wasn't there and she didn't have to deal with the reality of him. Or the possibility of it actually happening.

*Face it, girl. You're miles from it actually happening. With anyone.*

Her cheeks were warm, but she managed a normal tone as she asked, "Would you and Maddie like to come to a rodeo with me?" Sensing his hesitation, she added, "I need a bodyguard."

Way to spell it out, but it was totally true. She wanted someone with her who could take care of business. Make her feel safe.

Before he could answer, she added, "I'll give you and Maddie lessons for free if you'd do me this favor."

"We'll do you this favor and pay for lessons. I think Maddie would like a rodeo. When is it?"

"The second Saturday in June. Summit Lake."

"Close by."

"A purposeful choice." She cleared her throat. "In case I can't go through with it."

"I'll ask Maddie, but it's a yes from me."

Faith closed her eyes, drew in a breath, surprised at just how relieved she was at his quiet assurance that he'd go along to watch her back. "I appreciate it."

"Glad I can help." He sounded like he meant it, which made her feel all warm inside—even though she didn't want to react to him that way.

"Thank you." *I need to go.* "We can…talk at next week's lesson."

"Yeah. We can do that."

The warmth was beginning to flicker into a small flame. Why did this conversation feel so intimate?

*Because he understands.*

He was a survivor and so was she. Like it or not, that gave them a connection.

"Thanks, Drew. See you then."

Quickly, she hung up the phone, feeling spent. She'd taken a chance. It'd paid off. And she was already wondering if she'd made a mistake.

THERE WAS NO way Drew could have said no to Faith's request for backup, but a part of him wished he had. He was sliding into dangerous waters and needed to stop before he got too deep.

Before the recent traumas in his life, Drew had never considered himself a student of human nature. Examining his own thoughts and feelings after those events made him uncomfortably aware of not only his own weaknesses and fears, but also those of other people. He read nuance in tones and expressions he hadn't noticed in his previous life, when he'd been busy conquering the world.

Now he noticed things—like how Faith had done her best to sound normal, but still had a tremor in her voice when she'd asked him to go to the rodeo with her. His instincts had urged him to say no. To not get further involved. To keep things exactly as they were—pleasant acquaintances. Neighbors. Teacher-student. But that tremor...

He did not want to screw things up. Not when Maddie was so thrilled with the riding class.

She was now researching breeds of horses and trying to find room behind the cabin for an enclosure, because Pete was allergic to animals.

Drew had created a monster with the lessons. It felt damned good. So now he had to do his best not to mess things up with the instructor.

He rolled over in bed—his very lonely bed. He was thinking a lot about lonely beds and lonely cabins of late. After Lissa's death, he'd been frozen with grief and disbelief, then the explosion had added anger to the mix. When the focus of one's life was loss and anger, it was hard to move on. To think about opening up and letting another potential loss into one's life.

But with every passing day, he felt a little emptier.

He needed…something….and at the same time he was afraid of that something.

Hell, he didn't know what he wanted or needed, except to have his wife back in his arms. To hold the woman he loved during the night, smell her hair, be glad she was there with him. But as things were now, he might smell her hair, then knock her out of bed as he thrashed around in the throes of a nightmare. The possibility of hurting someone was all too real. It'd be one thing for Maddie to hear him flailing about and then see that aftermath the next morning in the form of one haunted, hollow-eyed man. But to have someone right there? Someone he might actually hurt?

Couldn't happen.

He was sentenced to a lonely cabin. Shared by none.

## CHAPTER EIGHT

DREW WOKE, COUGHING and gasping as his
lungs filled with smoke. It was only when
he stumbled sideways and his shoulder hit the
lamp that he realized he was half out of bed,
trying to run. Not the thing to do in a loft.

With a groan, he sat on the edge of the mattress, wiped the sweat off his forehead with
the back of his hand.

Nightmares were becoming night terrors.

He closed his eyes, focused on his breathing. The smoke had been part of the dream,
but his body was still coming to grips with
that. Deep breath in, longer breath out. Re-
peat.

*Okay. This is something you have to live
with. Cara was right about Maddie. You'll
have to find other ways to be together.*

And that felt a shit-ton like giving up.

So what the hell did he do? Try the drugs

again? Go through his day sick to his stomach and walking through a fog?

If it meant spending time with his daughter, then maybe that was what he had to do. He wondered, though, if Maddie would want a nauseous zombie for a father. Because that was what he felt like. The undead. Who was about to puke.

Another deep breath. Another long exhale. *Focus*. What was the trigger? Stress? Faith? Working toward a new chapter in his life?

He was traveling down a new road—one he hadn't expected to be on. He was attracted to a woman, who he sensed was attracted to him, despite their inauspicious beginnings.

Drew got to his feet and headed for the shower. He had a visit to make today—a visit he didn't mind making in his current cranky state. In fact, his sister might well have been the cause of the stress that triggered the nightmare.

Drew gave Deb a quick call before leaving the cabin, telling her he wanted to stop by for a few minutes. She seemed surprised—and she had good reason to be, since he rarely stopped by her place—then quickly invited him to the afternoon barbecue she was having that day for the neighbors.

Drew refused her kind offer, just as she'd known he would. Part of him wanted to say yes, just to see how she would respond to the prospect of introducing her cabin-dwelling, hermit brother to the neighbors, but he was in no mood to play games. Especially not with Deb, who was a master at game-playing.

When he arrived at the McMansion, he parked on the street, which Deb hated, but it was the fastest way into the house and that was what he was looking at—a quick in and out. Deb's pretentious home with its two-story entryway, parquet floors and curved staircases gave him the creeps. It didn't feel real or lived in, but if that's what his sister had wanted to spend her inheritance on, cool. He had put his half of the money away for the proverbial rainy day. At the time, he'd had no idea just how hard it was going to start raining in the not-so-distant future.

He jabbed the doorbell, steeling himself for the trip into Deb's domain. The door swung open a split second later.

"Drew!" Eric sounded as if he hadn't seen Drew in months, rather than weeks. "Glad you could come." He pointed toward the kitchen. "Head on outside. Deb's out there working on the tables."

"Drew." Deb used her happy-to-see-you sister voice as she set down the centerpiece she was about to place on the last of three long tables.

"Expecting a crowd?"

"Most of the neighbors," she said with an offhand wave before heading for the outdoor kitchen area. An outdoor kitchen in Montana kind of boggled the mind. She and Eric had sprung for a special retractable wall that dropped down, thus keeping out the snow and rain for a good part of the year. She opened the fridge, revealing an awesome display of craft and domestic beer. She put a hand on his upper arm, her expression growing concerned as she studied his face. "Are you feeling all right?"

"Fine," he lied.

"I think you might like this Toboggan Ale," she said, pulling out a bottle and presenting it to him as if it were a fine wine. The scent of roasting tri-tip hit his nose as he took the bottle. "Are you sure you won't stay for the afternoon? There are some people I'd love for you to meet."

He managed a smile as he shook his head. The backyard was supremely manicured and since Eric spent most of his time in his insurance office, Drew was certain that a service did the work. And that a caterer had supplied most of the lunch. The salads and desserts he'd seen in the fridge weren't exactly the kind that were thrown together by a casual cook.

She really wanted to impress the neighbors. More than that, she wanted to impress the world.

"I assume you have a reason for stopping by?" Deb gave him a pointed look. "Because you never do that."

"Yes. I do have a reason. Where in the hell do you get off discussing me with Cara?"

Deb put her hand to her chest. "What did she say?" she demanded, as if she were the wronged party.

"She said nothing. I just found out that the two of you talked, and I want to know what you think you're doing."

"I'm not doing anything, Drew. You're overreacting."

She made it sound as if he did that a lot.

Which he didn't. His one blessing was that he managed to defuse his anger—during his waking hours, anyway.

"No. You upset Cara, and that's not right."

"I had no intention of upsetting her. I simply asked about you."

"And whether I should be living in isolation on the mountain."

Deb's eyes narrowed. "I thought you hadn't talked to her."

"I talked to her husband."

"I can't help being concerned."

Drew let out a breath, set his untouched beer aside. Deb raised her chin in a small jerk and he rolled his eyes.

"Drew, you have misunderstood my intentions. I want you and Maddie to live together as father and daughter. As you *should* be living. But that cabin is not the place for a child. It's remote and she won't be anywhere near her friends."

"Since when are you concerned about Maddie?"

"I know what it's like to be a teenage girl. It wasn't that long ago, you know." Her expression became serious. "Eric and I saw the cutest little place for rent on the edge of town.

It has a big shop and frankly, it would be perfect for you. We…contacted the realtor for more information. The packet's in Eric's den, if you'd like to see it."

He did not.

"You're looking for places for me, Deb?"

His sister's expression grew stubborn. "We just happened to see it, and because of the shop, it seemed perfect for you."

"I'm not paying rent right now." He and Lissa had signed a long-term lease with Deb, who received a monthly check from him. He imagined that his sister was kicking herself for not asking more now that rents were shooting up in town.

"Grandfather always got snowed in for weeks."

"I have a plow for the little tractor."

"What little tractor?"

"The one I bought from Pete." Granted, it needed work, but it was usable. He wouldn't get stranded for long. "Here's the deal, Deb. I like the cabin. I'm not there because I'm being antisocial or trying to isolate myself. I'm there because being there makes me feel good, okay? I remember good times with Grandpa and good times with my wife. I want to live there with my daughter, and I want you to butt out."

Eric appeared in the doorway, then came to an abrupt stop as he caught the expression on Drew's face.

"Think about your daughter," Deb urged. "If you moved to town, you could do a lot more with her. And she could do a lot more with her friends. You're being selfish."

"The cabin is less than ten miles from town. Maddie can do all she wants with her friends. And I'll have a much better idea what she's doing because I'll be the one chauffeuring her to and from."

"You're being unrealistic. You need to think about this."

"Don't talk about me. Don't try to find me places to live." He got to his feet. "I hope you have a good time impressing the neighbors. I can see myself out."

"Drew…"

He stopped at the sliding door. "What, Deb?"

"Eventually, you're going to see that I'm right. And that I was only trying to help."

"When I do, I'll give you a belated thank-you."

DURING THE NEXT riding lesson, Faith did what she'd been unable to do the previous week. She took hold of Drew's calf with one hand and his foot with the other, and maneuvered them into the correct position instead of trying to talk him through it. She'd touched people daily when she'd been helping Jenn with her equine therapy, but touching Drew was different. Made her feel self-conscious.

"Like that," she said as she took her hand away from his leg. His calf muscle was like a rock. A warm rock.

"Thanks." He gave her a rueful look, but there was a watchfulness in his expression that made her think that her casual attitude hadn't fooled him. He knew it was hard for her to touch him.

But did he know she'd enjoyed the feel of his hard muscles beneath her palm? That touching him made her insides go wobbly?

Damn, she hoped not. Faith had never been shy about going after what she wanted—in her old life. Again, this was different. She was different.

She folded her arms over her chest as she sent father and daughter around the arena. Maddie was a natural. Drew not so much, but he gave each lesson his best. The difference was that Maddie was here to learn about horses and become a rider; Drew was here for his daughter. He seemed to enjoy the horses while working on the ground, but he did not enjoy being in the saddle. He stiffened up, so the horse stiffened up and nobody had a good time. Except Maddie. She had a ball.

"Can we lope yet?" the girl asked.

"Next lesson," Faith promised. "If you can do all of your balancing exercises at a trot."

"Youch."

Youch, indeed, but Faith was a firm believer in mastering each step before moving on. And regaining her life had made her a believer in celebrating small victories. After the lesson and the cooldown, Maddie went into the barn to play with the kittens, leaving Drew and Faith leaning on the fence looking out over the pasture.

"How long will you keep this up?" Faith asked without looking at him.

"The lessons?" She nodded, and he said, "For as long as I need to."

"You're not very comfortable. You need to relax."

"It doesn't feel natural to be on an animal

that can change his mind about what he wants to do at any given second."

"These animals won't do that."

"So you say."

She rested her hands on the rail, one on top of the other. "Yes. So I say."

"I have a hard time giving up control. It's like I've had so much wrested away from me that I don't want to give up what little I have left—especially to a half-ton animal."

Faith let out a breath that was almost, but not quite, a laugh. "We look at horses differently."

"And probably life, too."

"No. I think we're kind of similar there."

"Do you have nightmares?"

"I did. But not anymore." She brought her cheek down to rest on her hands. "How badly hurt were you in that explosion?"

"I was lucky. My vehicle was at the tail end of the convoy. Concussion, broken ribs, punctured lung."

"Did you lose friends?"

"Three." She didn't say anything, so he did. "My wife had died only a few months before. I was so numb that, in some ways, the accident felt like more of the same. People I cared about getting hurt and dying. And in other ways, it was an outrage that made me feel targeted by the fates."

"You must have been so angry," she said softly.

He gave her an odd look. "Yes. I was. I went off a few times in the hospital. It's not unusual with a head injury. But I wasn't hurt that badly, so that symptom faded."

"To be replaced by bad dreams."

"Yeah. I guess."

"More things you can't control."

He frowned at her. "Is this part of the lesson package?"

Her face grew warm, but she held his gaze. "No."

Now he flushed, then looked out at the grazing horses. "I'm self-conscious. Since moving back to Eagle Valley, you're the only person other than Pete I've talked to."

"Because I'm broken, too?"

"You aren't broken. You're strong."

"Yeah?" she said. "You haven't seen me try to go to a rodeo yet."

"Hey." Maddie popped out of the barn just then, startling Faith. "Since you guys are talking, can I see the goats before we go?"

Drew looked back at Faith. "You're still mowing with goats?"

"No." Her blush was starting to feel permanent. "I mowed the grass with my newly repaired lawn mower. The goats just tidy up along the edges."

"They're behind the house," Maddie said helpfully.

Drew nodded. "Go see goats. Do not try to bring one home." He let out a breath as Maddie smiled and headed toward the house. "I'm toast on this kitten deal. How long until they can leave the mom?"

"I think about two weeks."

"Great." He glanced over his shoulder to see if Maddie was out of hearing range. Turning back, he asked, "What happens when you go to a rodeo?"

"Well, not much happened the first time. I paid my entry and then couldn't find the courage to go."

He gave a considering nod. "The second time?"

"I made it to the rodeo, got out of the truck to unload Tommy and promptly had a meltdown." Despite having Sully and her pepper spray with her.

"What kind of meltdown?"

"The hide-in-your-trailer-and-cry kind. Not very pretty. It took me a while to compose myself to the point that I could drive." Her mouth went hard at the memory. "You know what brought it on?" He shook his head. "Someone stepping on gravel behind me. It almost sent me into orbit." She'd been instantly back in the moment when she'd heard her assailant approaching.

"Of course it did."

"It's hard to go to a rodeo and not hear gravel. Or smell concessions or manure or beer breath. All of those things set me off."

"As much as before?"

"I don't know." She glanced at the ground, rolled a small rock beneath her boot. "When I called and asked you to come with me, I thought I could do this. Now I'm having second thoughts."

"Have you got your saddle back?"

Her chin came up. "No. He won't pick up my calls or answer my texts."

"Do you need that saddle?"

"I *want* that saddle. I was on a waiting list for a year to get it."

Drew looked down at his hands, which

were lightly resting on the pole fencing. "I think you can do this."

"I don't want to melt down in front of Maddie."

"Then maybe you and I can go alone."

Faith frowned at him. "Will Maddie be okay with that?"

Drew looked guilty. "I didn't tell her yet."

"Why?"

"I wanted to make sure you were really going, so I wouldn't disappoint her."

Faith stepped away from the fence and ran her hands over her hair, bringing them to rest at the back of her neck. "Very forward thinking of you."

"Yeah. I know some of the pitfalls now."

"I'd like to try to go…if you're still in."

He gave her a look that made her insides tumble. "If you have a meltdown, am I allowed to touch you? I mean…will it make it worse?"

"I don't know." Her words were barely audible. They both looked over to where Maddie was crouched in the flowers, laughing as she patted the goats, who were play-butting her hands.

Drew pulled his attention back to Faith,

and slowly lifted his hand to place his warm fingers on the side of her face. Faith forgot to breathe.

"That…doesn't feel bad," she said.

He frowned a little as he cupped his palm to her cheek. In response, Faith brought a hand up to rest on his solid bicep. Yeah. This was okay.

It was also slow and gentle, and she'd known it was coming.

Drew turned his hand over to draw the backs of his fingers from her jaw to her chin in a slow caress. Nerves came alive in every part of her body before he let his hand drop back to his side.

"Well," Faith said when she finally found her voice. "Now we know you won't send me screaming off into the night if you touch me. As long as I'm ready for it."

The sound of Maddie's boots on the gravel drive made her jump, probably because she'd been so focused on Drew. They turned together to see her coming back their way.

"We should go." His voice was low, just a touch uneven.

"Yes." Faith moistened her lips. "I have things to catch up on."

"I have exterior siding to attach and three weed whackers to repair."

Faith gave a sputtering laugh, thankful that he'd lightened the moment, and Drew smiled back at her. A cheek-creasing, take-her-breath-away smile. "I'll see you on Friday then."

Somehow, she found her voice. "Yes. Friday."

DURING THE WEEK that followed, Drew threw himself into building Maddie's room. He also read up on nightmares. Again. After recovering physically from the explosion, he'd tried all the strategies he'd read about—rewriting endings, meditation, dream journals. Only the drugs had helped reduce the severity of the dreams, and they pretty much ruined him during his waking hours, regardless of how the doc adjusted the dosage.

*But you can have your kid with you.*

That was almost worth fuzzy days. He could have Maddie. He'd be fog-headed, but he wouldn't scare her to death.

Five short years. Then she'd be gone. He had to do something.

At one o'clock on Friday, he pulled into his

usual parking spot near Faith's barn. She'd taken the day off to go to her rodeo, and he didn't ask if Deb knew he was going with her. He doubted she did. Faith didn't seem to like his sister much. Go figure.

Faith came out of the barn leading Tommy, her black-and-white paint horse. She opened the trailer and tossed the lead rope over the horse's neck. He walked inside as if it was totally normal for a horse to step into a glorified tin can. After shutting the trailer door, she lifted a hand to Drew in greeting, then disappeared around the side. He ambled over and found her standing on the running board tying the rope to an upright bar on the trailer. She jumped down and dusted off her hand.

"How you doing?" he asked.

"Good. So far."

"You look like you did when you saw me walk into the café that first time."

She gave him a startled glance. "That bad?"

"Close. Are you worried about a meltdown? Or having me along to witness the meltdown?"

"Both."

"It's not like I'm going to judge you," he

said softly. "That would be a case of the pot calling the kettle black."

"Which is why I asked you to come," she admitted before squaring her shoulders. "I've been dying a thousand deaths since yesterday. Time for that to end."

"Agreed." The urge to take her in his arms, tell her he was here and everything was going to be all right was almost overpowering. Instead he jerked his head toward the truck. "We should get going."

"Yeah." She made her way to the driver's side as he walked around the back of the trailer.

She was already in her seat, facing straight ahead when he got into his. "I'm glad you didn't tell Maddie," she said.

"Me, too."

"And…I'm glad you're here with me." She turned her head to give him a candid look after putting the keys in the ignition. "Just don't let me lean on you too much. I need to learn to handle this on my own."

"I'll be the red handle you pull in case of emergency."

Faith bit her lip, but the smile broke through.

"Thank you." She shook her head and turned the key, still smiling a little.

Drew forced his gaze forward, doing his best to tamp down the growing feelings of both attraction and protectiveness. He was getting to the point where he wasn't certain where one ended and the other began, and that could easily get him into trouble if he didn't watch himself.

SUMMIT LAKE WAS only fifty miles from Eagle Valley, and Drew kept up an easy conversation as they drove, which was remarkable, since, as Drew had once told her, he wasn't a talker. But he seemed determined to keep Faith's mind off her upcoming trigger-fest. They talked about general matters—movies, television, books. Superficial topics that kept her from dwelling on her past.

The rodeo started at five. There would be no dark parking lot. No overnight stay. And she had a pretty good size bodyguard. But the smells would be there.

Faith's heart started beating faster as she pulled into the rodeo grounds, but it always beat faster when she arrived at a competition.

*You can do this. You can't let what that jerk did to you run your life.*

There weren't that many rigs parked in the competitors' area. She'd purposely picked a smaller venue for her first outing—fewer witnesses that way. Drew was silent as she reached for her door handle. No last words. No pep talk.

She let herself out of the truck, he did the same and they met at the hood. "What's first?" he asked. Faith drew in a deep breath, felt her muscles tighten. The scents she associated with that night were there—concessions, grass, manure, animal. The only thing missing was the metallic taste of the gravel dust she'd sucked into her mouth and lungs as she'd fought off her attacker.

Drew touched her hand and she jumped, then stared at him as his warm fingers wrapped around hers. "Smells are the worst," he said. "When I smell diesel exhaust, it takes me straight back to the scene. Scorched anything…"

Faith tightened her grip on his hand, stared into his cool blue eyes. "How do you deal?"

"You know that trick about identifying things close to you?"

"I use it a lot." She was using it now. Dark hair, gray shirt, blue eyes.

"That." He squeezed her hand. "And having someone close by."

"You have someone close by?"

He smiled a little. "Most times they aren't even people I know. I just look at them, pretend they're friends."

"And it works?"

"I don't have to do it that often. And…I've never told anybody about it."

"You need to talk more." Although he had talked a lot today.

He surprised her by saying, "You might be right."

She pulled her hand out of his warm grasp and settled her fists on her hips. "I need to go to the office."

"Want me to come?"

Her gut said, *No*. Her mouth said, "Yes." She wasn't going to screw this up. She was going to take advantage of the fact that she had someone willing to be here with her. Someone who might not be there the next time. If there was a next time.

Drew waited outside while she checked in, then walked with her back to the truck and helped her unload Tommy. Then it was a waiting game—but not that long of a wait, because she'd purposely gotten there late, after the rodeo proper had begun.

"I need to warm him up," she said after Tommy was saddled. "I'll be fine. I'm pretty sure I'm over the hump."

As long as she didn't encounter something unexpected. Boots on gravel, the sudden appearance of a large guy. Her senses were on overload, but so far, so good.

"Can I watch you warm up?"

"As opposed to watching the rodeo?"

He gave a careless shrug. "I've never been to a rodeo."

"How long have you lived in Montana?"

"All my life."

She gave a short laugh. "You have no excuse." He made a face at her and she smiled. It felt good to razz him, helped her ease back a couple of ticks toward normal. She swung up into the saddle—her practice saddle, rather than her custom saddle, thank you, Jared—and motioned toward the small practice arena where other competitors were trotting circles. "I'll be over there."

"And I'll be close by."

Faith turned Tommy and walked away, trying not to think about how good those words sounded.

DREW HADN'T BEEN lying when he'd said he'd never been to a rodeo. His family had been more suburban than Western, but he had watched rodeo events on television and had a passing familiarity with them. Barrel racing was the second to last event, and Faith spent most of the time between the halftime entertainment and her time slot warming up her horse. He wondered if she always spent that much time on warm-up, or if she simply wanted to keep busy, keep her senses focused on anything except for possible triggers.

When the barrel racing started, Faith rode up to him and told him she was going to the gate and to listen for her name. Less than five minutes later, she was announced in the hole. Then on deck. And then she was up.

As Faith made her run, Drew got the feeling that unlike the other contestants, she was holding her gelding back, focusing on making the sharpest turns possible before finally turning on the heat and sending the gelding home. She raced through the gate, then pulled Tommy to a stop. The horse bobbed his head, took a couple nervous steps, then started walking normally as Faith rode him toward the trailer.

"Hey," Drew said before he came up beside her horse, alerting her to his presence. She glanced down at him. She was panting a little, as if she'd been doing the running. "How do you feel?"

"Like I just got a small piece of my life back." She didn't smile and Drew had the feeling she was coming down from an adrenaline high. A moment later, she dismounted and started walking beside him, leading her horse, her gaze fixed on the trailer.

"Are you okay?"

"Yes. But I'd like to leave now." She shot him a sideways look. "Before something happens. I want this to end well." She stopped and he automatically stopped, too, but wasn't prepared for her to reach up and touch his face, very much as he'd touched her that day Maddie had been playing with the goats. A small army of shock waves marched through his body.

"I owe you," she said.

"You don't owe me."

Faith gave a noncommittal shrug and started walking again. When they reached the trailer, Faith expertly swapped out the bridle for a halter and tied the gelding to the metal ring welded to the side of the trailer. Then she turned to face him. "Yeah. I do."

Her eyebrows came together as she took a long moment to study his features, making him wonder what she saw. A guy past his prime? A guy who didn't have as good of a handle on life as he should? "I don't think I would have made it through warm-up if you hadn't been here. I kept thinking something was going to happen. Then I'd remind myself that you were here. I couldn't see you, but I knew you were here."

His heart twisted a little. And because there was no way he couldn't touch her, he once again traced the backs of his fingers down her smooth cheek. Her lips parted and he wanted so badly to kiss them.

"Drew?" She swallowed before she continued. "Do you think something could happen between us?"

The question slammed into him. It was one thing to think about it, to idly fantasize despite the reasons it seemed impossible. Another to have to face the matter dead-on.

"I…" He frowned fiercely. Shook his head, but he didn't necessarily mean no. "If it were to happen with anyone…"

"I'm not proposing," she said. "I'm just asking. Because I don't like wondering."

"Faith…"

She waved her hand as she took a step back. "That's okay."

It wasn't.

She started uncinching the saddle, but he reached out and stopped her with a touch of his hand on hers. Her gaze jerked up. "I was married for twelve years. I dated my wife through college. I haven't been with anyone else." He found himself shaking his head again. "More than that, I'm not a guy to get hooked up with."

"How about a guy to heal with?"

"What?" He was frowning so hard now he was getting a headache.

"To heal with. We understand each other. We're both isolated. We don't have to be." She glanced at the ground, pulled in a long breath, as if steeling herself. Then she raised her chin, very deliberately took his face in her hands and pulled his mouth down to hers. From somewhere in the distance, Drew heard a low whistle, but he was too stunned to process.

Faith's soft kiss ended too soon. Ended before he had the opportunity to explore her mouth, feel her body against his. When he opened his eyes, she wasn't smiling.

He settled his hands on either side of her hips, letting his fingers splay wide over her firm curves, wondering what the hell he was doing, then deciding her didn't care, as long as he could kiss her again. But before he could lower his head, there was a loud bang and a shout on the opposite side of the trailer and Faith crashed into him.

A second later a horse trotted by, dragging a long lead rope with a kid running a few strides behind it. The boy gave a diving leap and caught hold of the rope, ending the escape attempt.

Faith let out a shuddering breath and brought her forehead down to rest on Drew's chest. "I thought he had me for sure," she murmured before stepping back. Drew pulled her back into his arms, holding her loosely, needing the contact, even though he was half-afraid of it.

"Let's go home," Faith murmured.

"Yeah. Let's."

Even though he was also half-afraid of what might happen when they got there.

# CHAPTER NINE

DREW DROVE HOME while Faith stared at the highway, wishing she could fall asleep. She was mentally exhausted but still too hyped up on adrenaline to have half a hope of nodding off. They both had a lot to think about, so there was no conversation, superficial or otherwise.

She'd made it through a rodeo. She'd kissed Drew Miller. She wouldn't have thought twice about doing either two years ago, but tonight both were noteworthy events. Drew hadn't spoken since they'd gotten into the truck, and even though he'd started to kiss her back before she'd pulled away, she had a feeling he hadn't welcomed her kiss. Yet another complication in his already complex life.

Faith didn't want to be a complication. And that meant she needed to backtrack.

"About that kiss," she said when they were almost home. "And about my question." He glanced over at her. "We don't have to go there again."

"By 'go there,' you mean…?"

"I don't want lessons to be awkward."

"Thank you."

She felt a stab of disappointment at his answer but shoved it aside. Some things simply weren't meant to be. "I think there's an attraction there," she continued, wondering why she was seemingly unable to stop herself. "But we're in rugged places. Both of us."

"Yes."

"And it would be hell if we messed up our lives even more. Especially since we do seem to be doing each other some good."

Drew gave a nod instead of answering, then slowed the truck as they reached Eagle Valley city limits. He turned off the highway onto the road leading to the Lightning Creek Ranch, his jaw set, his expression hard. Faith shifted her gaze to the glove compartment.

She shouldn't have kissed him. Now he'd probably have a nightmare and it'd be her fault.

But the memory of his mouth on hers, the pressure of his lips, the way he'd tasted…

She wanted more.

After Drew parked the truck and trailer, and Sully bounded out of the barn, ready to resume his bodyguard duties, she expected Drew to get in his truck and drive away to safety. But no. He waited until she'd unloaded Tommy.

"I'm okay now," she said after he closed the trailer door.

"I know."

Faith frowned a little as she led Tommy past him and then released the horse into the pasture. When she turned back, Drew was still there.

He rubbed his hand across his forehead, as if prepping for an unpleasant task, then dropped it back to his side. "We *do* do each other some good."

Faith swallowed as adrenaline started to spike again. "I think so."

"And there's a level of understanding between us."

"Yes."

"I don't want to lose that."

She wasn't certain she'd heard right. "Me, neither. I shouldn't have kissed you."

He gave a short laugh. "Well, that didn't make things easier." He began to close the distance between them, taking slow, mea-sured steps, as if he didn't want to spook her. Faith swore she could feel the warmth of his body before he was close enough for it to be physically possible. Or maybe it was her own body feeling like it was ready to burst into flames.

He took her face between his hands, just as she'd done to him a little more than an hour ago, his touch light. Gentle. "I'm not ready, Faith. Not for anything more than something physical. And those things often end poorly."

"I know."

But it didn't keep her from wanting him to do that physical thing. Although…

She moistened her lips. "I haven't done anything since the attack. Kissing you was the first sexual thing I've done."

"You need to stop telling me these things," he muttered in a hoarse voice.

"And I trust you…so I guess I thought… you know."

Drew gave a low groan. "You're killing me."

"Not meaning to."

He let out a long breath, shook his head. Stepped back. "Give me a little time on this. Okay?"

"Yeah. Sure."

"You're a beautiful woman, Faith. Your ex was an idiot."

"He also has my saddle."

Drew gave a laugh that he turned into a cough. "And you know how to lighten a moment." He leaned forward and pressed his lips to her forehead. "Not where I want to put them," he said. "But it'll have to do for now."

DREW RARELY KEPT anything from his daughter, but he didn't tell Maddie that he'd gone to a rodeo with Faith. If Faith hadn't kissed him, if he didn't have so much to process, if the trip hadn't been sexually charged, he would have told her when he'd picked her up the following day for their time together. But using the excuse that he didn't want to hurt Maddie's feelings by leaving her out, he failed to mention he'd already been to a rodeo when he asked if she wanted to watch Faith run barrels at the Eagle Valley Rodeo the next weekend.

"Are you kidding? Yes, I want to watch her race."

"Maybe Pete and I can come along," Cara suggested as she set a pot roast on the table. Once or twice a month, Drew stayed for a Sunday dinner after dropping Maddie off. Tonight was one of those nights.

"Sure," Drew said. "I hear it's kind of fun." And didn't he feel shifty? "Actually, I *know* it's kind of fun. I drove Faith to a rodeo last Friday."

Maddie's mouth fell open. "You went without me?"

"I had a reason."

"What was that?" she demanded. Cara also seemed interested.

"It's complicated." Now Cara's eyebrows were practically touching in the middle. Drew met her gaze and said, "She had a bad experience at a rodeo and hasn't been to one for over a year. She didn't want Maddie there in case she broke down."

"Yeah? What kind of bad experience?" Cara set the gravy next to the roast.

"She was assaulted."

Now Cara's mouth dropped open and Maddie frowned. "How?"

"A guy mugged her." But he looked at Cara as he spoke, silently telling her it was more than a mugging.

"Like knocked her down? Stole her purse? Or worse?" Maddie asked.

"Knocked her down. Some people came by right after and the guy ran off," Drew said, glad he didn't have to lie. "But it scared her bad. She didn't want to go to the rodeo alone, so I went with her."

Maddie continued to frown down at her potatoes.

Cara lifted her eyebrows and shook her head. "There are some sickos out there." She leveled a gaze at Maddie. "Which is why curfews are a good thing."

Always a teaching moment. He remembered Lissa doing the same thing when Maddie was little. He missed her. Felt guilty for being alive when she wasn't. More than that, he felt guilty for starting to *feel* alive. For experiencing flickers of hope and happiness. For thinking about sex in a serious way.

Of course, his subconscious had punished him that night and he'd woken up to a destroyed bed and barely made it down the mountain to pick up Maddie this morning.

Were the nightmares tied to Lissa? To stress? To guilt?

All he could do was soldier on and hope he hit upon the answer.

Before it was too late for him and Maddie and anyone else who might show up in his life.

CARA AND PETE decided to go to Missoula for a big shopping trip instead of the rodeo, so Drew and Maddie drove to the rodeo grounds on the outskirts of Eagle Valley alone. When Drew had graduated high school, the rodeo grounds were at least a mile out of town. Now the city limits abutted the parking lot.

"Have you ever been to a rodeo, other than the one last week?" Maddie asked as Drew found a parking place.

"Last week was my first."

A guy in full cowboy regalia led his horse by and Maddie stared after him. She turned back to Drew and asked, "Where do you think Faith is?"

He pointed to a field beside the parking lot that was packed with trucks and trailers. "I suspect that she's over there."

Maddie suddenly pointed. "There's Tommy."

"Great. Be careful walking behind the horses," he said as they started toward Faith's trailer. There were a lot of animals tethered in the competitors' area, and the space between trailers was sometimes narrow.

"I know. Faith has talked about that."

There was no sign of Faith as they approached, but the door to the small tack room at the front of the trailer was ajar and Maddie pulled it open.

Faith gave a yelp and whirled, then let out a shaky breath when she recognized the girl. She pressed her hand to her chest and swallowed hard.

"I'm sorry," Maddie said. "I should have knocked."

Faith waved a hand. "No. I'm always jumpy before I compete. You're fine."

Maddie met Drew's gaze, then looked back at Faith. "I hope you win today."

"I'm not trying to win yet. I'm just getting back into the swing of things."

Maddie frowned. "Kind of like practicing?"

"Yes. It'll take a while before I'm winning again."

"Did you used to win?"

Faith's smile became more genuine. "All the time."

"Then the bad thing happened?"

Faith's startled gaze jerked up to Drew's. "I told her that the guy tried to mug you."

"You must have been really scared," Maddie said.

"I was." Faith looked at Drew again, then said in an overly bright voice, "I need to finish saddling up."

"Can I help?" Maddie asked.

"Sure," she said. "Get the bridle with the silver on it."

Maddie disappeared into the tack room and Drew said in a low voice. "I had to tell her something to explain why I went with you, but I didn't want to scare her to death."

"I'm fine with what you told her. It works. I just don't want her to look at me differently."

Drew was well aware of the feeling, and could appreciate that Faith didn't want to be defined by victim status any more than he did.

Maddie came out of the tack compartment with the silver-studded bridle. "It was under some other stuff."

"Thanks for digging," Faith said. She bridled Tommy, then checked her cinch. Maddie wandered a few yards away to inspect the horses tied to the trailer next to hers.

"We're going to watch from the rail if we can find a spot," Drew said. "That way if you need me, I'll be easier to see."

"If you go over there," Faith pointed to an area between the announcer's stand and the main gate, where there was a small, three-tier set of bleachers, "you might be able to get seats without going into the main stands."

"I'll try to do that."

Faith swung up onto Tommy's back and gathered the reins. Drew moved closer and put a light hand on the top of her boot. "Good luck. Maddie and I will be close by."

She bit her lip as she looked down at him. Her green eyes were wide and wary, and he wondered if it was because of him or because of the demons she was trying to beat into submission. "That means a lot."

"Are you okay?" he asked.

"Still coming down from being startled," she confessed.

"Some bodyguard I am."

"It happens. More often than I'd like."

One corner of her mouth tilted up. "Not a big deal."

She pointed her chin to where Maddie was watching a girl saddle her pony. "And since *you* also have a bodyguard here, I won't ask you for a kiss for luck."

With that, she turned her horse and rode toward the field where other riders were warming up. He watched her go and realized he was still smiling.

MADDIE SEEMED OVERWHELMED by the sheer number of horses, cowboys and cowgirls as they walked the grounds before the rodeo started. When they came upon the mounted drill team waiting near the entry to the arena, Maddie's mouth dropped open. The horses were covered in glitter and spangles, with fancy bright pink blankets under their saddles that matched the riders' bright pink satin shirts.

"How do you make the glitter stay on your horse?" Maddie asked a woman nearby, forgetting her shyness.

"Hairspray," the lady answered with a smile.

"Really?"

"Just spray it on the horse's rump, then spread the glitter."

"What about the hooves?" Maddie pointed to the black glittery stuff there.

"That's a roll-on. You can find it online. A lot of Western stores carry it, too."

Maddie narrowed her eyes thoughtfully. "How do you become part of…whatever you are?"

The woman laughed. "You look for us online. We're the Rhinestone Rough Riders."

"Cool! Good luck with your performance."

"Thank you," several of the women called as they began moving their horses to line up at the gate.

"I need a horse," Maddie said in a thoughtful voice as they made their way to the three-tiered stands that appeared to be reserved for the crew that worked the arena as well as family of the competitors. No one questioned their right to be there—the beauty of a small event—so Drew and Maddie settled in.

Maddie loved the rough stock, just as Faith had predicted, laughing at the clown who entertained between events, and after the trained dogs performed during the halftime break, she told Drew that maybe she needed a terrier, too.

When the barrel racing started, Maddie was on the edge of her seat. After the first contestant, she sat back a little. "I want to run barrels."

Drew put a hand on the back of her neck. "I was afraid of that."

"I could do it…with a lot more lessons. Good thing Faith lives close to us, huh?"

The next barrel racer charged into the arena, her horse nearly losing its footing as it rounded barrel number one, then kicking up divots as it regained its balance and headed for the next one. Maddie was back on the edge of her seat. The third barrel went over, and she let out an audible moan of disappointment.

Faith was announced on deck and Maddie craned her neck to see her. Drew was tall enough to see over the heads of the people around them and he easily spotted her on her distinctive horse in the waiting area outside the gate. Unlike a lot of the other horses, Tommy stood stock-still, looking as focused as the woman on his back.

"There she goes!" Maddie leaned so far

forward, Drew was surprised she didn't fall off the bleacher seat onto the lady in front of her.

Tommy didn't charge into the arena as quickly as the previous horses. His turns were smoother, more fluid, and when he raced to the finish line, it wasn't with the desperate need for speed Drew had seen in the other competitors.

"She's still conditioning him," Maddie announced to no one in particular, and Drew found her need to defend Faith touching.

"She did good," Drew said. He jerked his head toward the trailers. "Want to go see her, or do you want to watch the bull riding?"

"I want to go see Faith."

FAITH FULLY EXPECTED Drew and Maddie to remain in the stands for the bull riding, but instead they met her at the trailer not long after she tied up Tommy.

"Wow," Maddie said. "He's sweating."

"Nerves," Faith replied as she uncinched the saddle.

"He didn't look nervous."

"He keeps a lot inside. That's one reason he's such a good horse." Faith dragged the saddle off his back, then jumped a mile as she turned. Drew was there. Right *there*. Where she hadn't expected him to be. He took an automatic step back, a frown creasing his forehead, then he slowly reached out for the saddle. She let him take it before wiping her hands down the sides of her pants.

That was twice.

"I thought it was bad to keep things inside," Maddie mused as she grabbed a brush out of the bucket on the running board and started brushing Tommy's flank.

"I guess there's a happy middle ground," Faith said, grooming Tommy's other side, her nerves still humming from being startled. She didn't like having men behind her—even ones that she trusted. "You don't want him to be dancing and impossible to control, but you don't want him to fall asleep waiting for his turn."

"How much does a barrel horse cost?" Maddie asked.

"Well, Tommy cost $8,000 and he's about a third of what a low-end proven winner would cost you."

Maddie's mouth dropped open. "Eight thousand?"

"I got him young, so he didn't cost as much as he would have if he'd been older."

"Eight *thousand*?"

"You don't have to pay that much, though. Some people get lucky and get a good horse for a whole lot less. Other people like to buy a horse that will put them in the money."

"But you didn't."

"I couldn't afford to," she said with a laugh.

"Then it's okay to just buy a regular horse and teach it to run barrels."

"And there are a lot of other things you can do with a regular horse. Things that don't cost as much as following the rodeo circuit. If I only had one horse, I would get a trail horse."

"I want a barrel horse," Maddie said. "A cheap one."

"I'll keep my eyes open," Faith promised.

Maddie headed off to the ladies' room before they started home, leaving Drew and Faith truly alone since he'd arrived at the rodeo. He put his hands into his back pockets, a troubled expression on his face.

"I'm sorry I scared you. Sorry Maddie scared you."

"Hey. That's the stuff I'm learning to deal with."

"I know. Doesn't make it any easier to watch."

She tilted her head. "Gee, Drew. It almost sounds as if you care." She'd been trying for light, trying to defuse the tension that was making her feel stiff and awkward, but it didn't come off that way. And now it was too late to do anything about it.

And then she didn't have to, because Drew reached out and gently pulled her into his arms, cradling her against him. "I'm sorry," he said. "Won't happen again."

She laid her head against his chest, felt his heart beating under her cheek. She was tempted to lift her face so that he could kiss her, but Maddie would be back soon and Faith wasn't about to risk upsetting his daughter, so instead she pulled back, and Drew's hands fell away from her. He wasn't ready for a relationship, and she didn't know if she was capable of one.

But it had still felt damned good to be held in his arms.

## CHAPTER TEN

ON SATURDAY MORNING, Drew picked Maddie up from her friend Shayla's house, where she'd spent the night. Grazing in the pasture were three horses and Drew wondered which was the "good one" that Shayla's sister didn't share.

"The white one," Maddie informed him when he asked on the way out the driveway. "But even though Bailey was gone, I couldn't ride it. Aunt Cara said that I'm not allowed to get on any horses until I've had more lessons."

"Good idea," Drew said dryly.

"I wish we could drive to the rodeo with Faith."

"Yeah. Things just didn't work out to do that." As it was, they were following Faith so she could drive alone. Another step in her plan to regain autonomy.

"Maybe the next rodeo."

"Maybe."

For not being a horse guy, this rodeo thing was rapidly becoming part of his life…as were his feelings for Faith, which he didn't know what to do with. She was still fighting demons and he couldn't guarantee that he wouldn't present her with another.

No…he was damned certain he would present her with another.

It was hell when you wanted to protect someone and you were one of the threats. But there was one simple way to not be a threat—keep his distance. As difficult as that was becoming.

They drove to the highway, where Faith was waiting with her truck and trailer. When he pulled up beside her on the turnout, she waved at Maddie, then pulled onto the road. Drew followed and settled in for the two-hour drive to Clovis.

"Dad…are you ever going to get a girl-friend?"

Drew shot his daughter a startled look. "Why do you ask?"

"Shayla says that her mom says that you're

really good-looking and she thinks you should get back in the game."

Drew pulled his gaze back to the road. "I see." Did he know Shayla's mom? Had he gone to school with her? Did he want women he didn't know discussing him?

"I think it would be weird for you to have a girlfriend."

"Yeah. I can see that." Drew's heart was beating a little harder. "I think it will be weird when you have a boyfriend."

"Dad!"

He smiled over at her, hoping it looked more genuine than nervous. "I'm not ready for a girl-friend." Maddie seemed mildly relieved. "But if I ever do get back in the game, you know you'll always be number one in my life…and that I will never stop loving your mom."

Her mouth worked a little, then she gave a quick nod. He reached over and gave her knee a reassuring pat.

"Sometimes I kind of forget what she looks like," his daughter confessed. "I have to look at pictures. And she's all frozen in them."

"But…you remember what she felt like, right? The way she made you feel?"

"Yeah."

"That will always live in you. Through everything."

"For real?"

"Yeah."

"So how can you love someone else if you will always love Mom?"

"My mom told me that hearts are elastic. They just stretch to make room for more love." It had seemed corny at the time, but now he was glad she'd said it.

"Huh." Maddie frowned down at her hands. "I guess that's true." She looked back over at him. "Do you like Faith?"

"I do. She's a nice woman."

"I think she likes you."

Drew gripped the steering wheel a little tighter. "If she didn't, I don't think we'd be following her right now."

Maddie looked like she wanted to say more, but instead she focused back on the road, leaving Drew to feel as if he'd dodged a bullet.

DRIVING TO THE rodeo alone was part of Faith's weaning process. First, she'd drive with Drew behind her, and then, eventually, she would go to the rodeo alone. Not that she had any big hankering to not have Drew come along, but she was realistic enough to recognize a roadblock when she saw one. Or two.

By his own admission, Drew wasn't ready. She wasn't going to push. It wasn't her place to push. She'd be happy with their friendship, grateful that he'd helped her move forward. Shown her she didn't have to be afraid of big guys on general principle.

When they got to the rodeo, Faith eased her truck and trailer in between two others, then unloaded Tommy. She'd just gotten him tied to the sidebar when Maddie came skipping up.

"Dad said we had to park with the normal people."

"The spectators?"

"I guess." She grabbed a brush and started working it over Tommy's smooth coat. "Are you going to ride faster today?"

"I might put on a little speed."

"Aunt Cara used to run track. She explained to me why you can't make Tommy go too fast, too soon."

Faith ran the brush down Tommy's legs. "She's right. I didn't know I would be competing this season, so I didn't condition him enough."

"I want to learn to run the barrels. If I keep coming to lessons, can I learn?"

"Sure. It just won't be next week or anything."

"I know. Dad says I need to learn patience."

"I'm behind you, Faith."

Both Maddie and Faith turned at the sound of Drew's voice, and even with the warning, Faith gave a small start.

"I let Maddie off at the edge of the competitor's area before I parked."

"With the normal people," Faith supplied. He frowned at her and she smiled back innocently. "Maybe you guys should get seats before the rodeo starts. I'm going to take my time warming up." She gave Maddie a serious look. "You don't want to miss the rough stock. Lots of cool cowboys there."

"My daughter doesn't need to be ogling 'cool cowboys,'" Drew said with mock sternness, making Maddie roll her eyes.

"Come on, Dad. We'll get good seats, so we can watch Faith win. She's going to let Tommy run today."

Drew met Faith's eyes, raised his eyebrows.

She nodded, then gave a small who-knows shrug, and his lips tilted up. Silent communication. Yes, she was going to let Tommy run. No, she probably wouldn't win.

After Drew and Maddie headed for the stands, Faith finished saddling Tommy and headed to the practice arena, where she walked him along the rail. Just…walked. Her thoughts weren't nearly as jumbled as the first two times she'd done this. And now she didn't need to think about what it would be like to kiss Drew, as she had at her first rodeo, to keep herself from panicking, cutting and running.

Now she knew.

Which meant she could distract herself by thinking about the actual experience.

Rodeo was a small world and some of the people she knew from her past life rode up to say hello, give her an encouraging smile. Everyone knew what had happened to her— why she'd stopped competing—but no one referenced the event or asked how she'd been, perhaps afraid she'd give a real answer.

Her two closest rodeo friends, the ones she'd left at the bar when she'd gone back to the campsite early, had both quit rodeo, moved across the country. She got the occasional email or text, but they'd moved on with their lives and their Montana rodeo summers were a thing of the past. Neither of them had been on track for Nationals. Neither of them had wanted it as much as Faith.

She didn't want Nationals anymore. She just wanted to be competitive in her state. To run for fun and to earn enough money to pay for her gas. To feel free again and not caged in by one asshole's sick action. That would be gold.

That would make her feel like she had her life back.

Faith started trotting Tommy in circles, loosening him up, helping him flex and bend. Judging by the loudspeaker, her event was about thirty minutes away. She'd just finished with a circle and started Tommy along the rail when a woman rode by. Faith jerked her head around as she passed.

That was her saddle.

*Her* saddle.

She turned Tommy and caught up with the woman, who gave her a frowning glance. "Hi. Are you a friend of Jared Canon?"

"Maybe."

"You're riding in my saddle."

"What?"

"That's my saddle."

The woman let out a scoffing breath. "No, it's really not," she said lightly.

"Then why are my initials on the back of the cantle?" There was absolutely no mistaking the saddle as hers with the small sterling letters set in the leather. "And there's a date stamped into the underside of the left fender."

"He bought it used."

"He stole it from me, and FYI, I'm taking him to small-claims court unless he can come up with a bill of sale with my signature on it." *Please pass that message along.*

The woman urged her horse forward, and Faith pulled Tommy up, her heart beating faster after the confrontation. She wasn't going to chase the woman down. But she was getting her saddle back. First, she'd make her run, and then see about the saddle. Except if Jared was here, he'd make a getaway as soon as the barrel racing was over—and he discovered that Faith was competing against his ladylove.

If he did, he did. She'd been serious about small-claims court when she'd first mentioned it to him, and she was even more serious now.

Tommy started dancing when she slowed him to a walk and she made an effort to relax her tight body. It was making her horse edgy, but anger felt surprisingly good. The woman might have been unaware of how Jared got the saddle, but she knew now. And Faith hoped she gave Jared what-for over it.

As Faith continued to warm up, she kept an eye out for Jared at the rail. When her event was called, she still hadn't seen him, hadn't spotted his vehicle. She calmly lifted Tommy's reins and urged him toward the waiting area. She was number ten in the lineup. Her stolen saddle was number two. Her saddle, and the woman sitting in it, set the bar to the event with a time of 17.071. A high bar. One Faith was fairly certain she wouldn't be reaching, but she'd give it her best shot.

After sliding to a stop just outside the gate, saddle-woman rode her dancing horse past Faith, both her chin and her color high. Despite her tremendous time, she looked angry.

*Good.*

Faith's name was called and she rode Tommy into position. Somewhere in the stands, a twelve-year-old girl was rooting for her. And maybe her dad was rooting for her, too. She took a breath, then sent Tommy forward. He crowded the barrel on the first turn, dropping his inside shoulder. Faith raised her own shoulder on the next turn, putting her weight in her outside stirrup and engaging his outer leg. Perfect turn. Followed by another, then Tommy stretched out to his full length as he raced home.

17.399. Not a winner. But maybe second.

Faith worked to bring her breathing back to normal as she rode Tommy halfway to her trailer, then got off and walked, her legs feeling heavy after so much time in the saddle.

She switched the bridle for the halter, tied Tommy up, unsaddled him and carried the tack into her trailer compartment. She climbed inside to lift the saddle onto the rack, then jumped a mile as someone stepped into the trailer, pulling the door shut behind them.

"You bitch."

For a moment, she thought her heart was going to explode. It seemed to swell in her chest as her frozen brain tried to grab hold of reality. *Trapped*. She was trapped with no escape and this angry guy, who'd once been her lover, was between her and the door.

She pulled in a shaky breath, tried to calm the reactive side of her brain so that the other side could operate. "M-move aside, Jared." She croaked out the words as she reached behind her to find some sort of weapon. Unless she beat him to death with a halter, she had nothing.

"You just had to tell Tara about the saddle."

"I…"

"What?" he asked darkly. He moved forward in the small space and Faith pressed herself back between the saddle racks and the trailer wall. Oh yeah, her heart was going to beat its way out of her chest. "I told you I'd buy the damned thing. I saw your times in the last two rodeos. You don't need it. You're done with serious competition."

Her hand kept groping and finally curled around the riding crop. She lifted it off the hook. "Get back, Jared."

"Oh," he said with a sneer. "Am I scaring you? Are you still 'dealing' with shit?"

She was about to raise the crop when the trailer door slammed open, and a big hand landed on Jared's shoulder, yanking him outside.

He gave a startled yelp as he tumbled backward, and gave another more strangled one as Drew hauled him to his feet and pushed him against the trailer, his hand on Jared's throat. "What's wrong with you?" Drew growled at the man. "Shutting her in like that."

"I… I—" Jared gave a strangled cough, clutching at the hand on his throat.

"Let him go, Drew."

At first Faith didn't think he'd heard her, but then he glanced over his shoulder and she was stunned at the stone-cold look on his face. Her lips parted as her throat went dry. "Please," she said. "Before Maddie gets here."

His daughter's name seemed to bring him back. He let out a shaking breath, then slowly let go of Jared, who practically crumpled to the ground.

"You're in deep shit, man." Jared's voice was rough.

"Keep the saddle," Faith said. "I'll write you a bill of sale. Tell Tara I'm a liar."

Jared got to his feet, stumbling a little in the process, and once he was a safe distance from Drew, he said, "I'll sue your ass for assault."

"I'll do the same," Faith said.

Jared's angry gaze swept toward her. "I never laid a hand on you."

"You trapped me. Wrongful imprisonment."

Jared rubbed his hand over his throat, shooting Drew a cautious look.

"Don't give him the saddle," Drew said.

Faith shook her head. "Keep it," she told Jared. "Just…leave. Now."

"Mail me the bill of sale?"

Drew made a step toward him and Jared jumped, then turned and hurried off, shooting a nervous look over his shoulder before disappearing around the nearest trailer. Drew pressed his fingers to his forehead, then turned to Faith. "Are you okay?"

She slowly shook her head before dropping her chin to her chest. "Not right at this moment."

He was breathing heavily, his chest heaving. "I might have handled that wrong."

She looked up. "You think?" She scanned the grounds behind him. "Where's Maddie?"

"Ladies' room. We agreed to meet here, then I saw that guy follow you into the trailer."

"Here she comes." Faith raised her chin in

the direction of the stands, where Maddie's bright pink shirt shone like a beacon. She was still a good distance away—far enough away for Faith to escape. There was no way she could fake a smile or act like everything was all right. "I need to go."

"What do I tell Maddie?"

"I wish I knew."

"I can't let you drive like this."

She tightened her lips. "You don't have a whole lot of say in the matter."

HE'D SNAPPED.

For the first time since leaving the hospital, he'd lost control, and Faith had not only been there to witness it—she'd been the catalyst. When he saw that guy sneaking up on her trailer, then quickly stepping into the tack room and closing the door, his only thought had been to get Faith out of there. To save her.

Oh, he'd saved her all right, but at what cost? To himself? To her? The woman who'd told him she trusted him must now see that she didn't even know him.

And he had no idea what to do about that. His head told him to do nothing. To leave Faith alone, let her work this latest trauma out without adding to it. His gut told him that at the very least he needed to make sure she was all right.

"Are you okay, Dad?"

"I'm…uh…getting the beginnings of a headache."

"Maybe you have what Faith has." Maddie had accepted Faith leaving suddenly because she wasn't feeling well, and she'd kept a close eye on her trailer a couple of car lengths ahead of them since they'd left Clovis. Faith drove just under the speed limit, so he'd been able to catch up with her.

"Yeah. I think I do." A big case of reality sucks.

What kind of man was he, to lose it like that?

Although…his mouth hardened at the thought…he would have done almost the exact same thing before the tragedies in his life. He wasn't one to let guys pick on women. Or anyone, for that matter. But he probably wouldn't have choked the guy down.

He owed Faith an apology. And he owed it to her to take a step back in their relationship.

"Are you good with us not working on the

room tomorrow?" Maddie asked, breaking into his thoughts.

He glanced her way. "We'll have lots of weekends to build." Maddie's invitation to a birthday party at the local pool was an excellent reason to not build together, and Drew was relieved. He had no idea what his night was going to be like. What shape he'd be in in the morning. "And I think I might pass on Sunday dinner, too."

"I'll tell Aunt Cara that you're coming down with something."

"I'll tell her myself. But thanks."

Faith left the highway, turning onto the Lightning Creek road, and Drew continued to the other end of town, to Pete's house.

"Dad's not feeling good," Maddie announced as Cara came out onto the porch.

"Nothing serious, I hope?" She pushed the hair back from her forehead with the back of her hand.

"Just a headache right now. I'm going to take it easy tomorrow and pass on dinner."

Cara smiled. "Cool. Then Pete and I can have a date night."

Date night. How long had it been? "Yeah.

Well, I need to hit the road. Maddie stayed off horses and all went well."

"How'd your girl do?"

"My girl?"

"You know… Faith. Did she do well in her event?"

"She came in second."

Cara gave an approving nod. "Good for her. Tell her hi from us." She gave him a smile, then disappeared into the house.

His girl. He should set the record straight, confess that he'd scared the crap out of her by coming unhinged, but instead he headed to his truck, dialing his phone with one hand before starting the ignition. Thankfully, Faith picked up.

"Are you home?"

"Just got here."

"Are you okay?"

"I'm better than I was." He heard her clear her throat. "How are you?"

"Not homicidal, if that's what you're asking. I'm…sorry about losing it." Sorry and afraid it might happen again. "I…just wanted to check in. Make sure you're okay."

"Sully's here. Tommy is in the pasture. I'm heading for bed."

*Don't have nightmares.*

"Will you be all right?"

"Yeah, Drew." She sounded weary. "I think I will."

WHEN FAITH CLOSED her eyes and concentrated, she could perfectly picture the stone-cold look on Drew's face as he'd gone after Jared. And she wondered what he might have done if she hadn't been there to stop him.

There were facets of the man she hadn't been aware of and she found that discovery unnerving. Had her instincts been wrong? She opened her eyes to stare up at the ceiling. The yard lamp gave off just enough light for her to make out the fixture, the molding where it met the wall. Beside the bed, Sully snored softly. Everything was just as it had been the night before...except that tonight she probably wouldn't sleep.

She'd had a freaking awful scare. Now that she'd calmed down, she was able to look at things more rationally. Jared wouldn't have hurt her physically, but he'd been trying to scare her, to hurt her mentally. As their relationship had progressed, he'd shown a lot of ego, had a hard time laughing at himself, but she'd told herself that no one was perfect. He had good points. A lot of them. Unfortunately, those hadn't shown after the attack, when being with her had apparently become troublesome, limiting and inconvenient. Jared hadn't been in her corner.

Was Drew?

She didn't know. The cold look on his face. Could he take a knife, slice off some woman's hair?

She hated that she'd just thought that.

Faith squeezed her eyes shut again, felt tears welling. Her attacker had been violently proactive. Drew had been reactive. Someone he knew, someone he cared about, had been threatened.

That was different…right?

Different or not, it had still scared her.

The next morning, Faith wrote up her fake bill of sale, with its fake date, and put it in the mail to Jared as promised. After what had transpired, she didn't want her custom saddle, didn't want to recall how reality had slammed into her when Jared had closed that tack room door, trapping her.

Didn't want to remember how it had shaken her confidence. As she'd driven home, she kept telling herself that she couldn't put herself in a position where things like that could happen. And she couldn't keep dragging Drew to rodeos. He'd been to three. Enough.

Could she go to a rodeo alone after this last incident?

Her logical side said it wouldn't happen again.

Her anxious side said, *What if it did?*

Then logic had waffled and said, *Okay. Jared and his lady friend might well be at your next rodeo. Maybe you shouldn't go.*

The outraged-at-feeling-like-a-victim side said, *Take a chance. Go.*

Then anxiety said, *No freaking way. You were in that trailer with your back against the wall. Remember?*

And what about Drew? She still had to figure that one out before lessons. Which gave her six days. For five of those days, she could hide out in her basement office. Mindlessly do her work and regroup. Consider her next move in her recovery.

And stop thinking about Drew, which was impossible, which was in turn frustrating.

Drew and frustration. The pair went hand in hand.

*What about Drew and fear?* her small inner voice asked. *Are you afraid of him? Or of what happened?*

*Or, more specifically, what might have happened?*

Drew had done what a lot of guys might have in the same situation. He shouldn't have laid hands on Jared, but Jared shouldn't have trapped her in the tack room. Drew had been protecting her...just as she'd asked him to when she'd invited him to travel with her.

## CHAPTER ELEVEN

MADDIE WAS SUBDUED at lessons, almost as if she knew that something was up between her dad and her instructor, so Faith made an extreme effort to act exactly as she had before the Clovis rodeo, which might well have been her last. She was still debating that matter.

She and Drew had had no contact during the week, except for his text asking if lessons were still a go. She'd written back, Of course, and received a Thanks in response. After that—nothing. Which meant she'd had a lot of time to think without being influenced by his presence.

And she'd come to some conclusions.

After brushing the horses, they tacked up and mounted. She called Drew over and firmly put his leg in the correct position, telling herself that at this moment in time, he was just a student. But that didn't stop her nerves from jangling long after she'd sent him on his way along the rail. She shoved her hands into her back pockets and watched as he pushed down through his heels. "Better," she called.

"Thank you," he said loud enough for Maddie to hear, apparently also trying to put on a good face for his daughter. Had he had any repercussions from the situation with Jared?

Dare she ask?

She did not.

"Reverse course and trot." Drew was becoming a master at posting, and his balance had increased significantly. When he pulled Freckles to a stop, he always patted her, then ruffled her thick mane—even today, when he'd drawn so far into himself it was surprising he was visible to the naked eye.

She'd been nervous about lessons, nervous about seeing Drew for the first time since the rodeo, wondering if her gut instincts would fall in line with her rational thought processes. So far, so good…on her end, anyway. Her nerves had nothing to do with fear of the guy she was teaching to go over cavalettis at a trot. They were how-is-this-all-going-to-play-out nerves.

Once the lessons were over, Maddie made her usual trek to the barn.

"Can Maddie really have a kitten?" Drew asked.

Faith, who'd been feeling awkward about having their first private conversation since the rodeo incident, blinked at him. "She can have all she wants."

"Thank you." No smile. No warmth. Just... thank you. He headed into the barn after his daughter, but Faith stayed where she was, listening as father and daughter debated kitten pros and cons, while thinking that he'd come up with a most effective way to avoid a conversation with her.

Finally, Maddie said, "This one and...this one." A moment later, she came out holding two yellow-and-white kittens, grinning from ear to ear. "These ones."

Faith smiled. "They're yours. Do you need a box?"

Maddie glanced up at her dad as a realization struck. "We have to go to town and get stuff. Kitty litter and food and—"

"I already did that."

Maddie's jaw dropped and Faith's came

close. Drew shifted, appearing uncomfortable. "I wanted to surprise you."

Maddie threw an arm around him, while keeping the two tiny kittens cuddled close against her chest with the other. "Thank you!" She was practically dancing as she headed for the truck.

Drew watched her get in, then glanced at Faith. "Thank you again." His tone made it clear there would be no further conversation. No exchanging of thoughts, feelings, insights. None of that.

"Glad to do it. Now I only have to find homes for the other four."

"Wish I could help." He gestured toward the truck. "I'd better go." If he sounded any more wooden, he would have been sprouting branches.

She called Sully and walked toward the house without turning back. Crazy how one incident could change things so radically—the way she looked at him, and, she suspected, the way he looked at himself. She pulled open the screen door as his truck pulled out of the driveway, then allowed herself a look in that general direction.

He might think this was over, but it wasn't. At least not until she'd had a chance to address the matter.

"Ow, ow, ow…"

"Just let her climb, Dad."

"I don't think so." Drew bent down to detach the tiny kitten from his pant leg. How could he have lived his entire life without playing with a kitten?

Drew's family had never had pets. His mom was allergic and, came to find out, Lissa—lover of all things furry—was also allergic, like her brother. It had been rough on her not to be able to cuddle every little creature who crossed her path—until she had Maddie. Then she'd given up mourning her lost furry cuddles and focused on her baby. She'd been a hell of a mom. She'd had to be, since she'd ended up being both mom and dad to Maddie for months at a time.

As soon as they'd gotten back to the cabin, Maddie had promptly announced that the yellow kitten with white spots was Rosalee and the white kitten with yellow spots was named Cecily. Together she and Drew prepared kitty litter boxes in both the house and the shop, put down food and water, made little beds. Then Maddie spent the rest of the day cuddling and playing and nurturing while Drew put insulation into her bedroom.

He was surprised that the recent stress in his life had not culminated in another room-wrecking nightmare. Maybe that was a sign that the dreams were gone for good. Right?

Sure. That's how things work in the real world.

He *was* working on cutting the self-pity. Yes. Life had walloped him. He felt cheated in some ways, but he was totally blessed in others and that was where his focus would lie.

The blessings.

His biggest blessing was in the living room playing with kittens, and she hadn't seen him lose it at the rodeo, so yeah. Blessings.

After lunch and another kitten play session, they went to work on the siding, Drew on the ladder and Maddie handing him boards.

"What's wrong with you and Faith?"

"What?" Drew missed the nail completely and almost hit his thumb.

Maddie gave him an impatient look that clearly said, *Don't play grown-up games with me.*

So much for pretending things were normal. Before he could wrap his tongue around a fitting answer, Maddie said, "I like her. I hope you guys aren't fighting."

"We're not fighting."

"You're not friendly, either. Not like before. I don't get it."

"Faith had stuff on her mind."

"She seemed really happy at the rodeo last week…until she got sick."

His daughter had apparently been working through things, looking for connections. "A lot can happen in a week. Stuff we don't know about." *Other stuff that we do.*

Maddie glanced over at him as he started hammering again. "How much do you like Faith?"

Another near miss with the hammer, but this time he only bent the nail and his thumb remained in the clear.

"She's a nice person."

"That's all?"

Drew let the hand holding the hammer drop to his side. "What more do you want?"

Maddie shuffled her feet. "I don't know. Shayla said that since you're taking lessons

with me, you probably like her. I mean *like*
like her."

"Yeah. I get what you mean." Drew came
down off the low ladder. "And I can promise
you that when I signed up for those lessons
I had only two reasons—to spend time with
you and to get over my horse issues."

"What about now?"

"In what way?" How did he keep losing
ground here?

"Do you like her more now?"

Drew patted the hammerhead lightly in his
palm, decided to cut to the chase. "Do you
*want* me to like her?"

"I don't know."

"That's honest."

Maddie gave him a serious, wide-eyed
look. "I'm not ready for a new mom, but
Shayla says you're probably lonely."

Drew sat on the low retaining wall that kept
the mountain from sliding onto the small back
yard and patted the stone next to where he
sat. Maddie took a seat and leaned into him.
Drew looped a loose arm around her. "Don't
worry about me being lonely."

"But you're my dad and I need to worry
about you."

No. She'd had enough worries in her young life without adding his loneliness to the list.

He gave her shoulder a squeeze. "I'm doing okay."

"But someday you might get a girlfriend, right?"

"Someday. Maybe. I don't see it being any time soon." He hoped that was the right answer. It was certainly the truth. "And if I do, it won't affect how I feel about your mom. She was the love of my life. Nothing will replace her."

Maddie let out a little sigh, telling him he'd done okay.

He gazed down at Maddie's profile and she shifted her eyes to look at him without turning her head. "Are you all right?" he asked.

"I'm about to be a teenager, Dad. You know, that time of life when everything gets confusing and weird?"

"True. But you'll always be my little girl, and no matter what, remember that I'm here for you."

Maddie nodded. "Same thing here, Dad."

Drew laughed and ruffled her hair. "Should we get the last of the siding up before dark?"

"Yeah. One step closer to finishing my room."

Drew's breath caught, but she didn't say a word about coming to *live* in her room. Sometimes, after a bad night, he felt like building the room was an exercise in futility, but he needed this time with his daughter.

"Hey, Dad?"

He turned from the ladder. "Yeah?"

"Thanks for taking riding lessons with me. I really like them."

Which was why they were going to continue for as long as Faith would have them.

AFTER HIS CONVERSATION with Maddie, Drew couldn't stop thinking about the lessons, thinking about his unfinished business with Faith. If Maddie wasn't involved, and if she wasn't so keyed into the actions of the adults around her—the curse of being an only child—Drew would have let matters stand. He wouldn't have pulled into the Lightning Creek Ranch on Wednesday evening after helping Pete replace the wrinkled panels in his Jeep. But the lights were on in Faith's house, he was worried about his daughter and he figured, what the hell? Maybe they could hammer out a new understanding before the next lesson.

He knocked on the door and her dog gave a few throaty barks. A few seconds later, Faith pushed aside the curtain and then pulled open the door.

"This is a surprise."

"Yeah." He dug his hands a little deeper into his coat pockets. "Can I come in for a few minutes?"

"Sure." She stepped back, swinging the door wider.

"Thank you." He stepped inside her warm living room, took in the book and the glass of wine on the table next to the overstuffed chair. "The kittens are doing well," he said as a way of starting a conversation he had no clue how to have.

"I'm glad to hear it." She motioned toward her wineglass. "Want some?"

"Better not."

"All right." She folded her arms over her chest, waited for him to dive in. He didn't know how, so he did the equivalent of a conversational cannonball.

"I scared you at the rodeo."

"Anyone would have been scared. I was

just…more scared. But I'm glad you were there." She rubbed her upper arms as if warming them. "Honestly? A part of me is glad you did what you did to Jared, even though I think in some ways it was scarier for you than it was for me."

He felt his barriers, which were already firmly in place, rise just that much more. "How so?"

"You fear losing control of things. I imagine losing control of yourself is the scariest thing of all."

How could he say she was wrong when she was right on the money? Losing control terrified him—but he hadn't expected her to clue in on that. Not while she was dealing with her own issues. And then, instead of allowing him to reply, she floored him by saying, "I want things to be the way they were before."

Story of his life, but her stark admission still brought him up short. He knew exactly what she meant. She wished they could go back to the flirting and the sense that maybe they could help each other out, instead of triggering one another.

"I can't be the kind of guy you need, Faith."

She let out a breath as she raised her eyes. "What kind of guy is that, Drew?"

"A normal guy with a minor amount of baggage." How could she claim she didn't want a man with minimal baggage? Everyone wanted that. "Here's the thing—grabbing that guy felt good. He was hurting you. I wanted to hurt him. And that in turn hurt you. Vicious circle."

"What's the solution, Drew? Are you going to isolate yourself? Stay far away from me? Send Maddie to lessons with her uncle?"

He gave her a dark look. "Isn't isolation *your* first instinct in time of trouble?"

"This isn't about me. It's about you *and* me."

"There is no you and me." If he'd hoped to put her off with his blunt statement, he failed. Faith was easily frightened—by sudden movements, being approached from behind, certain smells—but she didn't seem to be one bit frightened of him.

"No," she agreed. "But there was a beginning."

"I told you I wasn't ready. I wasn't kidding."

"And that," she said softly, "is something I must respect. As long as it's the truth."

He scowled at her. "What does that mean?"

She dropped her arms to her sides. "That means I can accept you not wanting a relationship because of *you*. But not because you're afraid of what that relationship might do to me."

"That's a legitimate concern."

"Yes. But I should have a say in what I am or am not willing to try to deal with. You shouldn't decide for me."

"I trigger you," he said roughly.

"Not *you*, Drew. Not anymore."

"My actions, then." His expression softened as he studied her face, took in her wide green eyes, the lips he'd once kissed...wanted to kiss again. "I'm sorry I scared you at the rodeo. I *am* afraid of losing control. I want to be friends."

"Friends."

He nodded.

She dropped her chin. Shook her head. "Any chance we can keep an open mind? I was kind of looking forward to healing."

"Friends, Faith."

She lifted her chin, looked him square in the eyes. "I don't know if that's possible...but I'll try. For Maddie's sake."

FAITH GOT HOME late on Thursday. Debra had needed some misfiled records for an important alum at the very last minute, and it had taken Faith almost an hour past quitting time to find them. She could have said no, could have gone home. Could have dealt with passive-aggressive Debra the next day.

She chose to stay.

By the time she finished feeding the horses, a storm had started to move in across the valley, casting an eerie yellowish light over the fields. The wind came up suddenly, blowing the hay around the feeders and back into her face. She brushed it out of her hair with her fingers, then headed to the house. Once upon a time, she'd loved storms, but now they made her uneasy. All that energy. All that unpredictability...

No one knew the outcome of a storm until it had passed, and Drew had tried to tell her that his situation was similar. There was an element of uncertainty. Things he couldn't control.

Was that a deal breaker for her?

Was being a deal breaker even an issue when he didn't want to *have* a deal with her? Other than friendship?

Honestly? She didn't know if she could play the part of a friend, when she still felt a wild physical attraction toward the man. When the bond felt deeper. When she thought about him in the early hours of the morning after something startled her awake.

She'd just started reheating pasta for dinner when her phone rang. A speak-of-the-devil moment as Drew's name appeared on the screen. She answered it before the second ring.

"Faith. It's Drew." There was an odd note to his voice. A hint of desperation that made Faith's heart beat just a little faster. She knew the sound of an emergency.

"What happened?"

"I—do you have any baby shampoo?"

Certainly she hadn't heard right. "Baby shampoo?"

"If you don't, that's fine. I'll go to the store, but you're closer…and I think the store closes at seven." It was six-forty.

"I have baby shampoo."

"And I have kittens covered with motor oil. Can I come down and borrow it?"

Motor oil? Faith pressed a hand to her head. "I'll bring it up."

"Faith—"

"I'm coming up. I want to see these oily kittens." She ended the call and headed for her bathroom. A few seconds later, she had her coat on and was out the door. Instead of getting into the four-wheeler, she got into her truck and started up the mountain. Kittens covered with motor oil. How?

Well, they were kittens.

When Faith pulled to a stop in front of Drew's cabin, he instantly opened the door. He held two sad-looking kittens in the one hand, their little oily bodies staining his T-shirt. "Thank you."

"I can't say no to a kitten emergency. What happened?"

"Before I took Maddie home, we put the kittens in the shop to play. I never dreamed they'd find my used oil container. Knocked it over. Maddie is going to kill me."

Faith reached out to take a greasy kitty away from him and held it up. The little cat mewed in distress, her ears sticking out sideways, her oily fur spiked, giving her a punk-rock look. "Maddie doesn't need to know," Faith said.

Without waiting for an invitation, she

moved past him and took the kitten to the kitchen sink, then changed her mind.

"The bathroom basin will be smaller. Easier to fill and empty."

Drew crossed the living room and opened the door to a bare-bones bathroom. But it had a basin that was perfect for washing a kitten. Faith started the water running—warm, but not too warm—then turned to Drew. "Got some hand towels?"

"Two clean ones. I haven't hit the laundry this week."

Sounded about right for a single guy.

Thunder rumbled outside as she dunked one kitty in the sink and it started to howl. "I hope you don't mind me taking over."

"They were your cats until last weekend."

"Not really." She held out her hand and Drew poured shampoo into it without her having to ask. They made a decent cat-washing team. "Like I told you, Mama showed up a few days before giving birth in the barn. She's not mine, so the kittens aren't mine."

"She's wild?"

"She's cautious."

"Aren't we all."

Faith frowned at him, then continued soaping up the kitten. When she was done, she rinsed the baby and then handed her off to Drew, who started rubbing her dry with a hand towel while Faith tackled kitten number two.

"Is this Rosalee or Cecily?" She knew that Rosalee was yellow with white spots, but she was playing the game, making inane conversation, distracting herself from the man standing so close to her.

It took Drew a moment to say, "Rosalee... I think."

Once the second kitten was washed, Faith handed it off to Drew, drained the basin and dried her hands on the edge of the towel that Drew was using on the first kitten. Without a word Drew handed the second one back to her and she grabbed the other hand towel. Silently, they dried the kittens.

Thunder rumbled in the distance, but the storm no longer concerned her. She had bigger issues at hand. Drew met her eyes with his cool blue gaze, but despite his distant demeanor, she had a feeling he was anything but cool. He wanted her as much as she wanted him.

But he wasn't going to let go of the iron-clad hold he had on himself.

"I need to go." Her duty was done. The kittens were okay. Drew was okay. She was about to shatter. Her kitten started to purr, the sound of its little motor overly loud in the quiet cabin.

"Thank you for coming."

She rolled her eyes at his stilted words as thunder rumbled in the distance. "Not a problem, Drew. Glad to help." Her kitten started squirming and she let it down on the wood plank floor. Drew also set his kitten down, and she promptly jumped on her sister. They seemed no worse for wear after their oil adventure and baths.

Drew stayed rooted next to the sofa as Faith walked to the door. She looked at him over her shoulder before opening it. "How do you feel about this friendship thing now?"

He pushed his hands into his back pockets. "I feel like it's going to be a struggle. And not because I don't like you."

She hadn't expected him to be so honest, and because he'd been honest, she couldn't come up with any kind of a return quip. "I guess we'll have to work at it."

"Yeah," he said dryly. "Maybe we could have coffee sometime."

AFTER SATURDAY'S RIDING LESSON, Drew took Maddie to Pete and Cara's place instead of to the cabin. Cara wanted to take advantage of the summer sales to help Maddie stock up on school clothes, and Maddie was excited to start building a new wardrobe. Yeah. His kid was growing up.

"That was a good lesson," Maddie said as they pulled up next to the shop.

"Yeah. It was." Even though they were moving beyond the things he wanted to do on horseback. He had the basics. He was good.

"I'm glad you guys are friends again."

*You guys* meaning he and Faith. They'd both put on Oscar-worthy performances during the lesson, and he hadn't lingered afterward. The goats had gone back to Jolie's place, and Maddie had kittens of her own, so there hadn't been much call to stay longer. Faith had asked about Maddie's kittens, and he'd told her they were doing well. Maddie never had a clue anything had happened to them. And as near as he could tell, she had no idea that he'd had a hell of a time keeping his eyes off Faith as she taught them the basics of loping.

That he wanted her in a way he'd never again thought he'd want a woman.

And she wanted him.

She knew about his issues. She still wanted him. Faith didn't seem particularly self-destructive—if anything, he would peg her as overly self-protective. But not where he was concerned. She'd wanted him to help her heal…to help them both heal. Together.

Was that possible?

He didn't know, but he couldn't get around the fact that he was waking up thinking about one particular red-haired woman every single morning.

When Drew drove back to the cabin, that red-haired woman was riding Tommy in the field, keeping the horse supple so he could bend properly when he rounded the barrel. There was a lot more to barrel racing than just running—and sometimes Drew had a hard time believing he knew things like that. Faith had kind of changed his life, and not in the way Deb had intended when she'd brought them together. He was still in his cabin on the mountain, although he wasn't as much of a hermit.

Didn't want to stay that much of a hermit.

But he also wanted to make sure he didn't inflict his brand of pain on anyone else—such as his daughter. Or Faith.

But Faith knew about it. Was willing to work around it.

Or so she said. She hadn't yet been subjected to a screaming man in the middle of the night.

There was a solution to that. A very simple solution.

Drew parked the truck and went into the cabin, standing for a moment in the silent interior. The kittens started across the floor toward him and he smiled as he sat. One of them started climbing his pant leg and he reached down to scoop it up into his hand. The little cat started purring and punching the front of his shirt. Amazing how the steady purring made tension abate. Not a lot…but a little. Cecily—or was it Rosalee? He'd have to get a refresher from Maddie—turned in a circle and made herself comfortable on his chest.

He lightly stroked the kitten with two fingers as he stared across the room.

Maybe he should call Faith.

Maybe they should talk.

FAITH FROWNED DOWN at her phone. "Coffee?"

Drew's voice was low and somewhat ironic as he said, "Isn't that what friends do? Have coffee?"

Faith was about to ask for a deeper explanation, then stopped herself. If he wanted to have coffee, she would play along. "Sure. Where and when?"

"There's a place on the lake."

"I know it." She'd driven by a time or two but had never stopped. Coffee alone in a swank shop just didn't cut it.

"Tomorrow morning. Maybe nine o'clock?"

Sunday morning coffee. With Drew. "I'll be there."

He said goodbye and ended the call, leaving Faith holding the phone and feeling like she'd stepped into another dimension.

He was taking this friends thing literally—and maybe that was the point he was trying to make.

She went out for the evening feeding, taking a largish cardboard box with her. One of her coworkers had responded to the Free Kittens ad she'd stuck on the bulletin board, taking all four to help with mouse control in her newly constructed barn.

"Your babies are going to a good home," Faith assured Mama Cat, who twined around her legs. "I know you'll be lonely for a little while, but trust me, this is a good thing."

With the babies loaded in the box, Faith closed the lid and carried them to the car. Five minutes later she'd changed out of her barn coat for her corduroy blazer, her rubber shoes for flats and she was out the door, ready to take the kitties to their new home.

Faith made a mental note to ask her coworker about open oil containers, which in turn made her think about Drew.

He wanted to have Sunday morning coffee. Go figure.

## CHAPTER TWELVE

DREW WAS WAITING for Faith near the coffee shop entrance when she drove into the small parking lot a few minutes early on Sunday morning. He opened the door for her, let her precede him to the counter where she ordered a brewed coffee with cream and he ordered the same, only black. The place was busy, with Sunday morning walkers and family groups meeting for coffee next to the lake. Drew found a table near the edge of the patio, under a tree, where Faith could keep her back to the wall and they could watch the people come and go.

Not that she was interested in anyone except the man on the other side of the table from her.

"When I was in high school, the lake was on the edge of town," Drew said as they sat. "The town has almost doubled in size since the time I left for the service."

The small body of water was now essentially in the center of Eagle Valley, with houses surrounding it on all sides. "This still feels like a small town to me," Faith said. "Maybe it's the lack of big-box stores." Missoula was close enough that Eagle Valley probably couldn't support big stores—which didn't hurt Faith's feelings. She liked the small-town vibe.

"Thank goodness," Drew said. "But the housing…that's something else." He shook his head, then pointed to the side of the lake where big houses on small lots were hugged up against one another. "That hill, Snob Nob…no one wanted to live there because of the problem with washouts. Look at it now. A quarter acre costs a year's salary or more."

She picked up her mug with both hands, holding it as she looked across the lake at the town proper. "It's still a nice place to live. I'm glad I landed here." For many reasons.

He glanced down at his cup. "I'm thinking of buying Maddie a horse."

Ah. The reason for coffee. She didn't know if that made her feel better or worse. Frankly, she'd had no idea what to expect from the meet-up. Yesterday they'd had a good lesson and had done a decent job of hiding their reactions to one another. Maddie had gone home smiling.

"That's a big commitment," she said.

"And Maddie won't be at home for all that much longer. She keeps reminding me that in five years she'll be heading off to college."

Faith's eyebrows lifted. "Somewhere close, I hope."

"I hope so, too." He pulled a paper out of his shirt pocket and unfolded it. Faith craned her neck to see it when he smoothed it out on the table.

"A horse sale?"

"Isn't that where people buy horses?"

"If they know what they're doing. It's easy to get burned."

"Oh." He pulled the paper back, refolded it.

"I'll keep my eye out. You want something reliable and those can be hard to come by. How much are you willing to spend?"

"Whatever it takes." Faith slowly lifted her eyebrows and he explained, "The beauty of living frugally."

"All right, then." She glanced down, not sure what to say next.

"Not to dampen the mood, but have you heard from your ex?"

Her gaze came back up. A horse. Her ex. "I mailed him the bill of sale for the saddle."

Drew's lips tightened.

"It's the best way to handle things," she assured him. "He disappears and I never have to deal with him again."

"Are you sure about the disappear part?"

She gave a small shrug. "He has no reason not to."

"Maddie said you're going to three more rodeos this summer?"

"They're smaller ones. I doubt he'll be there. He doesn't enter anymore, so he's probably just there to support his girlfriend." For as long as it's convenient for him.

"Do you want me to go with you? If I behave myself," he added grimly.

"I'm going to try to go alone." She needed to see if she could do it alone after her last trauma. Worst-case scenario, she would have a meltdown. But she didn't think that was going to happen—if she didn't put herself in a situation where she could be trapped. "It has nothing to do with what went on with Jared. I just…think it's time."

"You're sure."

"I'm taking Sully. I can put him in the horse trailer if it's hot, because it's not fully enclosed." He hated it, which was why she rarely brought him to rodeos with her before the attack, but it was the only option she could think of. "I have pepper spray." A possibly illegal taser.

It was obvious from Drew's expression that he didn't like the thought of her going alone, and equally obvious that he wasn't in a position to insist otherwise.

"I found homes for the other four kittens," Faith said. It seemed a good way to divert the conversation into more comfortable channels. "They stayed together, so the cat story has a happy ending."

"How did the mother cat take the loss of her litter?"

"She disappeared," Faith said. So not a totally happy story—at least not on her end.

"No kidding?"

"Yes. She was gone when I got back from delivering the kittens and she didn't show up this morning when I usually feed her. I guess my barn served its purpose. She raised her family and now she's gone. Too bad because she was a nice cat."

A group of women came onto the patio then, talking and laughing, and Faith instantly recognized them as faculty from the college. The Sunday brunch. Of course. The brunch that the associates, such as herself, were not invited to. Drew let out a low groan when he spotted his sister.

"Do you want to go?" Faith asked, pushing her empty cup aside. But it was too late. Debra caught sight of her brother, then her chin came up as she recognized Faith.

"Great," Drew muttered as his sister excused herself from her friends and headed over to greet them.

"Drew! Faith! What a surprise." She leaned down to air kiss her brother, who took the gesture with good grace, then straightened up to beam at Faith, who was thankfully out of range. "Do you come here often?" Debra asked Faith.

"No." She smiled after the monosyllabic answer.

"I live just up there. On the hill," Debra pointed toward the hill as if it were a badge of honor. "I come here quite a lot." She gestured at Drew. "But this is the very first time I've seen my brother here."

"What a lovely area to live," Faith lied to draw the heat away from Drew. She actually hated the boxy, ostentatious pseudo-mansions.

"Well, you two enjoy your morning." Debra bounced a look between them, as if she could get one of them to confess their relationship by putting them under sharp scrutiny.

"I should have known," Drew said as Debra headed back to the faculty group.

"How?" Faith asked as she scooted her chair back. Drew did the same and a few seconds later they were heading out the door.

He waited until they were out of earshot before saying, "It's pretentious. It's close to her house. It's her day off, too." He opened the heavy door for Faith. "I'm afraid of how Deb is going to spin seeing us together."

"She'll probably ask me to spy again."

"And what will you do?"

Faith smiled. "File a harassment claim." Drew gave her an appreciative smile and she went on. "I like my job, and I need the steady paycheck after a year of living on too little money. However, I am not kissing ass like I did when she first asked me to meet with you."

"You didn't want to help me?"

"I don't like to be manipulated into helping, and that was what Debra was doing."

"Imagine that. My sister manipulating."

"She's good with the public."

"Fake people often are."

When they reached Faith's truck, he stood back as she opened the door. She turned back toward him instead of getting inside. "What was the purpose of this coffee date, Drew? Because you don't seem like a coffee date kind of guy."

"Well…there's the horse."

"Yeah." She took hold of the open door with one hand.

"And I like coffee."

"There's that," Faith said.

"I wanted to meet in a neutral place to discuss friendship."

Her chin tipped up as she felt a little spark inside at the mention of friendship.

"And…healing."

"Healing." Sparks flickered to flame. He couldn't mean…? What else could he mean?

He shifted his weight and then shot a look

toward the patio, visible beyond the flowering bushes that lined the parking area. "My sister is watching us."

"In that case, let's not kiss goodbye."

"Yeah," he said in a low voice that kind of did something to her. "Let's save that for later. After we talk."

And the flame became an inferno.

"Well, I for one, cannot wait to have this conversation."

DREW STOPPED BY Pete's shop on his way home from the café, still chewing on what had transpired with Faith. Had he agreed to have sex or to just pursue the possibility?

The latter. Yeah.

Maddie was inside, helping her uncle change out the broken headlight on the Jeep. She pushed her glasses up on her nose as he came in through the bay door. "It's almost done, Dad. Just waiting for that one quarter panel that got lost in transit."

"Good to know." He was looking forward to having his old friend back. He'd been driving the Jeep since high school and missed jumping into it and beating around the mountains.

"I'm ready. Why are you so late?" Maddie cocked her head and Drew instantly felt shifty.

"Didn't Aunt Cara explain about my meeting?"

"Who has meetings on Sunday?" she asked. Pete met his gaze over the hood of the Jeep, obviously having the same question.

"I do."

"Anyone I know?" Maddie asked as she started for the bay door.

"Hey," Pete said as he came around the Jeep. "Before you go, I need for you to check out these paint chips for the Jeep. I booked the paint booth and need to order the paint."

Drew gestured to his daughter, thankful for Pete's save. "Come and look, Mads."

Maddie reversed course and came to study the chips glued to the cardstock. "That one," she said, stabbing her finger on denim blue.

"What about this?" Drew asked, pointing at the cherry red. His Jeep had been cherry red since high school.

"Blue."

Drew looked at Pete. Pete shrugged. "She's probably going to be driving it soon. You may as well go with the blue."

"Blue," Drew said, shaking his head. "Fine."

"It'll look great, Dad. Wait and see. Who did you have a meeting with?"

Pete put the back of his hand up to his mouth, pretending to rub his lips as he smiled.

"I'll tell you about it in the truck."

Drew waited until they were at the end of the driveway before he said, "I met with Faith." Before Maddie could ask why, he said, "I think I'm going to keep taking you to lessons, but I'm not going to take them anymore."

He honestly had decided that he'd gone as far as he wanted to go horse-wise. He was no longer intimidated by the animals. He could walk, trot and canter. Stop with one rein, back up and turn in a tight circle—not all at the same time, of course. He was in a decent position to buy his daughter a horse and understand something about them, and, of course, Maddie could continue the lessons and go much further than he ever could.

"But you've only had a few lessons," Maddie protested.

"I like horses now. Wasn't that one of the objectives?"

"And for us to do something together."

"I'll still come to lessons. I'll bring you, watch you, cheer your accomplishments."

"I don't know," Maddie said. She shot him a sharp look. "This isn't because you and Faith—"

"We're friends," he interrupted smoothly. But he no longer wanted to be her student. "It's just that I've reached my limit." Maddie gave a sniff and he said, "Remember when you decided you didn't want to do soccer anymore and Mom didn't make you sign up again?"

"Yeah."

"Kind of the same thing. You feel a passion for horses that I don't."

Maddie frowned at him. The soccer analogy seemed to be working. Maddie had been an adequate soccer player, but she hadn't liked playing the game enough to enjoy the practices or the competitions. She just liked being with her friends. That was the way he felt about riding lessons—he wanted to be with his daughter.

AT EXACTLY SEVEN o'clock that night, headlights flashed over Faith's front windows.

Sully let out a baritone bark and Faith's heart jumped.

Drew was here and it was very possible that her life was about to change. She was going to find out just how damaged she still was from the attack, and Drew might well find out the same.

He'd texted about an hour ago, asking if he could stop by. She'd said yes, and then, for the next fifty-nine minutes, she'd paced from room to room wondering what she *should* do and what she was *going* to do. The only answer she could come up with was to talk.

She'd dropped the gauntlet and Drew was picking it up.

That'd teach her.

When she answered the door, he didn't step inside immediately, almost as if he knew that once they were in this house, together, alone, with the door closed, things were going to change irreversibly.

"I found your cat."

"You're kidding." Not the opening she'd expected, but welcome all the same.

"I opened the cabin door and she shot inside. It took her about two seconds to locate her babies and when Maddie and I left them, she was curled up with them in their bed."

"That's crazy."

"I guess that's maternal instinct."

"I don't suppose you'd want to—"

"Keep her?"

"Yes."

"I don't have an issue with that. I'm just hoping she understands the concept of a litter box, since I left her inside."

"Well," Faith moistened her dry lips, "it isn't like Maddie would appreciate the family moving back here to the barn."

"No. I wouldn't like it much either."

"Really?"

"They're growing on me. What can I say?"

An uncomfortable silence followed. Faith was rusty in the personal relationship sphere of life. No doubt about it. And Drew, by his own admission, was out of practice, too.

He shifted his weight, hooking a thumb in his front pocket. "I…uh…came to discuss our friendship. Figure out a few things before we…go forth."

Maybe she wasn't rusty—maybe she just felt awkward because she'd never negotiated sex before. Did that make it less than it could be? Like…more clinical?

Faith let her gaze travel over Drew's body, his broad shoulders, hard thighs, flat abs, then brought it back to his face. And what she read there made her realize there was nothing clinical about this. They were trying to discover what they were capable of, she and this beautiful man. And that involved communication that she'd never needed before, but that they both needed now.

"What do we need to figure out?" she asked softly, tossing the ball back into his court.

"Do we *want* to go forth?"

The thought of not going forth made her feel a little desperate. How many more nights of frustration could she take? How many nights of not knowing whether she was capable of doing what she was fantasizing about?

"I'm just going to come out and say that it seems a shame to waste all this sexual energy." There. She'd just cut through a lot of bull.

"Is that a come-on?"

Her lips twitched. "Do I need to be more direct?"

He shook his head and he reached out to

slide his hands up her arms to her shoulders. But he didn't pull her any closer. "If I were to expend said energy, I wouldn't be able to spend the night."

The nightmares.

"I'm not asking you to stay."

"What do *you* want, Faith?"

"I want to find out if I can be touched." She glanced down, suddenly feeling self-conscious. "If I happened to find out that I can't or suddenly panic…well…you understand my situation."

"And I'd stop." His fingers tightened ever so slightly as he exhaled. "Why me, Faith? Is it just because we've both been through a lot of shit?"

"That's part of it." She drew in a short breath, then let go of the rest. "You're the first guy who's made me think about sex since that night."

"I'm honored." His throat moved. "So, we understand each other? What's possible, what's not?"

"You'll stop if I need you to. You'll leave afterward because you can't stay."

He gave a slow nod. "That pretty much sums it up."

She looked up at him, feeling beyond awkward. "What now?" she whispered. "Because I kind of feel like I'm in a training session."

He stepped back, letting go of her shoulders and putting a little distance between them before running a hand over the back of his neck. He looked as uncomfortable as she was. "This isn't like the movies where we rush across the room and passionately jump one another."

Faith lifted her chin a little. "I *want* to jump you."

His eyes narrowed as he dropped his hand back to his side. "Yeah?"

Faith's breathing went shallow, but this was no time to chicken out. It would kill her if he decided things felt wrong and left. "I'd like to walk over there and unbutton your shirt. See what you look like under that flannel."

"All right."

Faith's cheeks felt ridiculously warm as she moved closer to him and silently reached out to undo the first button on his shirt. She felt his breath catch as she worked the white plastic disc thought the buttonhole. Keeping her focus firmly on his shirt, not daring to look up at his face, she undid the next button. And the next. The shirt started to fall open, revealing hard muscles covered with crisp dark hair. Her downward progress stopped when her fingers hit his simple brass belt buckle. Her gaze dropped to the worn denim below and she saw that he was already straining against his jeans.

A good sign, that, and her body answered with a rush of warmth.

She pulled her gaze away from the evidence of his erection and moistened her lips as she took hold of his shirt, pulled the tails out of his waistband and then undid the last three buttons.

The house was dead silent, except for Sully's low doggy snores from the opposite side of the room. And Drew's slow breathing.

She watched the rise and fall of his broad chest as she spread the shirt apart. The man was solid muscle. Not bulky, intimidating muscle, but long corded muscles that begged to be touched. Explored.

He moved then, taking her hand and placing it on his chest, his warm palm covering her fingers, holding them against him, lightly trapping her. She felt no need to break free, no sense of panic. Beneath her hand, his heart beat a rhythm that seemed a lot slower than her own, but when her gaze strayed once again to the erection pushing hard against his jeans, she knew this wasn't a one-sided deal. Anything but.

"What else do you want to do, Faith?"

The raspy whisper gave her the courage to raise her gaze to his face and what she saw there made her flush. He was beautiful and he wanted her.

Faith had never been a cautious lover. Before. But these were new waters—she and Drew were feeling their way along…literally. The smoldering intensity in his expression gave her the courage to whisper, "I want to see you naked."

His heart kicked under her palm.

"And then?"

"I want you to undress me…put your hands on me…touch me in places I haven't been touched in way too long." She lifted her face, bringing her mouth closer to his. "I want you inside of me."

Drew's eyes flashed, but his movements were slow and deliberate as he brought his hands up to cup her face and then lowered his mouth to hers, his tongue gently exploring as they kissed.

Faith felt the heat building and her response became more assertive. She kissed him back, pushing her hands into his hair, then dropping down to his solid shoulders, his skin feeling deliciously warm and smooth beneath her touch.

He lifted his head, gazing down at her, then nuzzled her cheek, her jawline, her neck, making crazy shivers go through her before moving back and taking hold of the bottom of her T-shirt. Slowly, he pulled it up over her head and tossed it aside, his gaze dropping to her exposed breasts.

"I never wear a bra around the house," she murmured.

"Yeah…I kind of noticed when I came in."

Her nipples had gone on alert when he'd walked through the door, and she'd hoped he hadn't noticed. Now she was glad he had. He cupped his palm over her right breast, lightly squeezed and caressed, his thumb sliding over her nipple and almost sending her over the edge, before he smoothed his hand over her sensitive upper chest and repeated the movement with her other breast. Faith let out a shaky, shaky breath, and put a steadying hand on his arm as her knees went weak.

"I...haven't been touched in two years."

"Then this feels okay?"

She closed her eyes. "I'd really like to go to my bedroom now." The words came croaking out as he bent to run his tongue over the area his hands had just set fire to, sucking her nipples in turn. Faith clutched at his hair, a low moan escaping her lips.

Drew straightened and brushed the hair back from her face as she pressed against him, reveling in the feel of skin against skin. He took her hand, drew down to his erection, held it there.

"Yeah," he said roughly as his penis throbbed through the denim. "Let's go to your bedroom."

She took his hand, led him to the back of the house where she slept in the guest room. She didn't bother with lights as she led him inside, preferring the intimacy of darkness. She wanted to see him, every part of him, but right now it was more important to feel. Experience.

Drew made no move to turn on the lights. Instead he closed the door and started undoing his belt. Need spiked inside of her at the intimate sound, and Faith abandoned the idea of having him undress her. She began shucking out of her jeans, her panties. Drew kicked off his boots and they dropped with twin thuds near the wall. The belt buckle clattered as his jeans hit the floor. Then he reached for her in the darkness, gently pulled her closer, cradling her against him. His erection pressed against her and without any kind of conscious thought, she brought her hand down to circle him, hold his heavy length in her palm.

"Any time you need to stop, just say it. Or hit me. Or something."

She dropped her forehead against his shoulder. "I want to be on top." She had to be on top. She was afraid of being covered.

"Done," he murmured, tipping up her chin and bringing his lips down to meet hers in a sweetly sensual kiss.

"And I want to feel you in me. *Soon*." She said the last words thought her teeth as she gently squeezed his throbbing erection, emphasizing her point.

He gave a low laugh, which made her feel like smiling. "Almost done."

"Protection?"

"In the palm of my hand." He rustled the packet he held.

He must have had it in his jeans pocket. "You're prepared," Faith murmured.

"I gave this night a lot of thought."

"As did I." She released him and rose on her toes, taking his face in her hands and kissing him fiercely. She trusted him. She needed him. They'd gotten this far and she couldn't imagine going back. Stopping. Not until she'd had her way with this man. Felt him moving inside of her. Given him as much as she expected him to give her.

Somehow, they made it to the bed through the darkness without breaking the kiss. Drew eased down onto the mattress, gently pulling her with him. She stretched out alongside him and now that she no longer needed to worry about knees buckling, she started her own slow exploration of his body, caressing the hard planes, feeling his reaction, bringing him to the edge of control as she ran her tongue down the length of him.

He gripped her shoulders convulsively and Faith considered it a good sign that she didn't freak out. That it felt natural for him to hold her so tightly. But she didn't dare let him cover her. Instead she let him pull her up on top, where she straddled his erection, slowly lowered herself onto the blunt tip, let her head drop back as he slid inside of her, inch by inch.

"Are you okay?" he whispered in a thick voice.

She closed her eyes as her clit hit the base of his penis. "I am so damned good." She started to move, bracing her palms on her chest, loving the feel of his big hands holding her hips, helping her move as he thrust into her from below.

"Yeah. You are."

Faith bit her lip to keep from laughing as the tension inside of her grew, became almost unbearable. She slowed, trying to prolong the moment, because she had no idea if she'd ever get another and she wanted to savor every second with this spectacular man. His breathing became heavy and his motions more driven. He was losing himself, pumping into her, so Faith let go, allowed herself to burst, explode, shatter. And all the other words she'd ever read about sex. Oh, dear heavens. It wouldn't stop. And neither did he, until he gave one last thrust, his hips arching against her.

And then she fell onto his chest, collapsing into a boneless state and a heavy arm dropped over her. Which only made her feel safer.

When they caught their breath, Drew took her face in his hands and kissed her lips.

"I don't know what to say."

"We said it all earlier."

He let out soft breath that fanned over her skin. "I guess so." Lightly stroking her hair, he said, "Guess we'll play this by ear, huh?"

"Yeah." She propped herself on her elbow. "We'll keep talking. Right?"

"How else are we going to heal?"


HE'D BEEN WITH a woman who wasn't Lissa.

The *first* woman who wasn't Lissa. Drew hadn't known what to expect going in…awkwardness was a given. Except it hadn't been after those first few moments when it'd felt like they were in a negotiation session. And not after Faith had essentially taken control. He'd needed her to take control so he'd be certain he wasn't scaring her. Triggering her. By the time he'd climaxed, triggering was pretty damned far from his mind. All he could think of was how she was turning him inside out, making him feel things he hadn't felt in years.

*I love you, Liss. Always will.*

But as much as he loved his wife, he had to move on. If positions were reversed, he wouldn't want Lissa to stop living. If anything, he would have wanted her to grab more tightly onto life, because it was too short, too unpredictable.

This thing that had happened between him and Faith...it was a good thing. Even though he had no idea what anyone's next move would be. New territory for him, and likely for her, too. Faith had probably never had a lover who didn't hang around to make love to her again in the morning. And she'd never know how much he regretted not being able to do that. He hadn't had a nightmare in over two weeks, but he wasn't ready to take that chance.

But enough nightmare shit. He was feeling good. Had passed a milestone...returned to the land of the living.

He smiled a little as he got out of the truck. Afterglow. Not a bad thing. Leaving Faith alone in her bed...yeah. He hated that.

The mama cat met him at the door. He

thought she wanted to go outside, but she circled his legs, then headed back to the bed with the kittens. The cabin felt different with the cats in it. Warmer. Friendlier.

He shucked out of his clothes, climbed the steps to the loft without bothering with the generator. The moon shone in through the windows, giving him enough light to keep from killing himself. He climbed into bed, lay there staring at the ceiling. He was almost asleep when he felt a movement at the foot of his bed and jerked awake.

The mama kitty was there, creeping along the edge of the bed. She took his open eyes as an invitation and walked up his chest, butted her head against his chin, then settled.

All right then…

He'd never slept with a cat before. This was a night of firsts. He was smiling a little when he finally fell asleep, wondering if he might be lucky enough to dream of Faith.

The scream woke him. No smoke. No explosion. Just a blood-curdling scream that felt as if it had turned his lungs inside out. Drew sat up, striking out at his attacker. Another noise—this one a choked sob—and then his fist hit wood, jarring him into full consciousness.

Heart racing, he blinked into the darkness.

He hoped he hadn't hurt the cat. He swung his legs out of bed, then sat with his head cradled in his hands until his heart rate slowed. Once he caught his breath, he stood. Swayed. Freaking head rush. Hanging onto the bedstead, he waited until the fogginess cleared, then made his way down the ladder and turned on the generator. The lights went on and he began the search for the cat.

"Here, kitty."

His voice was thick, harsh sounding.

"Kitty?"

There was a movement near the sofa and he turned to see the mother cat staring cautiously out from under the side table, a kitten on either side of her. He didn't risk trying to pet her, reassure her. Instead he felt thankful that she was unscathed—that he hadn't flung her against the wall or anything when he was fighting his formless enemy.

He went to the sink and poured a glass of water. Three o'clock. The witching hour. He'd been home for fewer than four…and so damned glad he hadn't given into temptation and stayed with Faith.

But he was going to tell her about it. Friends,

lovers, whatever they were, he was going to come clean. It was only fair that she know everything he was up against. So she would know what *she* was up against.

Because, deep down, he didn't think she was looking at him as a rebound guy. He had a feeling Faith really liked him.

## CHAPTER THIRTEEN

As soon as Drew walked into her barn, Faith knew something was wrong. She put aside the pitchfork she'd been using to clean the goat pen and let herself out the gate.

"Is it Maddie?"

"No."

She let out a breath as the truth hit her. "You had a nightmare."

"Pretty damned good one, too. I don't know if that mother cat is ever going to come back into the cabin again."

Faith sank down on a grain bin, her shoulders slumping. "Do you think it's because of last night?"

Drew took a couple paces toward the pen she'd just left, rubbed his hands over his face. He was drawn and pale, as if he were suffering from a migraine or some other source on constant pain. Faith wanted to touch him. Comfort him.

She didn't know if he would allow it and she wasn't about to push things. He was here, with her, and that was a good sign.

"I've had a lot of nightmares that weren't tied to sex. Like…all of them until now."

"I just thought…" she dropped her chin, drew in a breath, looked up again, "…maybe anxiety. Or…guilt?"

He turned toward her, one hand still on the rough planks of the goat pen. "I thought about that. I feel sad that I've lost Lissa. But I don't feel guilty about having sex with someone who isn't her."

*Someone who isn't her.* Well, that was meaningful.

But it also put things back into perspective. They were two people helping each other back to the real world. Two people who could be forgiving and understanding because they had an idea of what the other had gone through.

Maybe sex with Drew was clinical. Maybe all they were doing was using one another. But when she thought about what they'd shared, that wasn't how she felt.

"Faith."

She looked up, met Drew's gaze with a frown.

He crossed the alley to the grain bin, took a seat next to her. "That was a shitty thing to say, and it wasn't what I meant."

"Lissa's going to always be part of your life," she allowed.

"And part of my past. I have to move forward. Last night I made a major move in that direction. Because of you."

He slid an arm around her, staring sightlessly across the dim interior of the barn. The thousand-mile stare Debra had told her about. But his hand was warm on her shoulder and he showed no sign of easing away. So Faith leaned into him, lapsing into her own thousand-mile stare. She didn't know where they were going. Only where they'd been. They were moving on from that.

She closed her eyes, inhaled his wonderful scent deep into her lungs. Just as certain rodeo smells would forever be associated with danger in the more primitive part of her brain, Drew's scent would be associated with safety. And a journey back.

She let out a sigh, and Drew reached down to tip up her chin and gently kiss her lips.

"I feel better," he said.

"And I understand how serious you are

when you say you can't stay." Faith swallowed dryly, then asked the hard question. "I have to ask—do you want to continue seeing each other?" She didn't want him to walk away, but if he needed to, she wasn't about to stand in his way. "What I mean is, is this arrangement one you can live with?"

"For now? Yes."

"In the future?"

"We'll reevaluate." Because that was the kind of relationship they had. A cautious day-to-day affair.

And for now, as she'd said, she was good with that.

DREW WASN'T HAPPY about Faith going to her next rodeo on her own, but she'd insisted. This was not only her first solo run—it was a way to prove to herself that she could function without Drew being there. It *wasn't* that she was falling in love with a guy who wouldn't let her into his life...much. He wasn't ready for a relationship. That was simply the way things were—the fact she had to accept.

They'd made love almost every day over the past week and a half. The body that had once triggered her now intrigued her. She loved exploring the hard curves of his muscles, the flat plane of his abs, the raised ridges of his scars. He'd told her he worked out to reduce stress. She didn't know what kind of effect his workouts had on his stress levels, but they had a most excellent effect on his body.

And even though there were things about her body that she would change if she could, Drew made her feel beautiful. If she occasionally wondered how she compared to his lost wife, she quickly pushed those thoughts aside, focused on the here and now. It didn't matter how she compared. What mattered was that they help each other move forward— because that was the point of being together, right? To find their new reality and not let the past eclipse their futures.

She still liked to be touched. That one discovery made her tenuous journey with Drew worthwhile. She smiled a little as she turned onto the highway. He liked to be touched, too. A lot. This fragile thing they shared was, by its very nature, destined to be short-lived. The euphoria of initial discovery would only last for so long.

And then...

Either a bond had formed that would sustain the relationship or that relationship would wither and die. She felt a bond with Drew. A deep bond of mutual understanding and... more.

She wouldn't put a name on it. That was asking for trouble.

The rodeo venue was small, and there weren't many participants, because there were bigger, richer rodeos on the same day in other parts of the state. But despite that, Faith was thrilled to win the event and be awarded enough money to pay for her gas. Always a big achievement in the barrel racing world. Gas costs ate competitors alive— especially when they were almost, but not quite winning.

She called Drew from the rodeo, told him about her win, and he promised a celebration when she got home.

He was waiting for her at the ranch house with a bottle of prosecco. He cracked it open while she showered, handed her a glass to sip while he gently toweled her off.

She laughed as she tried to sip bubbly liquid and maintain her balance as he worked the soft towel over her body.

"Multitasking," he murmured.

"You're good at it." She sighed as the fingers holding the towel strayed to places that probably wouldn't remain dry for long. In fact, they were no longer dry at all.

"You better put the glass down."

She smiled wickedly. "I'm not done."

"Then maybe I should finish you off."

Heat spiraled through her at his husky words, then she set the glass down and her hands were on him, unbuttoning, unbuckling, unzipping. Drew was magnificent when he was naked, and Faith could have happily sipped her prosecco and studied his body— except for the fact that she really needed his body. Now.

When they were done making love, lying in bed and sipping the sparkling wine, Faith told him about the rodeo and her win—although there wasn't much to tell. Tommy had run well and she'd come in first. Just as she used to, only in a much smaller venue.

"Can I go to the next one?" he asked, tilting his glass toward her.

"I only have one more entry. It's the day that Maddie has her junior high orientation."

Drew blew out a breath, propping a hand behind his head. "I can't miss that."

"I should think not."

Drew rolled over and gathered her closer. "You didn't see what's his ass?"

"No. And his lady wasn't there either." If Tara had competed, it had been in a different venue that weekend. Faith thought about scrolling through the standings, to see where her—make that Jared's—saddle had competed, but it felt too much like stalking. Too much like she cared. The only thing she cared about right now was that she'd done a solo trip after a big scare, and not only competed, but won.

And that she was here with a guy she was starting to care deeply about. She brought her hand up to stroke the side of Drew's face, loving the feel of the stubble beneath her hand. She felt him tense, which she hadn't expected, because it was too soon. They hadn't even finished the wine.

"You have to go."

He pushed back the covers. "Yeah."

Faith made no move to stop him. He'd had another nightmare a week ago, after sex, which had scared him, and then scared her after he'd shown her his bruised knuckles. It had also made her research nightmares. What she'd read didn't give her hope that Drew would be working through this matter easily. His flashbacks and dreams could haunt him for the rest of his life.

Faith got out of bed and grabbed her robe off the footboard, slipping into it as Drew went into the bathroom to retrieve his clothing. She leaned her shoulder against the doorjamb and folded her arms, watching him dress. She was getting better… Drew was not.

After buckling his belt and buttoning his shirt, he came to her, took her face in his hands and kissed her lightly. Faith walked him to the door without a word. He kissed her again, and then he was gone.

This was what she'd signed on for. Which sucked because she was damned certain she was falling in love with the man, and she saw a long, tough road ahead of her.

FAITH PASSED THROUGH Jared's hometown on her way to her last rodeo of the season. There was a good possibility he would be at the event, since it was close by, but at some point, she had to deal with challenges such as this on her own. Now was a good time to start. She wouldn't always be able to depend on other people as she'd depended on Drew to help her through her first few rodeos. The important thing was to watch herself, watch her surroundings. Be vigilant, but not paralyzed by what-ifs.

So easy in theory.

Unlike her last solo rodeo, Faith's heart was beating hard when she pulled into the Silverton rodeo grounds. The competitors lot was packed, but she immediately caught sight of Jared's dually truck parked at the far end of the field. Only one horse was tied to the trailer, and it wasn't the fancy palomino his lady friend had been riding when Faith had confronted her about the saddle. New lady friend? New horse? Or was Jared competing?

No matter. Faith was going to make her run, load Tommy and leave before the rodeo was over. She might even haul him home tacked up. Better that than risk another tack room mishap.

Faith kept her gaze fixed forward as she drove past the rig and parked as far away as she could get, on the opposite side of the field. The rodeo grand entry started as she unloaded Tommy. She saddled him and mounted, glanced over at the practice arena, then sucked it up and rode over.

*This is your life now. You can hide at home or you can tackle life.*

She chose to tackle life. She also had pepper spray in her pocket. The small canister dug into her hip as she rode, but better to feel safe than comfortable. As she entered the practice area and started walking Tommy along the rail, she recognized Tara riding ahead of her on the flashy palomino. Oddly, though, she was not riding in Faith's saddle.

Faith had done a lot of brave things today— but she wasn't going to subject herself to another encounter with the woman on the palomino. She was about to turn and head back to the gate when the woman swung a circle and reversed. She pulled up as soon as she recognized Faith.

"That really was your saddle, wasn't it?"

"I sold it to Jared."

The woman cocked her head. "That's what he said, but I keep wondering how come you were so bent out of shape seeing me riding in it. I mean…" she gestured with one hand

"…usually if you sell something, you don't go nuts when you see someone else using it."

"I bet Jared told you I was nuts."

The woman looked past Faith in the direction of Jared's dually. "He's told me a couple of things that haven't added up. I can forgive a lot of stuff, but lying isn't one of them." She shot Faith a hard look. "Please answer me this. *When* did you sell him the saddle?"

She wasn't going to cover for Jared, but she didn't want him pressing charges against Drew because she'd screwed things up by telling the truth. On the other hand, this woman needed the facts to make an informed decision regarding her future.

"After I saw you."

The woman gave a silent nod as her jaw muscles tightened. "Thank you." Her horse danced as a cowboy cantered by too closely, and she drew him up. When he settled, she said, "By the way, my name is Tara."

"Faith."

"I know." Tara's mouth flattened. "Can I ask you a personal question? One that will help me make an important decision?"

"You can ask. I may not answer."

"That's fair. Did you break up with Jared?"

*Oh, my.*

"I was attacked by a man at a rodeo. Jared couldn't handle the aftermath and he left me."

"I see." The words came out in a deadly tone.

"In Jared's defense, it wasn't an easy time for anyone. It's hard to know what to do around a person who's been through a trauma." She didn't want to defend her self-centered ex, but she had to tell the truth. Better men than Jared might have had difficulty dealing with her situation.

"That's a much better answer than the one he gave me—which was another lie." She drew up her reins. "Thank you, Faith. I'll see that you get your saddle back."

"I don't want my saddle back."

"Yeah. You do."

"No. I don't." Tara gave no indication of having heard. She rode the palomino out the gate, toward the dually, leaving Faith staring after her. Two years ago, she might have followed and argued the point. Two years ago, she'd been bulletproof.

Now she just wanted to make her ride and get out of there. If that made her a coward, so be it.

# CHAPTER FOURTEEN

THE OVERHEAD LIGHTS were starting to buzz as Faith rode Tommy to the gate, fourth up in a field of fifteen. If luck was with her, she'd be loaded and ready to go shortly after the event ended.

Tara never returned to the practice arena, but Faith saw her near the gate, waiting for her name to be called. Her horse danced nervously, but she barely seemed to notice as she watched the action in the arena, her expression even tauter than it had been during their conversation about Jared.

Something had happened.

Faith blew out a breath when Tommy also began to dance, and she made a conscious effort to relax. When her name was called, she made a serious effort to focus on the next twenty seconds.

But her energy was off, and that threw Tommy off. He turned wide on the first barrel, then squeezed in too close on the second. By the time he negotiated a perfect turn on the third, he'd wasted too much time. She would not be in the money tonight.

Wasn't the first time. Wouldn't be the last.

She pulled Tommy to a skidding stop outside the gate, then dismounted and started toward her trailer. She put one hand on her horse's damp neck as she walked, drawing strength from the gelding's presence. She wasn't alone. She had a horse, and a dog sitting in her trailer, waiting to ride home snuggled up in the passenger seat.

She also had something sitting on the ground next to her trailer. Faith stopped a few feet away, shaking her head as she realized it was her custom saddle. Well, that explained Tara's tight, angry expression. She must have had it out with Jared once and for all.

Faith skirted the saddle on her way to the rear of the trailer, where she opened the door, letting Sully out. The big dog shook himself then headed for the tires to do his business. Then he returned to keep a sharp eye on the surroundings as Faith unsaddled Tommy and then loaded him in the trailer. Only then did she approach the saddle, which she nudged with her toe.

She didn't know what she expected, but she did not trust Jared after he'd lied to Tara and confronted her in her own tack room. Sully cautiously approached the saddle, sniffed it a few times, then sat next to it, staring up at Faith.

Okay. A case of overreacting. Resisting the urge to simply leave it where it lay, she lifted the saddle and carried it to her tack compartment, tipped it inside and then closed the door.

"We're out of here," she told Sully. The dog gave a happy bark and bounded to the truck and waited for Faith to open the door. Sully's presence hadn't been enough to keep her from melting down last summer, but she had most of her equilibrium back, and the Airedale and the pepper spray in her pocket made her feel safer. She knew she'd never ever feel as safe as she once had. And maybe, in a way, that was a blessing.

She shot Drew a text before starting her truck, telling him she was on her way home. She pulled out of her parking spot and eased onto the road leading out of the rodeo grounds as a cheer went up from the crowd. The first bull rider had had a great ride. Excellent. And by the time the last bull rider rode, she'd be fifteen miles closer to home.

THE LIGHTS WERE still off at the Lightning Creek Ranch. The message from Faith had come in two hours ago, which was more than sufficient time for her to get home and turn on those damned lights. Drew knew he hadn't missed her, that she hadn't come home and gone to bed when he hadn't been watching, because when Faith was home, the back porch light shone all night. It was off, too.

She wasn't answering her phone, wasn't answering his texts. She hadn't wanted him to go to this rodeo, but how long was he supposed to wait before he did something?

He decided that he would wait five more minutes. If he didn't hear something by then, he'd go looking.

Three minutes later, he was out the door.

The night was dark. The moon hadn't risen and his anxiety ramped up with each passing mile. Where in the hell was she?

When he hit the junction where he could continue taking the state highway or turn onto the rougher county road that cut off miles, he turned onto the county road, the tires bumping as they hit gravel. There were a lot of dead spots in cell service between Eagle Valley and Silverton, but most were along the county road. If Faith had broken down, it was in a place where she couldn't answer his texts.

The cutoff wasn't that long—only five miles, but it was lonely, and as he crested each low rolling hill, he expected to see the truck and trailer stopped beside the road. Nothing. Maybe she was somewhere along the state highway. He started the descent to the river, rounded a corner, then slowed as his headlights cut across the dark truck and trailer pulled to the side of the road.

"Thank you," he muttered as he pulled to a stop.

The truck door opened and Faith got out. Sully tried to follow, but she closed the door, leaving him to press his nose against the window.

She didn't say a word. She crossed the highway and walked into his arms, laying her head against his chest. He closed his arms around her.

"How long have you been here?"

"Going on two hours. One of the trailer tires is destroyed. I didn't know it was flat until it was too late, and now I can't get the lug nuts loose on the spare. I didn't know how long I'd have to walk to get cell service, so I stayed here. With the truck." She smiled weakly. "You know, like they tell you to do in the wild."

He ran a hand over her back, then leaned down to take her lips in a quick reassuring kiss. "Scared?"

"I'm glad you're here."

She was scared, but wasn't going to admit it. Again, those boundaries he'd set up. He stepped back, wanting very much to kiss her again, but instead he jerked his head toward her trailer.

The spare was mounted on the side of the trailer, the bolts rusted from exposure to the weather. Drew took the tire iron and started reefing on the frozen lugs. Inside the trailer, Faith's horse gave a snort and shifted his feet, the hollow sound loud in the quiet night.

"Guess we're lucky it's not raining yet." Because, according to the forecast, it was coming. The first lug squealed free and Drew left the loosened bolt holding the tire in place as he went on to the next.

"How'd you do?" Nothing like a little conversation to break the tension. The drive had made him anxious and the thought of Faith spending the night on a lonely stretch of road or having to ask an unpredictable stranger for help ate at him. The second lug came free, and then the third. The fourth. Each one easier than the last as he channeled his anxiety into the physical act of removing the lugs.

When the last one was free, he left the tire in place and started working on the destroyed trailer tire. All that was left were a few black strips of rubber wound around the wheel. She must have driven for miles with the flat, which wasn't unusual on a trailer with dual tires on each side. The lone tire supported the trailer.

Drew's shoulders hunched as he loosened the lug in one mighty push of the tire iron.

He hated her being stuck alone out here.

He wasn't her guardian.

He'd set things up so he couldn't be.

He was thinking of loosening his rules.

*Yeah? Well, she might have some rules, too.*

So they'd negotiate.

He looked over his shoulder. "Do you have a jack for the trailer?"

"The kind you drive up on. I didn't bother getting it out when I realized that I wouldn't be able to get the spare off the trailer." She opened the tack room door and pulled out a low yellow double-wedge with a dip in the middle. He placed it in front of the good tire and Faith went to the truck, started it and slowly drove the trailer up onto the wedge. Tommy shifted inside, but the angle wasn't great enough to knock him off balance. The damaged tire started to spin as it left the ground, and Drew made a cut-off gesture as the good tire settled into the center dip.

Drew unscrewed the lugs, handed them to Faith as she came up behind him. He loosened the tire and started to pull it off, then stopped and wiggled the valve stem.

The damned thing had been sliced at the base. Cold anger shot through him as he sat back on his heels.

"What?"

"The valve stem has been cut."

Faith put her free hand over her mouth as she stared at the tire.

"Oh, man," she said lowly.

He looked over his shoulder at her. Her eyes were wide, her expression stricken. He got to his feet, took her shoulders in his hands. "What?" Because there was a what. He was certain of it. "Tell me, Faith."

She shook her head.

"Why?"

"Because," she said lowly, "I'm afraid of what you'll do."

He stared at her, stunned by her answer. "You saw your ex at the rodeo."

"No. But I talked to his girlfriend and then found my barrel racing saddle next to the truck when I got back from my run."

"Next to this tire by any chance?"

Faith gave a small nod, then reached out to put her hand on his bicep. Drew dropped his chin, his jaw muscles tightening as he fought to maintain his equilibrium. It wasn't like he could find Jared and beat the crap out of him. And, even if he could, he wouldn't.

That didn't make it any easier to tamp down the fury unfurling inside of him. Faith squeezed harder. He raised his chin. Met her gaze.

"We're contacting the sheriff's office as soon as we get to a place with service."

"And tell them what?" There was a catch in her voice.

"We'll make a report, outline our suspicions. There will be a record."

"And that's all?" she asked in a quiet voice.

He let out a shaky breath. "I...yes. That's all." He squeezed his eyes shut, tightened his lips. Tried not to say anything that would scare her. It was fricking hard. "I want to get you home."

"I want to go home."

He turned back to the trailer without touching her, focusing on steady breathing, a slow release of anger. She hadn't been hurt.

*She could have been.*

It was the trailer tire, not the truck. No danger of a blowout and losing control because of the double axle and extra tires.

*She'd been stranded. A woman who was afraid of strangers. Stranded.*

His blood pressure started to ratchet up, but again he focused on breathing while taking the spare off the side of the trailer, mounting the ruined wheel in its place. "You'll have to buy a new wheel. The rim's bent." His voice was rusty, but he didn't sound as if he were on the edge of murder. Good, good.

Faith's hand settled on his shoulder as he tightened the last lug and he went still. Closed his eyes again. A small shudder went through his body.

When he looked over his shoulder, there was something in Faith's expression that had him getting to his feet before he was even aware of moving, taking her in his arms, holding her tightly against him. She slid her arms around his waist, pressed herself against him, and there they stood, on the lonely country road in the middle of nowhere. Slowly rocking as they each sought silent comfort from the other.

FAITH PULLED HER truck to a stop outside the substation in Belmont and she and Drew went in to make the report of the cut valve stem.

"Do you suspect anyone?" the deputy asked after inspecting the damage, which was clearly deliberate. He was polite, efficient, and even though Faith knew there was nothing he could do based on suspicions, he made her feel as if he would honestly try to help.

Drew put a hand on her shoulder as she said, "I've been having difficulties with an ex-boyfriend." She went on to explain about the saddle and how she'd found it next to the tire with the sliced valve stem.

"What's the man's name?"

Faith hesitated, Drew patted her shoulder, and she said, "Jared Canon."

The deputy met her gaze in a way that told her he was familiar with Jared. As a friend? Adversary? It wasn't as if she could ask, but she wanted to know.

"Thank you." He closed his notebook with a flip of his wrist.

"I have no proof and I want no trouble," Faith said. "We'll run into each other again."

The deputy allowed himself a small smile. "I'll make sure that if you do, there will be no more sliced valve stems."

As they left the substation, Drew kept his hand on the small of her back, as if he needed to reassure himself that she was okay. He gave a small grunting laugh as they stopped at her truck and she frowned at him. He pushed back a few tendrils of hair with one hand. "Maybe official channels *are* better than beating the crap out of the guy."

"Is that supposed to reassure me?"

His firm mouth tilted up on one side. "Yeah. Because unless I'm reading things wrong, the good deputy has had run-ins with Jared before and he's going to make a strong suggestion that Jared keep his distance."

She had the same feeling. "Thank you for *not* hunting him down and beating the crap out of him. He lives here, you know."

"I'm not going to lie—if he'd been close by when I discovered the valve stem, I would have had trouble controlling myself."

"Do you think you could have?"

"Controlled myself?" She gave a silent nod. Drew frowned down at the ground as he formed his answer. "I'm going to say yes. Because that's the way I want things to be." He met her gaze, a deadly serious expression on his face. "It's the way *I* want to be."

## CHAPTER FIFTEEN

WHEN THEY GOT back to the Lightning Creek Ranch, Drew put Tommy in the pasture while Faith went into the house. He figured she was tired and cold and upset after spending two hours sitting on a dark road, then finding out that her ex had deliberately cut her valve stem. The fact that he'd messed with the trailer tire told Drew that the jerk hadn't wanted to see her hurt—just inconvenienced.

A woman alone at night.

Drew tamped down the flare of anger. Anger wouldn't do either of them any good. He needed to take care of Faith.

She was waiting for him in the living room and when he closed the door, she crossed the room to take his hand, lead him back to her bedroom. Once there, she began undressing him. She pushed him back onto the bed and he pried off his boots so that she could finish the job.

"Faith…"

"Shhh."

She stood and undressed, dropping her clothing in a heap. In the moonlight shining through the window, he could see her almost as well as if it had been day—her firm breasts, narrow waist. Her gorgeous full ass that drove him crazy. She walked over to the bed and put a hand on his chest, pushing him onto his back. But instead of situating herself on top of him, she lay beside him.

"I want to try the bottom."

He brushed her hair back from her forehead, frowning down at her. "Are you sure?"

"Would I be saying it?"

One thing he'd learned about Faith was that, no, she would not be saying it.

"Okay."

He moved on top of her, easing a knee between her thighs, pushing himself into her without putting any weight on top of her body. There was a good foot of air between their chests by the time he was all the way home. But when he started lowering his body, she put her hands against his chest and pushed, hard, her breath coming in a series of short, frantic pants. He instantly understood and rolled, taking her with him.

But instead of getting on top, straddling his chest, she pulled him toward her, so that they were lying on their sides, her thigh over his hip, still joined.

"Better," she murmured. A moment later, she slowly arched her back, pushing herself against him. Cautiously, he pushed back.

"Is that okay?"

Her eyes shut and a faint smile curved her lips. "Oh yeah." She reached down between them to touch herself, which always made him a little crazy, and he started moving faster, cupping her ass with one hand.

They came together, which he always loved, and collapsed in a tangle of damp legs and arms.

She let out a breath against his chest. "Not quite ready for that."

"It's been a long day," he murmured.

She laughed and snuggled closer. Drew pulled her toward him and closed his eyes. He didn't say anything, made no official announcement, but tonight he was going to try to stay with her.

DREW CAME ROARING up out of bed as the sky turned orange and the world silently disintegrated around him, metal falling from the sky but making no sound as it hit the ground close to him, hit his buddies. Hit Maddie. Then the noise came, building in intensity until it was deafening. He put his hands to his ears, trying to shut it out until he choked in a series of gasping breaths and the noise stopped.

His eyes snapped open and he blinked, but couldn't see. The sky wasn't orange. It was black. Then he heard the shuddering exhalation from across the room and reality slammed into him. Faith was plastered against the wall farthest away from the bed, her hands flat against the drywall on either side of her. She was panting, and even at a distance he could see how wide her eyes were, how terrified her expression.

He tried to say he was sorry. Sorry for being there, sorry for scaring her, but the words refused to climb out of his dry throat as he held Faith's frightened gaze. He needed to reassure her, but was afraid to go near her.

It took him several minutes to get his

breathing closer to normal, and for the pulse to stop hammering in his ears.

Finally, he was able to ask, "Did I hurt you?"

"No." The word barely escaped her lips.

"I could have."

"You didn't."

She crossed the room, cautiously approaching as if he was going to suddenly attack, making his heart break as once and for all he accepted his reality. She sat next to him, settled a light hand on his bare thigh, and he flinched. She pulled her hand back.

"I don't like to be touched afterward." His nerves were close to being on fire.

"Noted." She got to her feet. Put some distance between them before snapping on the desk light. It was then he saw the mark on her arm, a long red line that would bloom into a bruise.

"You said I didn't hurt you."

She grasped her arm with her free hand. "I tripped as I got out of bed. Hit the nightstand. You didn't hurt me."

Yeah? Would she have that mark if he hadn't come fighting out of his sleep?

"I can't do this."

She didn't answer. What *could* she say,

now that she'd seen him come unglued? Seen the stress of not being able to beat the crap out of Jared Canon manifest itself in a deadly dream?

He reached for his jeans, shoved his legs into them. He hoped the Airedale still whimpering on the other side of the door would let him leave unscathed.

"You don't have to go," she said. He gave her a look and she lifted her chin in response. "I'll make coffee. We can…talk."

'I'm not real good with words right afterward."

"We'll talk later."

He let his head drop in defeat. She didn't get it. "Faith… I told you before that I wasn't ready. This is why. Don't fight me on this."

Her expression crumpled. "You're saying…"

"Give me space." She started to speak, but he cut her off. "I've got to go."

"When will I see you again?" The question she'd never asked him before.

He shot a look at the injury on her arm. "It'll be a while."

He felt like a coward, but he had to get out

of there. For her sake. For his. She stood back, wrapping her arms around her middle.

"It's not you, Faith—"

She interrupted him with an angry exhalation. "Don't *say* it. Don't even think about saying it."

His jaw muscles tightened and then he yanked open the bedroom door. Sully fell back as he strode past the dog on his way to the front door. To his escape.

A sacrifice he had to make.

FAITH'S ARM WAS throbbing from where she'd hit it in her hurry to get away from Drew when he'd come rearing up out of the bed. Her only thought had been to put a lot of distance between herself and danger—and she'd tripped on the rug on the way.

She let go of her arm and rubbed the backs of her hands across her cheeks, smearing the tears that had slipped from the corners of her eyes. She wasn't going to cry. Or mourn. Or feel helpless and lost.

She was *not*.

Propping a hand on the wall, she let her head drop. Her heart was still beating harder.

He'd scared her to death. No way around it. No way to pretend it hadn't happened.

The question was no longer *would* he terrify her, but when?

Faith pushed off the wall and went down the hall to the bathroom. She switched on the light, took a long look at her pale reflection—pale except for her eyes, which were red-rimmed. She ran water, splashed her face, patted it dry.

Still no color.

Drew had come to her rescue because he cared for her. He'd stayed the night because he thought he could. And then he'd erupted...

They had a problem.

And convincing him of the *they* part might well be impossible.

Faith didn't try to go back to bed after Drew left. She iced her arm, drank a cup of tea, researched nightmares, convinced herself that any decision made in the dead of night after a frightening experience needed to be reexamined in the light of day. Drew was right. They needed time. Both of them.

And Faith got her time. The days passed by without a word from Drew, other than a quick call the morning after he'd had the nightmare, making certain she was indeed all right. After that—nothing. Leaving Faith in a quandary. Did she accept the inevitable? Put up a struggle?

She had nothing to struggle against, and that was made clear when Maddie's aunt called and told her Maddie wouldn't make lessons that week. She was taking a weekend trip with Shayla's family.

"Will she be continuing lessons?"

Cara hesitated a split second too long. "I don't know," she finally said.

"If she wants to continue, I can pick her up and drop her off."

"Why would you do that?"

The note of suspicion in Cara's voice irked her. *Why, to get close to Drew, of course.* Faith sucked in a breath and let fly with the truth. "Because I like Maddie. My horses get exercise and I get to teach. Maddie gains skills she might not otherwise have. That makes it a win-win-win situation." *Any more questions?*

From the moment of silence that followed her rapid-fire response, she assumed the answer was no. Maddie's overprotective aunt did not have more questions.

"I'm sorry if I got peppery," Faith said.

"No," Cara said instantly. "Maddie likes you, too."

She softened her tone. "Glad to hear it. Even if we don't continue lessons this summer, there's always next."

Cara cleared her throat. "Yes. I'll keep that in mind."

Faith thanked her and hung up, wishing she hadn't offered to pick up the girl. But Maddie liked horses and Faith could help her indulge her interest. She *liked* working with her.

*This isn't about you.*

Obviously, since she felt like she had no say in anything, and no way to get a say. Short of going to his cabin and poking at Drew with a stick, they were not going to have contact. Maybe it was good thing Maddie was taking a hiatus from riding lessons. Maybe Faith needed a break from the Miller family.

Maybe she didn't need any more reminders of how much she missed Drew.

*Yeah. Definitely a good thing.*

But while she was able to take a break from Drew, she was not able to take a break from his sister. Debra had been wildly preoccupied over the past several weeks. At first

Faith thought it was because of the applications and admissions they were processing, but she became even more distracted and distant as those slowed down.

That wasn't totally a bad thing. Faith did her job with few interruptions and next to no questions about her weekend rodeos...or Drew. It was as if Debra had given up on helping him—or, as Drew had said, she really was only interested in appearances. Whatever her reasoning, it seemed that Drew had worn her down.

Lately, Debra had spent less time in the office than usual as she attended meetings, both on campus and at the capitol as part of the various committees she served on, so Faith wasn't surprised to see her office dark when she came upstairs to drop off a printout of missing alumni files.

She gave the printout to Penny, Debra's associate, and headed for the door, only to step back as it opened. The woman who came in stopped when she saw the dark office, then glanced at Penny.

"Unexpected meeting," Penny said with an apologetic smile.

A pained look crossed the woman's face

before she said in a resigned voice, "I'll catch her later."

"Do you want me to have her call you?"

"I'll text. Thank you." She hurried back out the door, leaving Faith staring after her.

"Salesperson?" she asked, thinking textbooks.

"Real estate."

Faith's eyebrows lifted. "Is Debra selling her house by the lake?" The one she was so proud of?

Penny shook her head and reached for the phone. "Her second house. The one on the mountain." She started punching buttons and Faith bit her lip as she let herself out of the office.

Could Debra have two houses on the mountain?

Somehow, she doubted that.

DREW HAD JUST stopped by Pete's to pick up his Jeep when a text from Faith came in.

Call me.

Hearing her voice was going to ruin him, but he moved to the far end of the shop, out of earshot of Pete, who was cursing lightly under his breath as he tried to unjam a pull starter on a small pump. Drew dialed her number anyway.

"Hey," he said when she answered. He'd been right. Just hearing her hello made him want her.

"I heard something today. It may be nothing, but I thought I should pass it along."

Not what he'd expected. "What's that?"

"A real estate agent came by your sister's office. Apparently, Debra is interested in selling her second home. The one on the mountain."

It took Drew a few seconds to process. "You're sure about that?"

"Sure enough to call you," she said tightly.

"Shit." He rubbed his forehead. "Sorry."

"Yeah. I know. About a lot of stuff." She didn't sound one bit snarky. "I thought you needed to know."

He gripped the phone more tightly. "Thank you."

"Not a problem." She hung up without a goodbye, leaving Drew holding the phone and wondering what the hell he was supposed to do now, other than head over to his sister's house and have it out with her.

"What's wrong?"

He hadn't realized that Maddie had been sitting in the front seat of the old Trans Am Pete worked on in his nonexistent spare time. She hopped out.

"Just…some stuff with your aunt."

"Cara?"

"Debra." He wasn't surprised that Maddie didn't think of her first.

"What kind of stuff?"

"It has to do with the property lease. No biggie."

"She wants me to live in town."

Drew's chin jerked up. "What?"

Maddie shrugged in an uncertain gesture. "She stops at my volleyball games sometimes. She's friends with Shayla's mom."

"No kidding," Drew said in a deliberately light voice.

"They belong to some club or something. We don't talk much, but she did tell Shayla's mom that it's a shame you want me to live so far away from my activities."

And now he had an idea why she was doing that. *Son of a bitch.*

"I told Shayla not to worry. I'm never moving up there."

Drew's eyebrows went up. "Yeah?"

She lifted her chin in a stubborn gesture. "We haven't worked on the room in two weeks, and I really don't know why we're bothering, since you don't want me there."

Drew stared at his daughter as he scrambled for a foothold, tried not to panic. "It's not that I don't want you there. I've explained that."

"You won't even try."

The accusatory note in Maddie's voice killed him.

"Do you want to wake up hearing me yelling at the top of my lungs?"

"As long as you're not yelling at *me*, I. Don't. Care."

"You don't know that," he said in a low voice.

"Neither do you."

"Maddie, please…"

"If you wanted me around, you'd think of a way."

She slammed the car door and headed for the shop exit.

"Let her go," Pete said quietly. Drew had

practically forgotten he was there. "She's having some teen-itis lately."

"I should be the one dealing with it."

"Yeah? Well, that isn't how things are working out. Is it?" Pete crossed the shop, wiping his hands on a rag that he then tossed on the counter. "What's up with Deb?"

"I think she's looking at selling the cabin."

"You have equal interest, right?"

Drew leaned back against the workbench. "Yeah. She can't sell without me being on-board... I don't think. Maybe she can sell her half to someone, though. I don't know."

"You might want to see a lawyer."

Drew let his head drop back. "Yeah. I better."

"How bad are the nightmares?"

"Bad enough that I'm thinking about the drugs again."

"They destroyed you."

"True. But I could have Maddie there if I took them. You guys wouldn't have to deal with teen-itis."

"We're doing okay," Pete assured him. "There are moments, but all in all..." He gave a shrug.

"I have to do something. I can't have Maddie think I'm using the nightmares as an excuse to not be her full-time dad."

"Maybe she needs to experience one to see that you're speaking the truth."

"Yeah?" Drew said harshly. "You might want to ask Faith about that. Scared the crap out of her."

Pete studied the ground. "Is that why you aren't seeing her anymore?"

"Pretty much."

"She can't handle it?"

"Neither can I."

Pete turned to look at him. "That's not an answer."

"She was terrified."

"Still not an answer."

"I don't know if she can handle it. My guess is no. She has a little PTSD herself." He ground the words out. The last thing he thought he'd be doing was defending his relationship decisions with his late wife's brother.

"You don't want to know, because then you might have to accept another loss instead of choosing to walk away—which is putting you in a very bad mood, I might add."

"I'm saving us both some grief."

Pete merely lifted an eyebrow in a way that

Drew didn't like one bit. "You are sidestepping an issue. I'm not telling you to torture the woman with *your* PTSD. I'm saying let her decide what she's capable of. Maybe she won't be able to handle it. But let her make her own decision."

"And ruin me in the process?"

"Will you be any more ruined than you are now?" Drew gave him a deadly look and Pete put up his hands. "Done."

Drew dragged his palms over his head, bringing them to rest at the back of his neck. "I had two nightmares this week. I went from having one or two a month, to one or two a week. What does that tell you?"

"That you have unresolved issues."

"No shit."

Actually, he'd had one nightmare and the beginning of a second. The mother cat had landed on his bed, waking him up before the second nightmare had gone into high gear. It'd taken him over an hour to go back to sleep, but he'd made it the rest of the way through the night.

"I don't know what to tell you, man."

Pete knew everything. Knew that Drew had been to therapy, knew he'd tried a lot of mental voodoo to stop the dreams. Had even tried hypnotherapy the previous summer. Nothing worked except the zombie drugs.

Drew pushed off the workbench. "Not much to tell. I'll deal with Deb. Finish the cabin. Maybe try another therapist…and… I don't know…take Maddie with me?"

"Maybe that's the thing to do."

"I'd better go, see what my sweet sister is up to." And the best way to do that was to talk to her husband. Eric was rotten at keeping secrets once he was asked a direct question. The trick was to know when to ask him one.

Drew went to the door and pulled his Jeep keys off the rack, holding them up. "Thanks. I'll figure out how to get the truck later."

"Only fifty-six more lawn mower repairs and you'll have me paid off."

"I already gave Cara cash. Sorry, bud."

## CHAPTER SIXTEEN

DEB SHOWED UP five minutes late at the little coffee shop by the lake where Drew had arranged to meet her. When she sat down, he didn't ask what she wanted to drink or even how she was. He asked how much.

His sister blinked at him. "Excuse me?"

"How much, Deb? How much do you need to get out of difficulty?" Difficulty being his sister's favorite euphemism for the trouble she got herself into.

"Are you talking money?"

"Yes."

She folded her hands, studying him as if sensing a trap. There was none. "You have money." She spoke flatly, disbelievingly.

"Why is that so hard to accept?"

"You live rent-free in a rundown shack with no electricity and fix small engines for a living."

"I'll give you a lump sum."

"How can you afford to do that?"

He gave a careless shrug. "I invested my part of our inheritance. I have nothing to spend my money on." And he'd gotten a life insurance settlement after Lissa's death, which was currently in an account for Maddie. If this worked out, Maddie would be half owner of the mountain property and still have a small nest egg for college. He had a feeling that Lissa would approve.

She narrowed her eyes at him. "How do you know I need money?"

He had sworn to keep his brother-in-law out of it, and he was going to keep his word. "I might have a few issues, Deb, but I can still put two and two together. You live large. You want to sell the cabin—"

"How do you know that?" she demanded. Her eyes narrowed again. "Did Faith over-hear something?"

"Maddie is no longer taking riding lessons." He gave her a bland look, daring her to say that he and Faith spent time together for any other reason. He flattened his palm on the table. "So, Deb…how much?"

"A hundred thousand would help us catch up."

He barely blinked. "I'll write you a check."

Deb frowned at him. "I can get twice that much for my half of the land the cabin sits on."

"*We* could get twice that much, but *we* aren't going to sell. I'm buying your half of the property for cash. You have a sure thing, versus nothing. What do you say, Deb?"

"I say if you ever decided to sell the blasted thing, I'm out a lot of money."

He gave a considering nod. "If I sell, I'll give you whatever amount will bring us even. We can write that into the contract."

Her mouth opened, then closed again and she abruptly looked out over the lake. "How did Granddad know you were going to live in that cabin?"

"He didn't. But he did know that you would bulldoze it, given the chance."

Deb tapped her fingers on the table, making Drew wonder how much her perfect manicure cost. "Do you know," he said, drawing her attention back to him, "that you aren't that important in other people's lives?"

"What does that mean?"

"You think people are always looking at you. Judging you by how perfect your life is, how perfect your close relatives are, but you know what? You're never going to win with those people. Even if you manage to impress them, they hate you for it."

"For heaven's sake, Drew."

"You burned through a lot of money, Deb, and what did you get out of it? The thrill of being better than the Joneses. And debt. A lot of debt."

"You're a fine one to talk."

"About debt?"

"About mental hang-ups."

He leaned back in his chair, put his palms flat in front of him on the table. "I know. And I'm doing something about it."

"Therapy at long last?" Deb asked with a tiny sneer.

"Want to join me?" he asked.

"Why do I need therapy?"

He shrugged. "Feelings of inadequacy?"

She stared at him as if not fully comprehending his meaning. "I feel great about myself."

"Yeah. Me, too."

"It shows."

He shook his head. "You're my sister, Deb. I love you. I'll help bail you out of trouble. But you can be damned unpleasant at times."

Her mouth flattened to the point that her lips almost disappeared.

"Do you want the check, Deb?"

"I'm not in a position to refuse."

"It's a position you got yourself into. Frankly, you're lucky to be able to get yourself out of it." He smiled grimly. "Lesson for the future."

"Damn it, Drew." She swallowed and looked out over the lake again. "It wouldn't have killed you to move off the mountain."

"I like my privacy."

Which was edging close to a lie. He liked being in a place where he didn't hurt the people he loved, but he was rapidly coming to the conclusion that something had to give. He was barely keeping the lid on the bubbling cauldron that was his life.

DEBRA WAS IN a foul mood after returning from lunch. She strode down the basement hallway, heels clicking on the hard tile floor. She paused at Faith's office, glanced in as if she had a matter to discuss, then moved on to the room that housed the archives.

Faith let out a silent sigh of relief when she passed by again and the elevator door dinged. Drew's sister tensed her up. No two ways about it. Was Drew responsible for her mood? If so, how was *he* doing?

She needed to stop wondering things like that.

She put her head down, did her best to focus. Tonight, she'd go home and ride, then make a big salad, watch a goofy movie on TV. Ah, the life of the swinging bachelorette. Not that she was complaining. She had a decent job, was making friends in the department. Right now, they were go-to-drinks-on-Friday friends, but maybe that would evolve into more. Jolie Brody would have her babies in a few weeks and that would add some excitement to the ranch.

What was wrong with leading a semi-boring life? It beat having her hair cut off.

An involuntary shudder went through her.

Faith still had trouble treating that moment casually. Some things stuck with a person, just as Drew's traumas stuck with him. She'd sought out help—from him, no less—but he wasn't able to do the same.

*You can't force help upon a person until they're ready to receive it.* That was a given.

*But what do you do when you find that per-*

*son leaning against your truck at the end of the work day?*

Drew pushed off her truck and started toward her as Faith looked over her shoulder at the building she'd just left, wondering if Debra was watching her and Drew. So what if she was?

"Thank you," he said after coming to a stop a few feet away from her.

"Concerning Debra and the cabin?"

"Yeah. We worked things out."

"Really?" She couldn't keep the dubious note out of her voice.

"In our own way."

"I'm glad I could help."

"I stopped by because I wanted to tell you that if there are any repercussions from her—"

"She knows I warned you?"

"No. But she's no fool. If she decides you had something to do with it...if she starts dicking around with you, let me know."

"No," she said. His chin jerked up, but before he could speak, she added, "I'll fight my own battles, Drew. I don't need you to intercede."

"You did me a favor. I don't want you to get any flak over it."

"Now do me a favor and let me handle things on my own." He started to speak, and once again she cut him off. "Or is that a privilege reserved just for you?"

"Low blow, Faith."

"You never gave me a chance. Never asked if I could handle your issues."

"Your bruised arm answered that question for me."

"I tripped, Drew. It could have happened when I got out of bed in the middle of the night to use the bathroom."

"I don't think you would have been moving that fast."

"I guess that would depend on my fluid intake."

He scowled at her, as if she was making fun of him, which was the last thing on her mind. She pointed a finger at him as pent up emotions broke through her weakly shored barriers. "I was scared to death. I'd never seen you like that. But that doesn't mean I couldn't have developed coping strategies."

"You shouldn't have to."

She advanced another step. "Life isn't perfect, Drew. That's why I'm on the top when we make love. It's a *coping strategy*."

She was going to lose it if she kept talking, and she did not want to lose it in public with her boss's brother. "If you ever want to talk, you know where to find me." She brushed by him but he reached out and caught her arm, bringing her to a stop. The minute she stopped moving, he let go.

"Do you blame me for not wanting to hurt you?" he asked.

She shook back her hair as she raised her chin. "No. But when I'm in a relationship, I want to *have* a partner and I want to *be* a partner. I don't want one person making decisions for the good of the other." She searched his face, read uncertainty, pain and…stubbornness. "That's what you're doing, Drew. And I can't live with that."

DREW DROVE HIS Jeep past the Lightning Creek Ranch up the winding mountain road to his cabin—the sanctuary that he and his daughter would soon own. His daughter who was upset because he was afraid to have her live with him.

Wind blasted him sideways when he got out of the rig, nearly taking the door off. He got the door closed and kept his head down as he crossed to the house. When he turned on the generator, all three cats, mother and babies looked up from where they were nestled together on the sofa.

Drew rubbed a hand over his forehead, then crossed to the kitchen, where he'd just finished installing new cabinets. They weren't the ones Lissa had originally picked out. He'd gone to the showroom in Missoula, taken another look at the cabinets circled in the brochure and decided to go with something simpler, more in keeping with the minimalistic nature of the cabin. He thought she would have liked his choice. They looked nice.

He poured a glass of water, went back to the living room and sat on the sofa next to his feline roommates. A few seconds later, the cat and kittens started edging onto his lap, curling around each other as they made themselves comfortable. Drew idly stroked Mama.

How would Lissa have handled his nightmares? She was a strong woman, but was she strong enough to have dealt with him raging in the night?

Would he have tried to protect her by isolating himself?

Probably. It was the way he was wired.

But Lissa wouldn't have put up with that crap. She would have told him he had a daughter to raise and a wife to love. He closed his eyes as his hand settled on the purring cat. And every time they went to bed, he would have been terrified of hurting her.

Just as he was afraid of hurting Faith.

No easy answers. No hard answers, either. Just lots and lots of questions.

He started to nod off, woke with a start, then eased the cats off his lap and headed for the bathroom. A few minutes later, he turned off the generator and climbed the ladder to the half loft without bothering with the electric lantern.

Lissa was gone. Faith was there.

No easy answers.

Drew jerked awake as the weight landed square on his stomach, making him let out a low *oof*. He blinked into the darkness, trying to figure out what the hell had just happened. He was breathing hard, but not hard enough to be coming out of a nightmare.

He could just make out the mother cat sitting on the nightstand, blinking at him with her wide green eyes. No. He hadn't been coming out of a nightmare. He'd been going in.

And the cat had jumped on him. Just as she had a few nights ago.

Drew rubbed the tight muscles on either side of his neck, then lay back down. The cat watched him for a few minutes before gingerly stepping onto the bed and making herself comfortable at the foot, out of reach.

Coincidence that she'd woken him twice now?

Was it possible that because of that first nightmare, during which she'd almost become collateral damage, she now recognized the initial signs? And had decided never again?

Drew let out a choked laugh. Saved by a cat. But how often could he depend on that happening?

Drew woke with the cat still sleeping peacefully at the foot of his bed. Hell, *he'd* slept peacefully, despite the wind buffeting the trees around the cabin. He couldn't count on a cat to save him every time, but just knowing that waking before the nightmare could stave off the terror that followed was somehow comforting.

Maybe there was an answer. Maybe he didn't have to have to take the zombie drugs.

He sat up in bed, then did a double take at the clock.

9:00 a.m.?

He *had* slept. He pushed back the covers, being careful not to disturb the cat who stretched and then rolled over onto her back. The kittens, who didn't have the necessary skills to make their way to the loft, were still curled up on the sofa. Everyone had slept late today.

Probably a damned good thing he didn't have a regular nine to five.

He was making coffee when his phone rang. Pete. He answered while pouring water into the carafe.

"Got any big plans today?"

"Nothing I can't work around," he said in a dry voice.

"The windstorm last night did some major damage to the roof of the house. I have shingles everywhere. Any chance you can give me a hand patching before the rains come?"

"I'll be there in the hour."

"I appreciate it. The place is a mess and Cara got called into work because one of the other girls had a sick kid."

"I don't mind. It'll give me a chance to

make peace with Maddie." He hadn't seen her since she'd stormed out of the shop the day before.

"She's been helping me pick up shingles."

"See you soon."

Drew ended the call, put the coffee on and went in search of roofing clothes. Less than fifteen minutes later, he was on his way out the door, an energy bar in one hand and a travel mug in the other. He just hoped Pete didn't grill him until he figured a few things out himself.

He drove slowly down the mountain, not wanting another deer encounter, then picked up speed just after the Lightning Creek Ranch. Faith's horses grazed peacefully in the pasture. Freckles raised her head as he passed and he felt a bit of a pang. He really had learned some stuff. He could ride a horse. He'd fallen in love with the horse's owner, he had PTSD and his daughter wasn't ready for a new mother.

But he had a cat that had saved him from a nightmare.

He was almost to the fork leading to town when his phone rang and he pulled over to answer it. Pete again. But when he answered, it wasn't Pete.

"Da-ad!" The sheer terror in his daughter's voice made the blood drain from his face.

"Maddie! What?"

"Uncle Pete fell off the roof. He's not moving."

*Oh, shit.*

"Call 911, Maddie. Call them now. Ask for an ambulance." He stepped on the gas, easing the truck back onto the road, still holding the phone to his ear.

"I did. They're coming. I don't know how to call Aunt Cara. Are you close?"

Her last words were choked. He could barely make them out. "A couple miles away. Stay on the phone with me, okay?"

"Okay."

"Let me know when you hear the ambulance."

"They said it might be half an hour. Something about the crew."

Double shit.

"Hang tough, sweetie. I'm putting you on speaker so you can keep talking to me while I drive." He managed to punch the speaker button without disconnecting the phone. "Where is Uncle Pete? Which side of the house?"

"The back side."

The steep side. Why the hell hadn't Pete waited for him? Old asphalt shingles got slick as they started losing their sand coating.

"I was dumping the old shingles in the garbage when I heard the crash." She exhaled on a choking sob.

"Was he on the ladder or the roof?"

"The roof."

Drew was getting close. He could see the shop. He wanted to keep his daughter talking so she didn't go into shock.

"I'm almost there."

"I see you."

"Okay. Hang up now and I'll be there in a few seconds." He took the corner into the driveway a little too fast, J-hooked the Jeep but got it back under control before skidding to a stop. He leaped out of the rig and ran to where Pete lay on the far side of the house.

"Don't move him!" Maddie said. "The 911 lady said not to move him."

Drew put his ear close to Pete's face, heard him pull in a shallow breath. "He's breathing,"

"So…he's going to be okay?" The words

were barely out of Maddie's mouth before she turned her head in the direction of the highway. "Listen."

Drew heard it, too. "Hang on, buddy."

He remained crouched near Pete, talking to him in a low voice. Maddie hovered nearby before dropping to her knees next to Drew.

"It's gonna be okay," she murmured. "The ambulance is almost here."

The ambulance pulled to a stop and Drew took Maddie's hand as they stood, moving back to allow the two paramedics to move in.

"How long ago did he fall?" The younger guy asked Drew. Maddie pulled Pete's phone out of her pocket and checked the time.

"Almost twenty minutes ago," she said.

Pete groaned as the paramedics started working on him. Drew put his arm around his precious daughter and pulled her closer, tamping down the overwhelming feeling of helplessness.

"He's going to be okay," Maddie whispered as if she was willing it to be true.

"He's the toughest guy I know," Drew said.

Maddie swallowed loudly as Pete groaned again when the paramedics started loading him onto the backboard. She pressed her forehead into Drew's side. He wished with all his heart that she hadn't been there to see her uncle lying crumpled on the ground or being loaded into an ambulance, but one of the hard facts of life was that sometimes it was impossible to shield those you loved from harsh realities.

"We'll take him to Eagle Valley General, but given his injuries, I think they'll transport him to Missoula. Just so you know."

"I'll tell his wife."

Drew punched in Cara's number as the ambulance started down the driveway, its blue light flashing. Maddie leaned into him again and Drew closed an arm around her as he waited for Pete's wife to answer.

"I WOULDN'T GO in there." Penny muttered as Faith walked past her with the latest enrollment report, heading toward Debra's open office door.

"Why?"

Penny looked up from her computer screen. "Something to do with her brother and a roof and him not being able to take her call." Penny made a face. "I think there's a hospital involved."

Faith's heart just about stopped.

"I don't think he was the one who fell off the roof," Penny clarified. "But I would give Debra half an hour to cool off. She doesn't like it when things don't conform to her schedule."

"Yeah. I'm kind of aware."

Faith headed back down the hall to the basement stairs. As soon as she got to her office, she pulled her phone out of her purse and called Drew. "Are you all right?"

"Yes."

Relief slammed into her, but if it wasn't him, then who? Her heart started hammering again. "I heard someone fell off the roof."

"Pete."

Faith pressed a palm to her forehead. "How is he?"

"We don't know."

"Is Maddie there?"

"Yes." His voice was clipped. "Deb told you?"

"No. Her secretary warned me about her mood."

"It has nothing to do with Pete," he said grimly. "She's upset because she wanted to meet with me and her lawyer and hammer out some property details this afternoon."

Debra Miller-Hill was one hell of a narcissist.

She heard a hospital page in the background, closed her eyes. "I'm sorry this happened, Drew."

"Yeah." He sounded as if he'd totally shut down, and she could only imagine how Maddie felt.

"Dad…" Maddie's voice came in from the background.

"Just a sec, hon."

"I'll talk to you later," Faith said to Drew. He needed to focus on his daughter and Cara. The people he loved.

When she got to her office, she started pulling materials to be digitized, then after ten minutes of not being able to concentrate, picked up the phone and rang Penny. "I'm taking the rest of the day off as a sick day."

"I'll make it happen."

"Thank you." The beauty of a basement records job. There wasn't much that couldn't be put off a day or two. When Faith got to the hospital, she parked near Drew's newly repaired Jeep and went in through the emergency entrance. The hospital was small, so she had no difficulty finding the emergency waiting area—which was empty.

She went to the reception desk and discovered that Pete had been transported to Missoula for surgery. Faith thanked the woman for the information and headed back to her car. Was Drew on his way to Missoula? If so, he couldn't have gotten far. Maybe she could meet him, take Maddie and then he could be on his way. The girl didn't need to be smack in the middle of this trauma.

Faith dialed Drew's number as soon as she was back in her truck. She could tell from the noise when he answered that he was on the road and that the call was coming in over the sound system—which meant that Maddie could hear the conversation if she was with him.

"I called to see if I could help. I thought Maddie could stay with me."

"We're on the road to Missoula."

"I don't mind catching up with you."

There was the briefest of hesitations before he said, "That would be great, but I need to get Cara to Missoula."

"I'll meet you at the hospital there."

"If you don't mind the drive, it'd help."

She'd been prepared to fight more of a battle, to stand up to Drew's stubborn protective instincts, but he hadn't fought her. He'd accepted help.

The thought stayed with her as she drove just a mile or two over the speed limit all the way to Missoula. Once she hit the city limits, she pulled over and searched for the hospital address, then plugged it into her GPS. Not long afterward, she pulled into the parking lot and found a space. She was about to call him again, to tell him she was there, when her phone rang and Drew gave her directions to the waiting room.

There were several people there, but she barely noticed them as she crossed to where Maddie and Drew sat with a pale-faced Cara. Maddie was the first to spot her and she jumped to her feet. Drew also got up, putting a reassuring hand on Maddie's shoulder as Faith approached.

"I appreciate you coming." His voice was husky, edged with emotion. This had to be hell on him, hell on Cara and Maddie.

"I had to," she said simply.

Drew reached out to take her hand, leading her to the chair next to where he'd been sitting. Cara looked up at her and managed a smile.

"Thanks for coming."

"I'm glad to help," Faith said, before turning her attention to Maddie. "How are you doing?"

"Been better," Maddie said truthfully.

"She's holding it together," her father murmured.

They sat down, and Drew surprised Faith by once again reaching for her hand. Maddie settled in the chair on the other side of her father and leaned her head against his shoulder. And there they sat, a small blended family of sorts, waiting for news about Pete.

Faith closed her eyes, concentrating on the warm pressure of Drew's fingers, the strength she got from being near him.

She loved this man. No doubts there. Now the question was, would he allow himself to love her back? Let her face his challenges with him?

He'd accepted help today. A big step forward. Was it enough?

DREW WAS WORRIED as hell about Pete, who'd been unconscious for way too long in his estimation, but despite that, his stress level had dropped markedly when Faith walked through the door of the hospital waiting room.

He needed her, and that was a hard thing to admit, being the guy who handled everything alone. Her thumb moved over his in a gentle caressing movement that made him realize how fortunate he was to have her there after trying his best to shut her out of his life. She might only be there for the day, because of the emergency, because of Maddie, but he was still grateful.

And ready to talk. They had a lot to talk about. He squeezed her hand again.

Cara sat silently, staring into the distance, waiting for word on her husband. He knew better than to try to engage her in conversation, knew that the last thing she wanted was platitudes and assurances that Pete would be all right. The treatment room door finally swung open and both Cara and Maddie got to their feet as a doctor came into the waiting area.

"Maddie," Drew said in a low voice, and his daughter sat back down as Cara quickly crossed the room, meeting the doctor half-way. They talked for several minutes, then Cara turned and gave Drew a nod.

"He's going to be okay," Maddie said.

"Looks like it," Drew said, hoping he wasn't lying.

Cara and the doctor talked a little longer, then she smiled and nodded, before heading back to their small group. Drew let go of Faith's hand and they all stood. Cara let out a shaky breath before explaining the extent of Pete's injuries, ending with, "He's going to be all right—as long as he stays off roofs. If he doesn't, then he definitely won't be all right, because I'm going to kill him." But her voice was shaky with relief, making her last words more of a declaration of love than a threat.

"How long till he's released?" Faith asked.

"He broke his leg, so they have to pin the leg together, and operate on his shoulder. Monitor the concussion. They said two, maybe three days." She hesitated, then met Drew's gaze. "Maybe Maddie can stay with Shayla."

"We'll work something out." Drew reached out to give Cara a quick hug, releasing her as the sound of footsteps brought their heads around.

"Cara!" An older couple entered the waiting area and made a beeline for their daughter.

"Mom!" Cara headed across the waiting room to meet her parents, who huddled around her.

Twenty minutes later, Drew escorted Faith and Maddie out of the hospital, leaving his sister-in-law with her parents. Cara had assured Maddie that Pete would fully recover and that she'd keep her informed as to his progress. Maddie had taken her words to heart, and on the drive back to the Eagle Valley, she started to bounce back, asking about sending flowers and making plans for a get-well card shaped like a lawn mower.

Drew glanced in his rearview mirror to make certain he could still see Faith driving behind them. Cara hadn't needed his truck, so Faith had made the trip for nothing—unless one counted the fact that it made him realize how much he loved her. And how much he wanted to work things out.

If they could.

It went against the grain for him to bring problems into people's lives, especially a person like Faith who had her own issues to deal with.

And, of course, there was the matter of

how Faith felt. She hadn't said much after Cara's parents showed up, and Drew began to wonder if she'd come more for Maddie's sake than his. Maybe she was doing the good friend thing. The duty thing.

She'd said he hadn't allowed her to be a partner. He hadn't. He'd tried to take all the hits, protect her from his reality.

So what now?

She was going to meet them at the cabin after she fed her animals so that they could work out a plan for Maddie. Maybe he'd have a better feel for things then. He hoped he would, because right now his stomach was in one hellacious knot.

## CHAPTER SEVENTEEN

DREW'S HEART HIT his ribs when he heard Faith's truck pull to a stop outside the cabin. Would she give him a chance to be a partner, and not just a friend in need? Or was she done trying to deal with him? He went to the front door and opened it as Faith stepped onto the small porch.

"Hey."

"Hey," she echoed, giving him a quick unreadable glance before stepping into the kitchen carrying two grocery bags that he automatically took from her. "I thought you might want some food and I didn't know what you had. Last time I was here, food was kind of sparse."

"I hate to shop." He set the bags on the counter. Faith stopped on the opposite side of the small breakfast bar, took a long look at the new cabinets.

"I like them."

"Yeah. Not part of the original plan, but I liked them, too. So, I went with them." Small talk. He hated small talk.

"Where's Maddie?"

"Asleep."

She glanced in the direction of the loft, then started pulling fresh produce out of the bag. Drew put his hand on hers, and her gaze jerked up. "Don't tell me I shouldn't be here," she warned.

"I was going to tell you thank you for being here." He scooped up the carrots and celery she'd unpacked and carried them to the fridge. When he turned back, she was staring at him.

"I thought maybe I could cook with those now. Make a stew."

He pulled the carrots and celery out of the fridge, even though cooking was the last thing on his agenda, and she pulled out an onion and potatoes from the bag. "Do you have flour? If not, we can have more of a soup than a stew."

"I have flour."

Faith pulled out a wrapped package of meat and set it on the counter. Even though her movements were fluid and she was chatting away, Drew sensed her tension, saw how tight her jaw muscles were, how stiffly she held her shoulders. She was as tense as he was. "Any news about Pete?"

"He's in surgery."

"I hope it goes well." She started to unwrap the meat, but Drew put his hand over hers, startling her. Her gaze met his, wide and questioning, but he didn't say a word as he led her away from the kitchen to the leather sofa. He eased the sleeping cats aside to make room for them to sit. The cats were stubborn, so he didn't get a lot of room, but he guided her down next to him, wrapped his arms around her and pulled her close to his chest. It'd been a long time since something had felt so damned right.

"I missed you so much," she muttered against his shirt.

Drew stroked her hair, held her, kept his mouth shut. He didn't want to ruin this moment. Then he felt her pull in a jerky breath and knew he had to say something. "About tonight—"

Faith pulled herself upright, put her hand on his chest and looked him dead in the eye.

"I'm not leaving. Not if Maddie is staying with you. If something happens—"

He cut off her words with a kiss. A deep kiss, in which he did his best to communicate how damned fortunate he was to have her. To love her. To have another chance. When he pulled back, Faith stared up at him with a bemused frown.

"We're going to work out some coping strategies."

Her eyes went wide, then narrowed, as if she didn't quite believe him. So he explained. "I don't want to keep living like this. I feel like I keep dodging one bullet after another. I need to learn to deflect." He cupped the back of her head, brought his forehead down to touch hers in an intimate gesture. "I was operating out of fear. Fear of losing something else. It felt inevitable, so I beat it to the punch."

"You walked."

"I…" He cleared his throat. "I know that loss is a given, and there will be more. But avoiding relationships isn't protecting me. It's ruining me. If you're willing to give this a try… I totally understand that it might not work. I'd rather try than not."

She slid her hand up behind his neck, kissed him. "If Maddie's staying, so am I. I'll sleep on the sofa—unless Maddie is going to sleep there."

"She wants to sleep in her room."

The phone rang and Drew kept his arm around Faith as he answered it. "Yeah."

He listened as Cara gave him an update on Pete, who'd just come out of surgery.

"He's doing better than they expected," Cara said. "How's Maddie?"

"She's doing okay."

"Have you made arrangements for her to stay with Shayla?"

"She's staying here." Drew said quietly.

"Are you sure?"

"Yeah. I think we can work through this."

"I don't want Maddie traumatized."

"Faith is staying, too. Sleeping on the sofa. I think we'll do okay."

"Call me tomorrow morning. Let me know how it went."

Drew smiled a little. "I will, Mama Bear."

After he hung up the phone, he leaned his head against the sofa cushions, only to bring it up again as Maddie made an *ahem* noise from the loft. "Can I come down, or do you guys need a minute?"

Drew started to pull his arm away from Faith, when Maddie waved her hand. "It's okay. Was that about Uncle Pete?"

"He's going to be fine. They said he's a tough old bird."

Maddie broke into a smile and started down the ladder. "But I still get to stay, right?"

Drew nodded. "And if you don't mind, Faith is going to stay, too. Just in case."

Maddie gave a casual shrug and moved past them to inspect the stew ingredients. "Are we cooking?"

Faith got to her feet. "Now that Pete is all right, yes. I think we should start cooking." Drew ran a hand down the side of her thigh as Maddie pulled a package of Oreos out of the half-full grocery bag, then got to his feet.

"Yes. Let's start cooking."

THE CABIN HADN'T felt so warm and alive since he and Lissa had spent their weekends here years ago, plotting out their future. He'd thought his wife had been the sole source of the warmth, but now he understood that it was also love and togetherness that had made the place feel so special. A sense of family.

"The cat woke you up?" Maddie asked as she mixed the dry ingredients for corn bread.

"Twice. It probably won't happen every time."

"When it doesn't, we'll deal," Maddie said, sounding very much like Faith.

"You don't know what you're dealing with."

"I read up on it. The dreamer may appear to be awake while dreaming. Allow the dreamer time to recover after he wakes up for real." Faith and Drew exchanged glances. "Challenges make you strong, Dad."

Then he was approaching superhero status.

After the corn bread was ready to put in the oven and the stew was close to done, they went out to the shop. They brought in the twin bed that was still wrapped in plastic and carried it into Maddie's room. Drew hadn't thought to buy twin sheets, so Faith and Maddie made the bed with his extra set, tucking them tight around the smaller mattress.

Cara called as they were dishing up the stew. Pete would be home in two days—one day earlier than expected.

"Tell Uncle Pete I'm thinking about him," Maddie called.

"Did you hear that?" Drew asked Cara.

"Yes. And if this works…her staying with you…well, we'll miss her, but we'll be happy that you guys are a family again."

"Thanks, Cara."

A family. Drew settled a hand on the middle of Faith's back and she smiled over at him, but he could read the edge of tension there. They would all be a little tense until they met their first nightmare challenge.

"You know these things don't happen like clockwork," he said after they'd eaten and settled back in the living room. Maddie was watching a video on her tablet and Faith was curled up on the sofa next to him. "It could be weeks."

"Then I'll sleep on your sofa for weeks, or for as long as Maddie's here."

Maddie pulled off her headphones. "You better plan to sleep on that sofa for the next five years, because I'm moving into my room. Sully can sleep with me." She slid the headphones back into place and went back to her movie.

"I'm not going to ask for a five-year commitment," Drew said in a low voice close to her ear and his hand settled on her knee. "But a few nights would help. At least until Pete comes home."

She touched his face. "We'll take it day by day, challenge by challenge."

He shot Maddie a look, then dropped his head to give Faith a quick kiss, wishing he could do so much more. Maddie kept her eyes on the screen, but damned if she wasn't smiling when he looked at her again.

Maybe, just maybe, this would all work out—and didn't that feel better than assuming it wouldn't, as he'd automatically done before?

THEY'D TALKED ABOUT the nightmares for so long—almost two weeks—that when the first one happened, it felt as if they were performing a fire drill. Early intervention was the key. If Drew wasn't too deeply into the dream, Faith would wake him, as the mother cat had done. If he was already thrashing about, she'd stay clear and let the nightmare play out.

Mama Cat had been out hunting the first time Faith heard him stirring in his sleep. She climbed the ladder and, because he wasn't yet fighting or lashing out, took him by the shoulder, said his name and gave a shake before quickly moving back in case he was deeper into the dream than she thought. Drew jerked upright, blinking into the darkness, then collapsed back onto the bed, sucking in air.

"You okay?" he asked a few seconds later, still staring up at the ceiling.

Faith came closer and he reached for her. She was glad he didn't know how hard her heart was racing as he pulled her down to the bed, wrapped his strong arms around her. "Yeah," she said. "How are you?"

"Edgy...but not decimated."

She nodded against his chest, then because she was afraid she wouldn't leave if she didn't leave soon, she kissed him and made her way back to the ladder.

A door opened behind her as she descended into the living room. "Is everything okay?" Maddie asked from the across the room.

"Yeah, Mads," Drew called. "Everything is okay."

"Good. Then maybe you guys can get married." She stepped back into her room, closing the door behind her.

"She doesn't sound traumatized," Faith said weakly.

Even though Maddie had told Drew earlier in the summer that she wasn't ready for a new mom, she'd seemed to appreciate the fact that Faith spent every night at the cabin, which meant she could stay at the cabin in her new room. Faith had become her safety net, and, as the days passed, her confidante. Faith had learned about Shayla and the cute kid who'd moved in next door. The terrible possibility that Maddie might get Old Man Taggert for math, because he flunked *everybody*, and a shy invitation to help her shop for school clothes.

"No. That didn't sound like trauma." Drew exhaled, then he said, "Maybe you can come back up here…just for a while."

Faith didn't need another invitation. She climbed the ladder to the loft, settled on the edge of Drew's bed. He pulled her into his arms and even with the blankets between them, she could feel how much he wanted her as she nestled against him. "I'm not going to jump the gun, ask you to marry me, but maybe we can work in that direction. You know…think about it."

"Or I could say yes."

He stilled. "Or you could say yes."

She propped a forearm on his solid chest so she could see his face. "These are not normal circumstances, Drew. We are not normal people—but we're becoming pretty good at working out coping strategies."

He pulled her onto him, kissed her passionately. "This is my favorite coping strategy so far."

"Sex or becoming a family?"

"Family. Sex is a close second."

She smiled against his lips. "You're sure about that?"

"Never been surer of anything in my life."

*Six months later*

"I DON'T KNOW." Faith smiled at her husband-to-be. "A horseback wedding sounds like fun to me."

Maddie made an expansive gesture with both hands. "We can put flowers around the horse's necks and Faith can wear cowgirl boots under her dress. You can both wear cowboy hats, and Faith can have a veil come off the back of hers."

Maddie looked at Drew, then Faith, then Drew again.

"Uh-uh," Drew said.

Maddie rolled her eyes to the sky. "Come on, Dad. Loosen up."

"I'm loose, Maddie." He let out a breath, looked over at Faith for backup.

She gave a small shrug. She didn't care how they got married or where. She just wanted to be able to sleep with her man in the new master bedroom he'd managed to frame in before the snow fell. They'd spent the winter finishing the room on the inside and completing the rest of Lissa's planned cabin renovations—putting a larger window in the living room, a spiral staircase up to the loft, redoing the bare-bones bathroom.

It'd been a good winter in the cabin. And she'd only been snowed in once, thanks to Drew's plow, and when that happened, she'd called Penny, who'd told her that Debra wasn't making it to work either, because the trip across town on unplowed streets was too fraught with peril for her.

As for the nightmares…they still happened. And every now and again, neither Faith nor Mama Cat managed to wake Drew in time to stave off the terror. But the dreams were fewer and further between, and the important thing was that Maddie seemed able to take them in stride. The once-a-week family therapy was helping them all cope a little better.

"Fine. Horseback wedding," Drew muttered.

"It'll just be you and me and Maddie and Pete and Cara," Faith told him. Pete was almost fully recovered, and even though Cara had gone through withdrawals when Maddie had moved to the cabin, finding herself pregnant—despite being told she couldn't have kids—had helped ease the burden. Now Maddie was looking very much forward to a baby cousin, and Cara was over the moon as she turned Maddie's old room into a nursery.

"Maybe we should go whole hog and have it at a rodeo," Drew suggested.

Maddie's eyes went wide and both Faith and Drew started shaking their heads. "Kidding, Mads. I was only kidding."

"But you're not kidding about the horseback wedding."

"I'm not closing my mind."

Maddie grinned and flipped back the cover

of her tablet. "There are a ton of ideas on Pinterest."

"Great," Drew said.

Faith hooked her hand under his arm and led him to the door. "We'll be back in a few minutes, Maddie. I want to talk about the new horse corrals and barn."

"Take your time," Maddie called back absently.

What she really wanted to do was to get her hands on her man. Once they were outside and around the corner of the house, she took Drew's face in her hands and kissed him. Hard. He wrapped his arms around her, bracing his back against the building as he lifted her off her feet, kissed her back.

"You know I love you when I agree to a strange wedding."

"It's for Maddie."

"And me. And you." He set her back on the ground, bent to touch his forehead to hers. "Here's to the future, my love."

She lifted her chin and met his lips. "To the future."

* * * * *

We hope you enjoyed this story from
**Harlequin® Superromance**.

Harlequin® Superromance is coming to an end soon,
but heartfelt tales of family, friendship, community
and love are around the corner with
**Harlequin® Special Edition**
and **Harlequin® Heartwarming**!

Romance is for life, and these stories show that
every chapter in a relationship has its challenges
and delights and that love can be
renewed with each turn of the page!

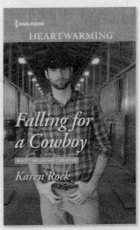

Look for six new
romances every month!

Look for four new
romances every month!

# Get 2 Free Books,
## Plus 2 Free Gifts -
just for trying the *Reader Service!*

STRS17R2

# Get 2 Free Books,
## *Plus* 2 Free Gifts—
### just for trying the *Reader Service!*

# Get 2 Free Books,
## Plus 2 Free Gifts—
### just for trying the Reader Service!

**YES!** Please send me 2 FREE Harlequin® Special Edition novels and my 2 FREE gifts (gifts are worth about $10 retail). After receiving them, if I don't wish to receive any more books, I can return the shipping statement marked "cancel." If I don't cancel, I will receive 6 brand-new novels every month and be billed just $4.99 per book in the U.S. or $5.74 per book in Canada. That's a savings of at least 12% off the cover price! It's quite a bargain! Shipping and handling is just 50¢ per book in the U.S. and 75¢ per book in Canada*. I understand that accepting the 2 free books and gifts places me under no obligation to buy anything. I can always return a shipment and cancel at any time. The free books and gifts are mine to keep no matter what I decide.

235/335 HDN GMWS

Name _____ (PLEASE PRINT)

Address _____ Apt. #

City _____ State/Province _____ Zip/Postal Code

Signature (if under 18, a parent or guardian must sign)

Mail to the **Reader Service:**

**IN U.S.A.:** P.O. Box 1341, Buffalo, NY 14240-8531
**IN CANADA**: P.O. Box 603, Fort Erie, Ontario L2A 5X3

**Want to try two free books from another line?**
**Call 1-800-873-8635 or visit www.ReaderService.com.**

*Terms and prices subject to change without notice. Prices do not include applicable taxes. Sales tax applicable in N.Y. Canadian residents will be charged applicable taxes. Offer not valid in Quebec. This offer is limited to one order per household. Books received may not be as shown. Not valid for current subscribers to Harlequin® Special Edition books. All orders subject to approval. Credit or debit balances in a customer's account(s) may be offset by any other outstanding balance owed by or to the customer. Please allow 4 to 6 weeks for delivery. Offer available while quantities last.

**Your Privacy**—The Reader Service is committed to protecting your privacy. Our Privacy Policy is available online at www.ReaderService.com or upon request from the Reader Service.

We make a portion of our mailing list available to reputable third parties that offer products we believe may interest you. If you prefer that we not exchange your name with third parties, or if you wish to clarify or modify your communication preferences, please visit us at www.ReaderService.com/consumerschoice or write to us at Reader Service Preference Service, P.O. Box 9062, Buffalo, NY 14240-9062. Include your complete name and address.

HSEI7R3

# Get 2 Free Books,
## Plus 2 Free Gifts—
### just for trying the Reader Service!

HARLEQUIN *Desire*